The Bayou Boys

omnibus collection

Voodoo Virus
Marsh Monster
Playhouse Phantom

Gregory E. Zschomler

Published by eyrie press, Vancouver, WA
Cover & interior design by Creativity-Unlimited

ISBN: 153275762X
ISBN-13: 978-1532757624

DEDICATION

To my dear children: Bethany, Isaiah, Josiah, Keilah, Micaiah, Jeremiah, Hezekiah, and Elijah who've adventured with me, with one another, and on their own. May the adventures continue!

And to my grandchildren: Aleric, Devereaux and Britt; may your adventures be grand and glorious!

CONTENTS

ACKNOWLEDGMENTS

Always, first and foremost, my editor and wife: Ruth A. Zschomler, MFA. Always and forever we are a team—in life, in love, and in literature.

For family and friends who have encouraged and supported me in this adventure called writing.

To my writing teachers and fellow author friends who have aided and abetted my humble pursuits.

And finally, to my Lord and Savior, Jesus Christ, who called me to be a voice.

A Note to the Reader:

I have journeyed far and wide across these United States. I have seen its mountains, forests, oceans, grasslands and cities, but nothing is quite as captivating as the deep bayou country of Louisiana. I've spent time on "dem by-yahs," wandered the rues (streets) of the French Quarter and Garden District, sat with Cajun folk in Houma, explored plantations, and listened to rollicking zydeco while consuming mouthwatering Cajun and Creole fare. It is from these experiences that I share with you a slice of the Crescent City.

You'll find unfamiliar Cajun or French terms (in italics), as well as quotes or other references that might need explaining, marked with an asterisk (*). These are defined at the back of each "book" in a glossary. Other terms you might have to look up in a dictionary (which never hurts for expanding your vocabulary).

Most of the places mentioned within these stories actually exist (though some poetic license has been taken by the author). If you ever plan to visit New Orleans, do look them up on the Internet.

1 COCODRIE BAYOU

Pete! Lookout!"
Bart yelled above the roar of our boat's outboard engine. His dark arm stretched toward the bow, pointing behind me, a look of horror on his face. Turning quickly, I was just in time to catch a face-full of wet, mossy fingers hanging low from an creepy cypress.*

Bart burst into laughter, "You are *such* a geek, Pete!" He'd steered the watercraft deliberately into the drooping grove of Spanish-moss laden trees.

"Ah right you dirty rat, you're really gonna get it, see," I said in my best movie gangster voice, and returned the prank with a playful splash of brackish* water into his smirking black face.

"Hey!" said Bart, sputtering from the surprise wash-down.

"Tell me you didn't have that coming," I retorted.

Bart laughed with me, "You have such a sense of justice, dude!"

Gingerly picking the tangled webs of moss from my wavy blond hair, I laughed maniacally.

"You're crazy, Pete. You sound like Vincent Price or something." Being a bit wacky helped break the journey's monotony. Time could pass ever so slowly in this sweltering maze of endless bayous.*

Gently weaving our small watercraft between clumps of twisted marsh grasses and waterlogged *bos coyo*,* I gazed out over the swampy expanse. A water moccasin swam under the shade of an overhanging root, its wake trailing behind. Brightly hued dragonflies darted about overhead. A bevy of other insects flitted about whining in the heat. The everhanging tentacles of the Spanish-moss swayed ever so lightly from the *chênière** in the late summer breeze as if beckoning travelers to some eerie, unknown fate that lay ahead.

The slight breeze didn't help much; it was still stifling. The humidity that hung in the air wore on a person like an invisible foggy coat. Visitors might find it oppressive — even over-bearing — locals were accustomed to it, but everyone agreed: summers in Louisiana are just plain 'muggy and buggy.' So, we were happy to be splashed; a little water on the skin actually felt good — real good.

The hottest part of the day was behind us now. We'd already been out of Houma* for nearly two hours and had spent most of it out in the open coming down the Houma Navigation Canal. *Good thing I've got that SPF 30 on*, I thought, pulling my wide-brim hat down to shade my fair-skinned face.

☠ ☠ ☠

We were now pressing deep into the confines of Cocodrie* Bayou — a haunting place known for its creepy mystery and strange superstition. A fuming, black cloud crept in front of the sun like a giant spider stalking across its web. We grew quiet.

This was Cajun* country and some of its stories could make your skin crawl. Zombies, the walking dead, floating caskets, voodoo magic, iridescent ghosts, swamp creatures, all kinds of spooky things. Not that I believed any of that mumbo jumbo. I've noticed that superstition has a real psychological effect on folks — the more they believe, the more the 'magic' works. And I figured it was either out-and-out superstition (and nothing more) or it was actually delving in dark spiritual things that messed up people who didn't have the power of God in their lives. Still, I felt somewhat uneasy about this journey. What if real sinister forces were at work — whether spiritual or physical?

☠ ☠ ☠

Bart and I both knew these bayous rather well. Some-how though, they seemed a more unearthly labyrinth in the now blackening Mississippi Delta* sky. It was late in the afternoon and beginning to cool off for the evening. I loved summer evenings here in Louisiana when the *mouche à feu** come out shining in the gloaming as we sit on the *galerie** sipping sweet tea.

Sure, there are the occasionally tropical storm and the infrequent hurricane, but usually there's plenty of sunshine and the regular, but passing, afternoon downpour. And, in the summer, the rains were as warm as they were quick; a person dried off after a rain as fast as a lightning flash. Well, that's an exaggeration, but it didn't take long.

"Looks like we could have another rainstorm," I said.

" *Fo' troo**,*" came Bart's reply, "That's what I'd 'spect, it *is* Louisiana, y'know."

As it got on toward evening we found ourselves a good twenty miles from home port. And, like I said, there were some creepy thoughts in my head. On top of that, we were out to solve a mystery — a mystery that began with the sudden disappearance of the long-time town character, Desmond Comeaux.

2 M'SU DEZI

We knew him simply as M'su* Dezi, an old coot who lived in the back-waters of these parts. He was an independent sorta hermit, if you will, who kept mostly to himself, but at such a volume that every-one around could hear. I remember distinctly our encounter with him just last month:

"Confoundit! Jus' my luck. What dat? No, I did *not* ferget to tie no aft line." He paused and turned his scruffy face sky-ward. "Huh? Oh, alright, is my fault den." Dezi's conversation was directed, it seem-ed, to no one in particular. Perhaps God. It was like he was talking on a blue-tooth cell phone, only he had none.

He was dressed in a worn pair of khaki shorts, a dirty wide-brimmed straw hat and a grubby, wrinkled New Orleans

8

Saints jersey. Typical. He liked the Saints and inquired about them often during the season.

"Tarnation!" Dezi continued mumbling while dancing a crazy jig that looked like he'd managed to get a mess of fire ants in his shorts.

"Hey, M'su Dezi! Howsitgoin'?" I called, watching him pull the wet mooring line from the water and tie it up to the dock as I sat down and dangled my feet in the water.

"Eh? Got a soggy line, that's what. Least I 'membered to tie the bow line. Wouldn't want to lose ol' Scum Bucket out to sea; git her swamped on some delta dad burn sand-bar or sum'tin'. She's my only transport, Peter, I say, my only transport."

"You coming or going?" asked Bart as he pulled the Third Day t-shirt off his back to soak up some rays. (I never understood why he thought he needed to — or even could — tan; his African-Indian heritage made him plenty dark.)

"Goin'. Goin', goin', goin' to Louisiana, my true love for to see..." sang Dezi, "gotta git my kicks on route sixty-six — route sixer sixer, yes sir. Them's old songs from way, way back, boys. Why, tarnation, you youngin's wouldn'ta been born yet. Course, I ain't that old neither."

Dezi laughed, slapped his leg and stepped into his bobbing dinghy. "Nope, I jus' sing 'um cuz I knows 'um. Hey, you boys wanna give me a hand with that there gear?"

"Sure," we volunteered together. Bart tucked his shirt into the waistline of his ratty cut-offs and I stood.

"Hand me that there parcel, son," said Dezi motioning toward a brown paper wrapped package sitting atop the stack of goods in his wheelbarrow. "Blazin' hot ain't it? Not as hot as was back in '97 though. That was a hot one — take the *joir de vivre** right outta ya. So chard* not even M'su Mosquito come a callin'. Shoot, they coulda sucked a man dry that year an' still been thirsty."

I gave the package to M'su Dezi, and he gestured at another — a blister-pack containing a hand-held, battery-powered blacklight (the kind of device that gives off ultra-violet light used to check for invisible hand-stamps at some amusement parks). *Odd*, I thought.

Next came an assortment of sacked fruits and vegetables, a hank of nylon rope and a rather large box of D-cell batteries. Bart handed him the last carton containing six shrink-wrapped propane cylinders and I grabbed his wheelbarrow.

"You got everything you need?" I asked Dezi.

"Shoot, I don't need nothin' but the love of God boys, but these'll come in mighty handy-like," returned Dezi reaching for the wheelbarrow. "I got mor'in a man could ever want out there in the bayous. Mor'in I could ever want. Them's *Bon Dieu's** playground, for sure."

"Yeah," said Bart, "I know what you mean. I..."

"Hey, you!" yelled a man down the wharf near Cahoui's* floating fish market-bait and tackle-convenience store. Looking up I saw two rough-looking men, one pointing in our direction. The store bobbed on the navigation canal tethered to the dock its neon cold beer signs jangling in the windows as the men walked hastily toward us down the pier.

"Well, gotta go, go, go. You boys take care, okay. What's that? Oh, yeah. *Bon heur** and God bless you real good. Throw me them ropes will you, *mon ami**?" Bart undid the aft line and I the bow. We tossed them into the boat.

"An' don't take no wooden nickels," Dezi added.

"You take care, too, M'su Dezi," I said. "Those bayous can be dangerous."
"*Bon heur!*" shouted Bart as Dezi pulled away from the dock.

"You bet," Dezi yelled back, "but I'm a keeping my eyes on the snakes that slither. An' I knowed ya can't stomp a snake with both feet in a bucket."

11

Whatever that means, I thought. "Later gator."

And he returned our traditional reply, "In a while crocodile." He was off; it seemed in more ways than one.

I looked back up the dock, the two men, now fifteen or so yards away, slowed to a stop. A gust of wind whipped up briefly and flapped at the shirttail of the shortest of the two men, revealing what looked like the grip of small handgun. They turned away and quickly walked back toward Cahoui's.

That was weird, I thought. *They must have wanted to talk to Dezi. And who were they?* I tried to place them in my mind. I certainly hadn't seen them before.

☠ ☠ ☠

Truth be told, M'su Dezi wasn't around all that much. He came into our little town of Houma, Louisiana twice a week to barter for the goods he needed — uh, thought might come in handy — in exchange for the catch he'd made trapping, fishing, or even diving in the bayous where he lived. He never traveled far into town from the docks. In fact he did most of his business right there on the water with Cahoui's. At least that was what was supposed to happen, but he hadn't showed up in town for close to three weeks now.

☠ ☠ ☠

It was getting on toward five-o-clock when we swung off the open water canal a few miles past Four Point and snaked our way east up the Cocodrie Bayou toward Dezi's place. It's not like we'd visited before, but my dad had pointed the place out the first time we cruised by together.

"Pete," said Bart, once again breaking the silence as we trolled in and out of the green, swampy passages, "there's not much going on here, *padnat.** I don't see a single sign that anyone has even come this way."

"Yeah, it may have been awhile," I agreed. "It's not likely we'd see much evidence this late in the ballgame. Dezi's probably the only one that keeps this channel open at all."

"*Fo' troo,*" added Bart.

Indeed, the duck grass*, magnolias*, and algae seemed to have been undisturbed for some time. It was a pretty sure guess that no one had taken a boat by this route for a good week at least.

Bart, sixteen and somewhat hefty, knew these waters like he knew his way to the kitchen in the dark. Not only did he know his way, he knew how to track. I hadn't really needed to remind him about what evidence a boat would leave in passage through the bayous. He was a pro exactly like his game-warden father, who often took him out on patrols in search of poachers and other riffraff. Seems the bayous were a haven for all kinds of outside sorts — outside, that is, of the law.

☠ ☠ ☠

Bart Davis and I were best friends, I suppose on account of our fathers being such good friends as well. Since my pa was Sheriff of Terrebonne Parish*, Warden Davis and he had the opportunity to work on many a case together, as had Bart and I. Besides, we liked to hang out together — camping, fishing, exploring — mostly outdoor stuff, but we liked movies and video games, too.

We often hung out at Arlow's Pizza with our other friends, as well — my girl Carla, Keilah, Dallas (the new kid from Texas), Reed, Will and Beth, mostly. We all went to the same homeschool extension and the same church. But, it was Bart and I who were tight, having grown up here in the 'ragged toe of the boot*' and knowing each other all our lives.

We had so many good times and adventures together; like all the times we got to go up in his Dad's surveillance chopper or out on the airboat to look for poachers.

We'd hunkered down together with our families in the Parish Courthouse basement when hurricanes Gustov and Katrina came barreling through. Or like the time we spent a week in a lighthouse on vacation together, stumbling upon a drug smuggling operation. Wow! That was our first mystery, but that's another story.

☠ ☠ ☠

"I can't figure it," I said, "he's been into town every Tuesday and Friday as faithfully as Pastor shows up Sundays to church."

"My dad says he's been comin' in all regular-like since before I can remember."

"That's just it, Bart, 'something's afoul in Denmark.'"

"You mean in De Cade,*" corrected Bart.

"Well yeah, but I was quoting Shakespeare."

"You pick the oddest times to swing into that drama stuff, Pete."

"You know me," I joked, striking a dramatic pose — my index finger in the air, "student of the stage, disciple of drama, thespian of theater, fanatic of film..."

"Yeah, yeah, save it for Broadway. They'll give you an Ollie one day."

"Oscar. That's Oscar, which is the Academy's honor for film, not the stage. The stage award is the Tony, while TV is..."

"Whatever, dude!"

Okay, Bart didn't share my drama interest, but otherwise, we were pretty much the same. Except, he can play the accordion; all I can play is my iPod.

☠ ☠ ☠

Generally, we spent the good part of our summers cooling off and kicking back down by the canal and, since that was where Dezi brought his wares to barter, we'd grown accustomed to seeing him. On more than one occasion he'd supplied us — our father's that is — with leads and useful information that helped them locate assorted fugitives, poachers, and the like. Could be, I suppose, a likely reason for his sudden disappearances. At least Bart and I suspected foul play; our dads seemed skeptical even though we told them about the two men on the dock from the day we last saw Dezi.

Actually, Dezi never was any trouble to regular folk and they didn't mind doing business with him either. He was as fair and square as they come. Yet, no one seemed to care that he hadn't been into town either. I guess that's why *we* were out looking for him. Crazy as he might be, he was actually a rather likable fellow and we sorta missed him even if no one else did.

3 VOODOO DRUMS

W hat time is it Pete?"
"Nearly six-fifteen by my watch. It'll be dark before too long." We'd have to be heading back within the hour if we were to get home before sunset. We were prepared — our camping gear on hand — to stay if need be, but I certainly didn't want to.

The bayous were beautiful by day. The brightly-colored, sweet-scented magnolias and fragrant, twisted pines mixed with the earthy and pungent damp smells of the forest floor made the bayous a unique and wondrous place. However, at night they can be quite un-settling. Wildcats and black bear roamed the twilight. Besides, I prefer to sleep in my air-conditioned bedroom on muggy days like this.

"That's what time I thought it was."

Bart was pretty good at telling time by the sun, or the stars for that matter. If we didn't find Dezi's place within the hour we would have to give up and try again tomorrow with an earlier start.

☠ ☠ ☠

"Look, Pete," exclaimed Bart, "that's it!" I wasn't going to fall for that again. I ducked low into the boat. "Pete?!"

Bart looked at me like I was a lunatic, but that expression changed quickly to one of understanding as he recalled his earlier charade.

"No, *fo' troo,*" he assured me.

"That's it all right," I said rising up cautiously for a look, "it's gotta be."

"Looks deserted."

"Yep," I agreed, "Let's have a peek. Pull the boat over to the quay there near Dezi's dinghy."

"You got it," said Bart, cutting the motor down to a near halt as we drifted slowly toward a levee* where a rickety makeshift walkway jutted precariously out into the marshy water. When we were a few feet from the landing Bart flipped the rudder, cut the motor altogether and our vessel swung in sideways up next to Dezi's boat, Scum Bucket. A gator lazily slid nearly silently into the water from the nearby bank.

Sitting in silence we studied the scene. Just ashore leaned Dezi's *cabane** — a small structure of assorted boards, tin roofing and canvas, moaning softly in the light breeze that moved spookily through the evening bayou. Squinting against the now magenta sunset, I surveyed the structure for signs of life.

"Looks like no one's home," Bart said, stating the obvious.

"If anyone *is* here, they're asleep — or dead," I muttered. It was all too quiet. Even the frogs and crickets were hushed, as if holding their breath for something creepy to happen. It seemed so, so... uninviting that I wanted to turn around right then and there and head for home, but Bart had other ideas. Before I knew it he'd leapt from the boat and began tying her to the dock.

"Come on, Pete," he whispered. I reluctantly followed, moving toward the shaky *cabane.*

"Why are you so gung-ho about rushing in where angels fear to tread?"

"What? You chicken?"

"Cautious. Okay?"

"Good," came his reply and he waved his hand in front of his nose, "Whew! Catch a whiff of that?"

"Excuse me," I said noticing a strong odor, "I had beans for dinner." But it wasn't me, it was the assaulting stench of a day-old, maybe a week old, catch of *gou-jon.** It didn't take long for a little fish to work up a great stink in the stewing swelter of these swamps.

Moving forward I noticed an assortment of crude wooden frames about the "yard" over which were stretched several different animal hides, mostly what looked to be nutria and rabbit. Soon we were standing silently outside the shack's small door. It was made of a flimsy and weathered aluminum roofing material rustily hinged to one side of a rustic frame. The 'door' banged gently in the breeze. I stood on one side of the entryway, Bart on the other.

At last I twitched my head toward the door and whispered, "Well, come on," I urged, "knock." Bart shook his head.

"*You* go first," he whispered.

"Who's the chicken?" I retorted. Still we made no move. Time ticked by and I grew impatient — the suspense was killing me. A few fireflies braved the growing dusk, dimly sky-dancing in the shadows of the underbrush.

Finally, heaving a sigh, I knocked meekly then called out, "Hello?" No one answered.

"Dezi?" said Bart in a half hollering squeak. A crooked smile turned up the corner of my mouth. Bart scowled.

I slowly turned the door back on its reluctant, squeaking hinges. Clicking on the flashlight I'd remembered to bring with me, I swung the beam into the opening and scanned the room.

It wasn't much to look at. I'd have said it wasn't much to sneeze at, but sneeze I did as the dust and must swirled in the heavy air.

"Bless you," said Bart.

A mildewing canvas hammock hung in the far corner of the shack. A dented and rusted oil drum stove sat against the back wall sporting a single metal pot that flaked blue enamel. Various canned goods, a couple of dented tins and an old soda bottle sat sparsely on a pile of three old-fashioned apple crates next to a stack of wood against the right wall. An assortment of fishing articles and animal traps hung from a smattering of hooks on the wall above them. An old-fashioned perk coffeepot lay on the tattered tarp floor.

In the center of the room stood a simple plank table next to another crate that likely served as a chair. On the table sat an unlit propane lantern and the hand-held UV lamp that Dezi had bought the last time we saw him. Against the wall on the left, near the ham-mock, sat a closed chest and another wooden box; these appeared to serve as dressers since a number of clothing items looked like they were trying to escape. On the wall above, hung a mirror shard and, of all things, what looked an awful lot like a framed, cobweb-ridden, college diploma to which I was curiously drawn. I ambled closer.

"Hey Bart, take look at this." He came to my side as I read aloud, "The Louisiana University Marine Consortium, Desmond R. Comeaux, Ph.D."

"Ph.D?!" exclaimed Bart, "Dezi holds a doctorate?"

"From LUMCON," I added. "Who woulda thunk?"

"I guess it's true; you really *can't* judge a book by its cover."

"*Fo troo*, dat," I replied.

Nothing else seemed particularly out of the ordinary — at least for an old hermit-coot-type. Bart sat down at the table and started tinkering with the lantern, at-temptting to light it with matches he'd found in a tin by the stove. Striking one, he coaxed the lamp to a dim glow. He blew out the match and I switched off my flash-light, walked over and leaned on the table next to him.

"What's this?" Bart pulled a scrap of paper from the tabletop. Shrugging, I leaned toward the light to read. I narrowed my eyes and peered at the note. I could see number sequences — most of them crossed-out — scribbled down the side of the paper. These were next to a single hand-scrawled word: 'trinity'. I was about to comment, but I didn't get the chance. The eerie hush was suddenly interrupted by a distant — but not too distant — drumming!

"Voodoo*!" I gasped. Bart quickly snuffed the lamp and leapt to his feet, clutching the paper scrap in his fist and jamming it into the pocket of his jeans. I clicked on the flashlight, covering most of the beam with the palm of my hand.

"Let's get out of here *vite, vite*!*" Bart exclaimed excitedly. I agreed with a hearty nod and we dashed toward the door and flung it open. Instantly, an intense heat and brilliant light washed over us. At the water's edge both boats were in flames! We'd not taken more than two steps toward the shoddy pier when two explosions — one immediately on the heels of the other — knocked us backwards. Showers of water and flaming debris flew in all directions as we lit hard on our backsides.

4 FOLLOWING THE LIGHT

Whoa!" exclaimed Bart, scrambling to his feet. I sat up in time to see the fragmented stern of my boat sink gurgling into the bayou. It heaved out a final hiss as the flaming piece was extinguished by the water. Small pools of gas and oil continued to burn on the surface of the bayou. Instantly, as if ordered to do so by some unseen captain, we simultaneously crouched low to the ground and dove into the scrubby foliage cover.

"My boat!"

"Gone, *padnet*," replied Bart, "to Davy Jones locker, I'm afraid."

"Duh. Someone torched my boat, dude! And the gas tanks exploded! And... Hey, what happened to the drums?" The percussion had ended as abruptly as it had begun.

"I don't know, but it might have something to do with *that*," Bart said quietly, motioning his head to a position off behind Dezi's hut. Through the twilight-shadowed underbrush I saw a single torch flickering in the distance. "You think *they* might be responsible for the drumming?"

"Yeah, and my boat, dude!"

"So, why didn't they come inside the *cabane*?" Bart wondered out loud.

"I dunno, must not have expected anyone to be here."

"Cuz they'd already abducted Dezi."

"Probably. So, what are we gonna do?"

"Lay low, I guess. Not much we can do. It's getting dark now."

"Fo' troo, and most of our gear is gone."

"Say," Bart volunteered, "there are a few supplies in Dezi's hut. We can commandeer, you know, abscond what we need."

"Borrow, huh?"

"Why not? We can pay Dezi back when we find him."

Neither of us moved and, for a moment, neither of us spoke.

"Ya know, it doesn't make sense, destroying our boats and leaving us behind," I said after a bit.

"No, it doesn't," Bart agreed. "Maybe they thought both were Dezi's. Maybe they'll come back if they figure out that one wasn't. I think we should stay put a

tad longer and see what happens, if anything."

"Sure," was all I could muster. It sounded like a plan to me and I didn't have one
of my own to offer. Besides, I really didn't
want to traipse off into a zombie ambush
or the clutches of some maniacal voodoo
queen. I certainly wasn't into a voodoo
*mojo**. Of course, I didn't believe in that
stuff. At least that's what I tried to tell myself. Maybe, it was...I don't know, maybe
demons were involved? I do believe in
demons. And angels. As a child of God,
would His angels protect me? I sent up an
unspoken prayer; Psalm 91:11 popping
into my mind: *"For he will order his angels
to protect you in all you do."*

☠ ☠ ☠

It seemed like the longest time that we
lay silently on our bellies watching the
torch gutter and wane into the distance. I
didn't like lying in the brush waiting to be
eaten by some swamp creature — a crock,
cat or coyote.

Bart blurted, "Let's roll!" and I nearly
jumped out of my hide.

"Dork! What are you trying to do? Give
me a heart attack?"

"What?"

"What?! It's all quiet like and I'm lying there all freaked out about zombies and gators and, you, you, you..."

"You, you, you're such a drama queen, Pete. You're sixteen years old; you ain't gonna die from a heart attack — at least not from a fright. Now what say we go after some answers?"

I growled and picked up my flashlight.

☠ ☠ ☠

Stumbling through the dark, we crept back into the old shack. Slipping inside, I clicked on the flashlight and once again scanned the room. I found an old fishing vest full of pockets and a creel nearby. Inside the creel I found a knife and an assortment of hooks, line and other fishing stuff. I emptied the creel of all but the knife and slung it over my shoulder and tossed the vest to Bart.

"Here," I instructed, "put some goods into this — anything useful."

Bart and I rummaged through the shelves. We collected a tin of *tasso**, a rusty can-opener, two good-sized pop-top cans of beans, a parcel of dried fruit, and an old jug of water that seemed to smell alright. From the table Bart grabbed the tin of matches. I found a length of rope near the hammock and another flashlight and, after checking to see that it worked, put it in the creel.

We drew near the door and peeked through the crack. I stuck my head out and surveyed the area, "Coast is clear — I think."

"Go!" Bart shoved me out the door. I stumbled once again into the brush and we both hit the soggy ground panting, my heart pounding wildly in my chest. *Was Bart sure about that heart attack?*

"Now what?" I asked as my nerves began to settle.

"Don't know," Bart replied, "wait I guess. Wait here, for now."

"We've *been* waiting, dude! I feel like I'm waiting for my demise — for some carnivorous creature to sneak up on me and use me as a nighttime snack!"

"Look," said Bart, "I gotta do some more thinking. Okay?"

I nodded, shrugged and sat. I could almost hear the gears of his mind turning over in the silence so I left him alone. I, too, was thinking. I was thinking we might die. I was thinking that I really didn't want to be here right now. I wished I was home safe in bed or, at least, in town — maybe at the pizza parlor or the arcade with the gang.

I thought back — back to last week's paintball outing: Will, Reed, Bart and I, took Dallas just to show him the ropes.

The girls went along, too, but decided to hang in the snack bar and feed themselves on gossip — which was not necessarily standard procedure (Keilah for one made Scarlett Johansson and Angelina Jolie look like pansies when it came to handling firearms).

"Whoop, whoop! I gotcha, I gotcha!" Dallas hooted jubilantly from behind an inflatable barrier.

"No you didn't; you missed me," I retorted. "Time out okay, I'll show you." I came out from hiding, hands up and turned to show my back side. He had indeed missed, splatting only a nearby obstacle. He poked his head out to look as I continued backing toward him.

"Ah, shucks!" he exclaimed in his southern drawl. I was now right in front of him.

"So," I said, turning, "do you feel lucky, punk?" and bringing my gun down from above my head, "Well, do ya? Huh?" Then quickly I added, "Time in!"

He leveled his gun and said, "Go ahead, make my day." And I did. I dived left, rolled and shot a volley of five rounds at his knees. Two connected. He managed to squeeze off a couple shots, but, again, they were both misses. I rolled behind another obstacle and instantly felt two stinging blasts on the small of my back.

"Gotcha!" It was Bart standing directly over me. "And why is that?" he questioned rhetorically, cocking his head. "Because, you know, I've always got your back, *bon ami**."

I whipped my feet around in a break-dance-like move and took his feet out from under him. He fell on top of me as a volley of shots whizzed over his head. "And, as usual, I've got yours. You're still in the game. That was Will. Now, take him out."

Bart rose to his feet and roared insanely above the pulsating Techno music, "Fire at Will!" Reed was already out; Bart would have Will down in a minute, so the rest of us went to join the girls.

"Hey, Cowboy, how'd you fare?" Carla shouted to Dallas as we came through the door.

"I felt like a shootin' duck," he replied.

"Sitting duck," came Beth (she was a stickler for detail), "that's *sitting* duck." Keilah and Carla giggled.

"I weren't sittin'," he retorted, "I was shootin'."

"He fought like a great army scout," I said in support, but the afterthought came to me and I added laughingly, "like Custer at Wounded Knee."

"Hey, I took out Reed, didn't I, Reed?"

"Yeah," Reed responded, "Dallas ambushed me while I was loading."

"You weren't loadin', retorted Dallas, "you was standin' there like a cow lookin' at a new gate."

"Okay, I was thinking."

"Yeah," said Bart, "your head wasn't really in the game, dude. Something wrong?" Will and Bart sauntered in, removing their gear.

"Ah, nothing serious," he reply, "I was just thinking about the recent zombie rumors that have been cooking out on the southwest side of town. Zombies are of..."

"Come now, Reed," said Carla, "you don't believe that stuff do you?"

"You scared, Reed?" taunted Will jokingly.

"Nah, just interested," answered Reed. "I don't believe they could be 'walking dead'," he indicated quotation marks with bent fingers, "but I do believe people see or have contact with something — something real."

Bart jumped into the conversation, "*Fo' troo*, I heard about the supposed sightings. It's only superstition, nothing more. The people in west parish are..."

"No," interrupted Reed, "I think there's something to it all — something scientific."

"Or spiritual," I muttered under my breath.

"You believe in little green aliens, too, huh?" said Carla to Reed, not hearing my remark.

"In UFO's, yes, but..."

And that's pretty much how it went. Reed was the intellectual sort, Bart and Carla — the skeptics. They could go on and on arguing about such things and often did. The rest of us drifted off to play the arcade games.

☠ ☠ ☠

So here we were — far away from all the usual comforts — out in the bayous. Our parents wouldn't be worried — they knew we could take care of ourselves — since we'd come prepared to "go camping" as we often did. We would not need shelter to-night unless it was to ward off the skeet-ers and whatever else roamed the night — wild boar, gators and nutria. Or, ah, zom-bies?

"Here," said Bart, handing me a hunk of *tasso*, "it's not Arlow's, but it'll do." *How'd he know I was thinking of pizza?* Arlow's was the main pizza place in town. Jake Mandingo, who named the place four years earlier when he'd opened it, never explained the name. When asked he just said, "Seemed right." Needless to say, a big slice of 'za would have hit the spot.

5 CAPTURED!

ome on," said Bart standing, "let's get a move on." I rose and followed him down the obscure path. The ground one can cover during daylight in a quarter hour turns to three-quarters in the dark. *Maybe the torch bearers wanted us to follow, I thought, maybe we were walking right into a trap. And what about those voodoo drums?* Like I say, I'm not superstitious or anything, but I'd certainly heard enough Cajun stories of the walking dead. The hoot of an owl sent shivers up my spine.

"You think there're zombies out here, don't you?" Bart asked. *Does he read my mind?*

"Never seen one, but maybe there's something to them. Could be demonic possession for all I know. Remember what Reed's been telling us about recent sight-

ings; and Sister Tee-Tee says they're *fo'
troo.* I don't think she'd lie. She's like a
saint and she's been around these parts a
good long time."

"Yeah, Tee-Tee must be like ninety
years old."

"And Cajun, too."

"But there can't really be 'walking dead'
can there?" I said looking for reassurance.

"Some say it's voodoo magic, others said
it's psycho-logical — a sort of hypnotism,
still others claim it's drug induced, but, in
my book, zombies are freaky however they
get that way."

"I'll say. Maybe they're dead folks walking around to save funeral expenses," I
joked. He didn't laugh and I added, "I was
thinking they might be demon possessed
people or some other manifestation of evil
spirits."

"Maybe," he said thoughtfully, "Do you
remember that story of the zombies that
came after old man DeBower up north of
here last month?"

"No, and you're not going to tell me it
now, either."

"Sister Tee-Tee said that maybe twenty
or thirty of them came out of the swamps
knocking on DeBower's door, moaning and
wailing and knocking; wheezing and hacking..."

"I told you, I didn't want to hear it,
Bart."

"He claims the zombies were bent on getting his 'secret elixir,'" Bart continued, "that is, the moonshine he's making. Anyway, they're knocking and banging on the doors, on the windows and on the sides of the house all the time wheezing out a low rhythmic chant, 'Devour DeBower, devour DeBower.'"

"Stop it, okay?"

"His dogs take off, tails tucked between their legs and yelping. DeBower's heart is pounding in his chest. He's sweating, cold, clammy, and he takes the shotgun down from over his mantle and loads two shells from the hutch drawer. There's a strong odor of rotting flesh in the air — hot and putrid. They're banging louder and harder. Chanting, chanting, chanting. He can see them through the windows — maggoty skin hanging from their faces, sunken eyes..."

"Bart, shut up."

"He blows out the first window and then the second and begins to reload, but now they're pouring through the..."

"Shut up! That's only a story designed to scare people to keep them from moon shining."

"Alright weenie," said Bart throwing his hands in the air, "but, you know, Sister Tee-Tee wouldn't lie and they did find De-Bower crazed and half-starved wandering through the streets of town."

"Outright lie, no, but Cajun's are known for embellishing the truth a bit. It was pro-bably just a sheriff's posse or he'd had a little too much of his own elixir."

"I suppose, but what about the story of the walking casket?"

"I don't need to hear any more, okay."

"Oh, you'll like this one. There's this water-logged casket that shows up at this lady's door and when she answers it the drip-ping casket chases her through the house and traps her in the bathroom. It's about to get her when she pulls some throat lozenges from the medicine cabinet to stop the coffin."

I chuckled a bit, "Yeah, that's better."

"Did you hear the one about...Man! What gives with these vines?" yelled Bart, tripping headlong and mashing his face into the mud next to a salt mound jutting from the forest floor.

"Shhhhh!" I shushed. He sloshed, then standing to his feet, we marched on as he cleaned his face on his sleeve. That put a damper on the zombie talk — at least for the time being — and I was glad for it. I smirked for a moment, thinking of his just desserts.

☠ ☠ ☠

As we pushed even further into the confines of Cocodrie Bayou, I wondered

what trouble lay ahead. The nearly full
moon rose up in the eastern sky and shone
from time to time be-tween the dark clouds
that rolled hauntingly over its face. Mostly,
when the moon wasn't hidden be-hind the
clouds, there was enough light to make
our way without the aid of the flash-lights.
Eerie shadows made the trek all the more
ominous.

We moved with caution — especially
when crossing a *float'on** — with as much
haste as we could muster in the soggy
overgrowth. There was only one trail and,
though not heavily used, it was easy to
follow — even in the growing darkness.
Thirty minutes passed by my best reckon-
ing and at last Bart, in the lead, came to a
sudden stop. I nearly barreled into him
and ended up giving him a 'flat tire' as I
stepped on his heel.

"Hey! Take it easy," he said in hushed
tones, fixing his shoe.

"Sorry."

"Whattya make of that?" said Bart
pointing ahead at...a head!

A head on a stick! I nearly lost my
lunch — both gasping and gulping, I put
my hand over my mouth. "Ugh. Let's get
out of here."

"You gonna let *that* bother you? Look,
it's not even real." Bart yanked the head
from its post; it was a mask and it was
masking something alright — a video sur-

veillance camera and it was pointing right at us!

"Uh, oh!" We both spoke in unison.

"Now, let's get out of here!" agreed Bart.

"I don' tink dat's a-what's going to happen, *moi ami**."

The deep Cajun voice wasn't Bart's. We both turned around fast as the sound of cocking guns split the night air. Time slowed instantly and our turn seemed to happen in slow-mo. The swamp critters all became silent. Before we made it completely around we were bathed in a bright searchlight. All I could see were light and silhouettes. Three men — big men, two of them with guns—stood outlined against the back-drop of the flood lamp's blaze.

"So, what you two boys doing out on a night like dis, all alone in the bayou? Taking a little moonlight stroll, perhaps?" The men laughed together.

My hands rose slowly into the air above my head. Bart's did the same. We'd seen far too many Westerns I guess. Maybe that was a good thing, knowing what to do when someone waves a gun at you. Anyway, no answers came to mind, so we made none.

"A'right den boys, let's get a move on, *vite vite.*" The middle figure, a tall, heavy-set man dressed in ragged jeans and a grimy muscle shirt, gestured to his right with the barrel of his gun as the other two moved toward us. As we turned and fell into line, the light turned with us, shone upon our backs and illuminated the trail before us, creating huge shadows dancing hauntingly upon the foliage above our heads. I felt the business end of a gun poke the small of my back so I got a move on, like the man said.

"Really now, what *are* you doing out here, boys? You wanna tell me or do I need to — shall I say — 'coax' it out of you?"

There was a shrouded threat in that word coax; I knew it called for an answer and a possible few flew through my mind. They all sounded crazy. They all sounded made up. All but the truth, that is, and I thought *that* might really get us in trouble. Never-the-less, the truth is what I told, though I really pared it down to the bare bones. While some Cajuns may be prone to embellishing their tales, I was partial to the truth and nothing but the truth — even if it wasn't the whole of the truth.

"We came out prepared to do some camping. We were hoping to meet a friend," I said, answering in all honesty — without all the detail.

Bart piped in with his two cents, "Our folks said we could and they know exactly where we are." *Oh, that's convincing Bart,* I thought, *why'd you go and say that? Now they know nobody knows where we are.*

"Oh, dey do, do dey?" A smile broadened across his face. "And who are you looking for? Perhaps I've already found dem." There was an oiliness about this big fellow that repulsed me. He made me nervous and he gave me the creeps. It didn't help that he and his goons were toting those guns either.

"We were looking for Waldo," Bart just had to run off at the mouth. "Have you seen him?"

"Bart, cool it, will y…"

"Both of you cool it!" barked the big men, "I know all I need to know. And I know a lot more dan you told me. But what *you* don't know is *what* I know and I'm gonna keep you guessing, but you'll know what I'm talking about soon enough. In the meantime, do me a favor and shut up." I wasn't going to argue and it looked like Bart got the clue, too.

6 A COMPOUNDING PROBLEM

We stumbled on for two or three minutes and soon arrived at a strange and shoddy compound surrounded by a tall — I'd say eight foot high — chain-link fence which had spirals of razor-wire crowning its top. Another surveillance camera hung over the gated entrance. Inside the fenced area stood three buildings and four army-issue style tents erected on raised wooden platforms. Two of the buildings were unpainted and rustic-sided with a hodgepodge of scrap building materials and roofed with rusty tin. One looked to be about the size of a two-car garage; the other less than half that size — maybe eight by twelve.

The third building, nicer than the others, was set off on the opposite side of the com-pound away from the others. It was finished and painted and looked to be a small stilted bungalow-style home. There were curtains covering the windows. I could see a warm glow of light showing through each them.

It had a small *galerie** upon which sat two mismatched rocking chairs. Numerous bundles of dried flowers, herbs, feathers, and an assortment of skins, heads and other parts of snakes and animals hung from the porch's open rafters swinging as if from gallows in the humid breeze. That indicated that the inhabitants of the bungalow were, more than likely, into making magic — voodoo, potions, *mojos**, *gris-gris** — who knew what?

Near the house was a sprawling chicken yard surrounded by, what else, chicken wire and containing a small coop. The yard was overcrowded with dozens and dozens of the birds, clucking and cackling while they scratched the bare, muddy ground. The conditions looked inhumane. A "fowl" stench wafted our way from the caged area.

The only other things within the compound were a mud-encrusted, camo-painted Jeep and about a half-dozen rusting industrial barrels that sat maybe a hundred feet or so from the middle-sized building. I was about to ask questions about what I saw when we arrived at the smallest building and our captors shoved us forcefully up the steps. I nearly fell, but managed to stumble forward and remain upright.

"Oh lookie, home," said one of the guards laughingly, the other joining in. "You're going to like it here. The rats do." That really set them off. *What was so funny?* I felt a shiver run up my spine. Bart glanced at me his dark eyebrows furrowed.

"Tie dese two up," commanded the big boss in the muscle shirt, "I'll be in my office. I'll deal wit dem later." He set off toward the bungalow. "So good to have some Guinea pigs drop in, just when you need them."

"Guinea pigs," laughed the larger of the two men, "squeak, squeak."

"Shut up," said the other as he fumbled with a ring of keys and then worked one of them into the rusty lock. It took him more than a few seconds so he grumbled at the other heavy, "Why don't you ever shoot this thing with some WD-40?"

"Ain't my job."

"Who's is it then? You think some lock fairy is gonna come by each night and wave a magic wand over it?"

"Why would we need another fairy around here when we've got you?"

"Why, I ought to..."

At that moment the lock groaned open and his attention was turned, but I think their mounting hostility was taken out on us. Neither of them asked us to move inside and they didn't wait even a second for us to do so. Instead I was grabbed by the hair and sent flying into the shack. Bart got a similar treatment. I knew complaining would only get me more of the same, so we both kept our mouths shut as the larger of the two men lit a nearby lamp, then lit a cigar from the lamp. He wedged the cheroot into the corner of his mouth and exhaled a stream of noxious fumes.

7 LOCKED AWAY

The inside of our new *'maison*'* wasn't much to sneeze at — it certainly wasn't the Ritz Carlton. There was a great deal of dust and disarray about the place as it was cluttered with an array of articles: garden tools, sacks, boxes, lumber, *et cetera, et cetera, et cetera*. I took it for their storage shed. *Great,* I thought, *I'll be stored away and forgotten like a broken lawn mower.*

"I'll take these," growled the cigar henchmen as he took my creel and Bart's vest, puffing on his stogie, "Now sit down." The smoke and dust motes gave life to the moon beams that pried through the cracks around the door and window, eerily illuminating the room in a bluish haze.

He gestured toward a couple of heavily worn, mismatched armchairs. We followed his order. The other thug went to a dilapidated writing desk that sat against one of the walls under a boarded up window, opened a drawer and removed a partially used roll of duct tape. "Hands behind you, through the rungs," he demanded. We complied as he pulled the tape out from the roll.

"Why are you doing this?" asked Bart, "We were just..."

"Shut up, ain't none of your business. You're trespassing," replied the guard with the tape. "Your mommies never tell you trespassing's illegal?"

"Well, yeah, but..." returned Bart.

"That was a rhetorical question. I said shut up or I'll tape up your pie holes, too."

The man began wrapping Bart's wrists in a figure eight of tape. I watched intently in silence as he then wound the tape a-round the rungs of the chair back. He cir-cled the tape around Bart's chest and the chair back, then over his lap and under the chair. Around and around he went. As he bent over I noticed a *gris-gris* fall from his shirt. The tiny pouch dangled from a cord around his neck. The amulet smelled of cinnamon — it was a charm intended to give the wearer success. *These guys were into voodoo!*

The heavy finished off by taping each of Bart's ankles to the chair's legs, then he moved to me, applying the same process. However, he ran out of tape before finish-ing the first of my legs. He'd wrapped it but twice when the paper began to show on the roll.

"Eh, that'll do," he said, tossing the cardboard roll aside on the already cluttered floor. Obviously housekeeping wasn't high on the list of priorities with these guys.

"Okay, Jean, let 'um rot in peace. *Vieus avec moi**, it's supper time," said the other.

"Yeah, I'm starved." With that the one called Jean doused the lamp and they both turned and left, slamming the door behind them. I could hear the rattle-snap of the padlock outside the door and their heavy boots on the steps as they descended.

I looked at Bart; he looked at me.

"Well, that's another fine mess you've got us in," I said, quoting Stan Laurel of Laurel and Hardy fame.

"Why do you always make light of stuff with weird sayings?" asked Bart.

"It's from the old black and white..."

"I know what it's from, 'Ollie'. You watch *way* too many movies, dude."

"Well, Will Roger's said, 'The movies are the only business where you can go out front and applaud yourself.'"

"Meaning?"

"Oh, nothing. It just came to mind."

"Okay, Brainiac, any way out of *this* come to mind?"

"Ah, well, Indiana Jones..."

"Sheesh!"

"Wait, wait. This will work. I'm going to push my way over to that lamp, knock it to the floor, take a broken shard of the chimney, tip myself over, get a piece of broken glass in my hands and saw through the tape."

I could see Bart's dumbfounded face as he recalled a similar scene from "The Last Crusade."
"Thank God for movies!" he exclaimed — I'm sure with genuine gratitude and reverence.

☠ ☠ ☠

I spent the next thirty-some minutes working at my plan. Pushing my feet against the littered floor I hopped my chair across the room, inching toward the kerosene lantern. I couldn't reach the lamp with my head as I'd planned; it was too far in on the table. So I worked my chair under the table and thumped my chair up and down until it jarred the table enough to knock the lamp over; it then rolled off the table in an arc and crashed to the floor. The acrid smell of kerosene quickly filled the small room as both reservoir and chimney broke. I silently hoped no one would light a match or somehow cause a spark.

I hopped my chair back from the table and rocked from side to side. Tipping myself over, I slammed to the floor bruising my shoulder considerably and nearly bonking my skull.

I fished around behind me, my hands straining against the bond of the duct tape, reaching through the slats in the chair toward the floor. I twisted, turned, shuffled and bounced as I searched blindly behind me for a piece of the glass. I was a bit grossed out when a cockroach the size of a small mouse scuttled by, all too near my face.

Finally, I got hold of a hefty shard and wriggled it into the duct tape figure eight between my wrists. That was all of perhaps ten minutes; the rest of the time was spent sawing through the duct tape. The glass was slippery from the kerosene and job seemed to take forever. My thumb cramped painfully.

"Are you going to take all day?" questioned Bart.

"No," I said, "I thought I'd hurry and slice my wrist open and save those hooligans the trouble of killing me."

"You dissin' on me, *padnet*?"

"Whatever gave you that idea?"

I was finally able to pull my hands through the rungs and rip the tape off with some ease and, considering the removal of my knuckle hair, some pain. I then worked on my feet and waist which went much more quickly. Scrambling up from the floor I then turned to release Bart. "Maybe, I ought to leave you," I said with a smirk.

"After we've come so far together, *mon cher**?"

I quickly cut through his bonds and Bart was up in a flash. He bolted to the door separating the two rooms and turned the handle. That door, like the front, was locked fast.

"Hmm, no easy way out," he said, "Looks like it's only that boarded up window."

I noted it was boarded from the outside, which was good. "No glass," I said, "maybe we can shove the planks off without much noise."

"Let's get to work, Pete."

I climbed up on the desk and set the soles of my shoes against the bottom board. Bart planted his back against mine and braced as I kicked. The board loosened. I kicked again and it flew outward. There was little sound as it landed softly in some bushes below the window. I leaned forward and stuck my head out. No one was it sight.

"All clear," I said after pulling my head back in. Moving to the second board up, I kicked it clear of the window as well. Now there was enough space to wriggle out between the bottom sill and the third board in the window. I crawled through and dropped to a crouch low to the ground next to the building. Bart followed me out and hunkered down beside me.

"Okay Pete, now what?"

"I thought we'd do a little song and dance — you know, something from 'Singing in the Rain'."

"Yeah, got an umbrella?" It was, indeed, raining. The wind had picked up as well. Possibly a tropical storm was moving in.

"No," I answered over the wind, "but this is *bon heur*; it will likely keep them inside. Let's see what's up in that other building."

We moved stealthily through the dark and pinned ourselves to the back of the larger building when we got there. All was quiet save for the sound of a chugging generator near the lighted bungalow. We slunk sideways until we were under a window and I twisted around and peered in. It was too murky inside the building to make anything out. I slid back down the wall.

"Too dark," I said, "Wish I had that flashlight."

"Should we try the door?"

"Why not?"

"Come on."

We crawled along the side of the building to-ward the door, keeping as close to the wall as possible. At the first corner Bart peered around the turn. It must have been clear because he moved on. At the second corner he hesitated.

"There's a camera over the door. It's not pointing straight down though," he said in hushed tones. "If we stay real close to the wall I don't think we'll be seen."

We edged closer to the door, hugging the wall. Bart reached up and tried the handle.

"Locked," he said.

"No keyhole though," I pointed out.

"Look here," Bart said gesturing to the wall next to the door frame. A keypad was attached to the wall.

"Oh, great!" I said.

"Yeah, we'll never break the code."

"Hey, how hard can it be? A key-code is usually only four digits."

"Well, let's see Einstein, twelve possible keys — zero through nine, including the splat and pound keys — hundreds of possible combinations, even if we knew what the four digits were that would be..." He glanced at the key-pad and tried a quick calculation in his head, "well, we can ignore the pound key — that's marked 'cancel' — and the splat — which is marked 'enter' — so ten to the fourth power — that only makes ten-thousand..."

"Shoot!" was all I could say. Well, I could have said something else. I mean I could have cursed I suppose, but I really saw no purpose in being coarse — it didn't honor anyone.

"Hey, hey! Wait. The piece of paper!" Bart dug into his pocket, "The sets of numbers. Dezi must have been trying combinations."

Pulling the note from his jeans and un-wadding it Bart read, "Nine, Two, Five, Four. That's the combination that isn't crossed out!"

"Well, try it," I encouraged.

Bart rose cautiously to his feet and, extending his finger, punched in the sequence and stabbed the splat key. There was a click at the door.

"Score!" I exclaimed under my breath, quickly turning the handle. It opened and we slipped inside.

Latching the door behind us, we moved carefully for-ward in the dark, scuffing our feet across the floor. I could hear nothing but our breathing and the thumping of my own heart — and the scuffing.

BAM!

I bumped into something and a light flickered on. The quiet was suddenly shattered by metallic whining! I nearly wet my pants.

8 THE LAB

As it turned out, I'd run into a desk and in doing so joggled a computer mouse which in turn brought a sleeping PC to life. The monitor flickered on and the hard drive began whining. Bart let out his breath.

The building's interior was now dimly lit by the soft blue glow of the computer screen. Looking away from the monitor my eyes adjusted to the eerie light about the room. Next to the desk were a number of lab tables forming an L-shape in the room's center. Mounted on the walls were various cabinets and, sitting on an array of foldable tables, a number of very large terrarium-like tanks. Two barrels, similar to those we'd seen outside were near a back door next to what appeared to be a large steel double-door freezer.

The tops of the lab tables were cluttered with an assortment of beakers, test tubes, Petri dishes and various other scientific paraphernalia including a quality electron microscope similar to the one in my Dad's crime lab. Other than a discarded pair of rubber gloves on the floor near a trash bin, this room was rather clean. We both turned back to look at the door. Hanging next to it were two yellow out-fits that looked like space suits with hoods and gas masks.

"Whoa!" said Bart, "what do you make of those, Pete?"

"Right out of *Contagion*, dude! We are in deep doo-doo."

"Yeah, I think you hit that nail right on the head," said Bart, "those steel cabinets near the back door must be incubators. Looks like they're growing something here."

"But what? That's the ten-thousand dollar question," I responded.

"I'll bet it can't be good. We ought to put on those suits, man."

"I think we'll be alright as long as we don't open anything up. Besides, it'd probably be too late anyway..."

"Yeah," interrupted Bart, "it'd have to be clean unless you had to put on the suits *before* you came in, right?" I think he was fishing for reassurance.

"Guess so," I hoped aloud as I wandered over for a look at the terrariums. I could hear a high-pitched whining noise as I approached. Looking closer I could barely make out a swirling cloud floating over the slimy surface of about four inches of putrid liquid. The vessels were giving off some heat.

"What'd you find?" asked Bart, coming over to join me.

"I don't know." I noticed a small tube lamp affixed to the lid of the tank I was peering into. I fumbled around for the switch and, finding it, clicked it on illuminating the container. It was filled with a thick, swirling cloud of mosquitoes!

9 CRACKING THE CODE

oly Moly Guacamole! There must be millions!" Bart exclaimed under his breath, "What kind of nut would intentionally breed mosquitoes? I'll bet they're hatching left and right in these things."

"Weird," was all I could say. I flicked off the lamp. Once again our eyes had to adjust to the dim light. "Breeding skeeters and cooking up who knows what else with this lab equipment?"

"I don't know, but I'll bet we can find out."

"What!? You're not going to open up anything are you?"

"No way! What do they always do in the spy movies, Mr. Spielberg?"

I thought for a moment then: "Look into the computer files," we said in unison as we dash-ed to the PC. Bart, who was the computer geek, sat in the chair and scanned the desktop for something that might be relevant. Aside from the basics — the Internet icon, the trash-can, 'my com-

puter' and 'my docs' — there were no spe-
cial file folders. The trashcan was empty.
Bart clicked the mouse over 'my docs' and
the window opened revealing the usual
folders: *my pics, my music, my videos*, etc.
— plus three others: *talisman, operation
airwave*, and *maria.*

"Click on that one," I said indicating
operation airwave," because it sounded
like something right out of a war movie.
Bart did so and the folder opened. It was
empty.

"Drat!" exclaimed Bart, not too loudly.

"Yeah, curses, foiled again."

"Don't tell me; that was from 'Dudley
Do-Right', huh?"

"You got it."

"O-kay," Bart said slow and drawn out,
rolling his eyes.

"So…"

"Listen," came the reply, "I don't even
know where to begin."

"Try the other folders?" I suggested
without hesitancy.

"Why not? That one was productive."

I was getting worried about the time
this was taking and the potential for being
dis-covered. Bart easily opened the one
labeled *maria*." It was full of text files that
ended up being email love letters to and
from a Maria and Fidel. The *talisman* file,
like the *operation airwave* file, was empty.

"Another dead end," Bart said with exasperation.

"You know," I said, "What we have here is a failure to communicate." I said it just like in "Cool Hand Luke."

"Yeah, well, go ahead, make my day," answered Bart.

"Hey, you're getting good at that."

"It's not what I need to be good at right now. What I need to be good at is..."

I interrupted because an idea came to mind, "Go back to that *talisman* folder."

"Why? It's empty."

"Maybe and maybe not."

"Oh, yeah, yeah. Hidden files."

Bart clicked the file then right clicked the window and scrolled down the menu to 'show hidden files' and clicked again. A folder popped up labeled *devotions*. We both looked at one another with raised eyebrows. Bart clicked the folder. It was empty, so he did the show hidden files thing again. Another folder revealed itself labeled *father*. It, too, was empty.

"This is a wild goose chase," whined Bart.

"I don't think so. Keep going," I urged, "a talisman is a charm that's supposed to bring good luck. I think we're on to something here."

The next hidden folder was marked *son*. The next, *holy ghost*. But, inside the *holy ghost* folder was an icon—an icon of three intertwined circles!

"I've seen that before, Bart."

"Me too, it's a Celtic symbol for God."

"Well, click it!"

He did and a dialogue box popped up that read:

LUMCON STUDY BIBLE
PASSWORD:

[   ]

"Okay, that's odd," I commented.

"Yeah, why would these guys have a study Bible—a password protected...?"

"No, no. A *LUMCON* study Bible."

"I thought that was lexicon?"

"Well, that *is* a Bible text, but LUMCON is a branch of Louisiana University — the one where Dezi graduated from, like on his diploma."

"Right. So?"

"Okay, letsee...what have we got?"

"Father, Son, Holy Ghost—the triune God..."

"Yeah, and that icon is a representtation of the trinity. Dezi has intentionally left a trail."

"Trinity," I said as it popped into my head.

"Trinity? What, from 'The Matrix' I presume?"

"No, from the scrap of paper."

"Scrap of...oh, yeah!" Bart realized that I'd meant the same scrap with the keypad code.

"Trinity!" we said in unison as the door swung open.

10 THE WALKING DEAD

Bart somehow had the wherewithal to hit the monitor's 'off' button, thus shrouding the room once a-gain in darkness. However, there was no time to hide, much less move. A gangly figure darkened the door-way and walked — more like shuffled — in. The light came on and we were sitting ducks — right in plain sight. I was sure we were about to die. But, it was Dezi!

"Dezi! Are we glad to see you," Bart exclaimed. There was no response. Dezi moved mechanically forward, shuffling past us as if we were invisible. His wiry frame — marked here and there by open running or scabbed over sores — shambled along until he came to one of the cabinets near the skeeter breeders. Opening it, he reached inside and withdrew two items — a syringe and a vial. He closed the cabinet and turned back toward us, staring blankly toward the door.

"Dezi," I said quizzically, "Dezi, it's me and Bart." But again he made no response and continued blindly toward the door in that slow methodical cadence, his lesions shining with a pus-like substance oozing from them. He switched the light off and went out. Bart and I just looked at one another.

"Oh, man!" I said, "I am totally creeped-out."

"He's, he's, he's a z-zombie!" Bart whimpered.

☠ ☠ ☠

We sat there for a moment, unnerved. Finally Bart spoke, "Look, we can't do anything about Dezi right now, but we do need to follow this lead." He switched the monitor back on and typed "trinity" into the password box and hit enter. The window disappeared and another took its place:

LOADING

After what seemed like forever the screen flickered and yet another window opened revealing a notepad text message. I began reading it aloud in hushed tones.

> You have come this far because you have
> somehow discovered one of the mes-

sages I have left. Hopefully you are friendly to our country — a tried and true American patriot. This is my genuine hope because the country that you and I so love is in grave danger. Homeland security and the lives of possibly millions are at stake.

In reading the following you will come to see this and I pray that you will follow the instructions I give. Download this file along with the entire Operation Airwave folder and get them to the authorities immediately. There is not much time, if it's not too late already.

First of all understand that a severely deranged mind is behind this horrific plot. Lucien Péralte is an illegal from Haiti. His mother and sister lived near New Orleans before Katrina, but they died in the aftermath when aid was delayed. Following Katrina, the Cuban government offered to send 1,600 medics, field hospitals and medical supplies to the U.S. to aid the victims, but the U.S. government would not allow it.

Péralte blames the government's slow response, their denial of aid from Cuba, and discrimination for the death of his family. He and his minions — a small army of mostly drug-controlled Haitian/Cajun thugs and a brilliant, but disgruntled, Cuban medical/bio-scientist named Fidel Gonzales Ortega — will stop at nothing in their hate for America. I do not believe any of these "terrorists" are acting on the sanction of their governments. However, they are dangerous. They have created a deadly virulent strain of the West Nile virus...

What followed was a lot of technical jargon and statistics which I didn't understand and quickly scanned to:

...the virulent form (WN-V) that these terrorists have created is far more potent and will kill in far, far greater numbers. <u>They expect that more than one in fifteen who contract the disease will die!</u>

The virus primarily lives in and affects birds and equine animals and is transmitted from host to host by mosquitoes. Humans also contract the disease through mosquito bites. The intent of these terrorists is to inject chickens with the virus and then have an army of mosquitoes feed on the fowl. The mosquitoes will rapidly spread the virus.

<u>The terrorists have also created a vaccination</u> — the formula is also contained in these files.

<u>This virus, kept and being manufactured here, must be destroyed! This is highly hazardous and must be done by trained professionals. You must get word to the proper authorities! Do so immediately and do NOT get caught!</u>

I have been discovered and do not believe I will make it out alive. It is up to YOU to save us all. These terrorists mean business. You may be our only hope.

Good luck and God bless. The fate of
America depends on YOU!

~Desmond Comeaux,
PhD.

P.S. I have also seen additional handiwork
from these madmen. It seems they are
able to control a small army of henchmen
by means of a drug concoction that
numbs their minds and makes these
forces pliable in their hands. However,
many do not last long due to physical
damage these chemicals cause. I suppose
it doesn't matter to them as long as they
control these minions.

"I...I..." Words failed me.

"I know, me too," said Bart, "What do
we do?"

"I have no idea, other than that we have
to get out of here, get Dezi and, somehow,
get back to our Dads."

"We've got no boat, remember."

"But, we have a Jeep. You saw the..."

"No, no. I saw it, but using it would call
attention to us. So far, no one knows we've
escaped. I think.

"Unless Dezi does."

"Yeah. And, if we *are* discovered the
terrorists might accelerate their plan. We
have to get away undetected, even if we
have to leave Dezi behind."

"But, but, if he's under this drug, he
may die!"

"He must have known the risk; we have to get to the authorities. That's what he would want, I'm sure. Quick, see if there is a disk in the desk and let's download this file!"

We both tore through the desk drawers. We found no disk, but I did find a jump-drive and jammed it hurriedly into the USB port. The window popped up and I quickly copied all three file folders to the drive. Removing it, I stuffed the device into the front pocket of my shorts and Bart shut the computer down by holding in the power button. Five seconds and it was off; once again we were plunged into dark-ness. We had to get a move on, but we had no plan.

☠ ☠ ☠

"Look," said Bart, "we can't go back the way we came as we have no boat. There is that Jeep outside, which means we're close to a road — probably Four Point or 57, but we don't know which one or even which direction to go. We start that Jeep and we're heard. Though they will have no way of pursuit, they may, as you said, ac-celerate their plot. Even so, soon we will be missed, if we aren't already. Foot travel is too slow — even if we knew which way to go. I'm just plain out of options, *moi ami.* You?"

"There's got to be something."

"And?"

"Uh," I was thinking like crazy, and then BAM, a thought jumped into my head, "do you remember in *Star Wars* when Han Solo breaks into the prison block with Chewy and Luke and he blasts the com panel and then...oh, that won't work, we don't have blasters. How about Clint Eastwood in..."

"This is serious, dude!"

"Look, I'm thinking, okay!"

"That's dangerous."

"Danger is my middle name."

"Right! Look, Pete, we're *in* danger and, quite frankly, I'm tired of danger. I want to get out of here — alive! This ain't no Bond movie! We aren't the dynamic duo and the Force doesn't surround us and bind us together. We are in deep voodoo doo-doo, dude."

"That's it!"

"What?"

"Bond."

"Sheesh! You are absolutely out of..."

"No, no! We *do* let them know we're here. We let everyone know we're here."

"Are you crazy?! Wait, let me rephrase that: You *are* crazy."

"Crazy is as crazy does. You saw all those barrels out there, right?"

"Yeah."

"Did you see what was written on them?"

"No."

"Flammable."

"Flammable?"

"Flammable."

"Flammable! Yeah!" Bart paused, "And?"

"Duh! That generator out there means gasoline. It's like this, see…"

11 THE PLAN

I visualized it differently than it played out. The idea was to occupy the terrorists, protect the lab — making it inaccessible — and send up a huge signal flare. We would distribute the barrels around the lab building, dig moats, fill them with whatever it was that was in the barrels, set the moats aflame and high tail it out of there in the Jeep. That was how I pictured it anyway. It was too lofty of an undertaking, though. Too much time and work required.

First of all, there would be no moats since they would take forever to dig. Without moats there was too much danger that the wall of fire I envisioned would not be contained and could spread dangerously close to the lab. And secondly, the barrels were way too heavy to move. The Jeep was parked precariously close to those barrels. That meant we would have to move the vehicle away — *if* we could. Then we'd have to start the barrels ablaze and then crank the Jeep over. In so doing our captors might get distracted and think the Jeep went up in the inferno. That, we decided, could all take place in a fraction of the time. Though not ideal, it was our only hope.

Now, how to start the fire?

☠ ☠ ☠

We crouched below the eastern window looking out at the barrels. "Got a light?" I said.

"Uh, those would be in the creel they took."

"Okay then."

"What are our assets?"

"Our what?"

"Our assets — that's what Wesley, a.k.a. the man in black, from the *Princess Bride* calls the stuff around you that might be of use."

"Might be matches in here in the lab; there are Bunsen burners."

"Matches won't work. We'd have to get too close."

"You're right. Hey, I *did* see some extension cords hanging by the back door. There had to be a couple twenty-five-footers and maybe a fifty-footer at least."

"And," Bart was seeing the light, "all we gotta do is cut an end off one, twist the two leads together, set that end in the fuel, string the cords together and plug the other end into a socket..."

"The resulting short will spark and ignite the gas," I said, finishing the thought, "and ka-bloowee!"

"Okay Pete, you get to work on the ignition wires and I'll check out the Jeep."

With that Bart slipped carefully out the door and I flipped on the computer, turned the monitor toward the back of the building and waited for the machine to churn back to life. After what seemed like eons the monitor flickered on, providing some illumination. I quickly moved to the back wall and grabbed the extension cords. I threw one on the workbench and dropped the rest on the floor near my feet as I rummaged through the work-bench drawers in search of a knife.

In the third drawer I came to I found a bunch of junk including a couple of razor blades. I took one and proceeded to saw through the end of one of the cords. It wasn't easy, hurt my index finger and took a while. I'd finished the cut and was stripping the first of the two needed wires — the third, the green ground, wasn't necessary — when Bart dodged back in the door, giving me a start.

"No good," he volunteered, "there are no keys and I don't know how to hot-wire."

"What?! You haven't seen 'Grand Theft Auto'?"

"No, Mr. Hollywood. I suppose *you* have?"

"Of course," I said, peeling the casing off of the second lead and twisting the pair together. "But," I added, my eyes well-adjusted to the dim light, "there's a little something that might be useful swinging next to your noggin."

Bart, turned to the right and saw what I'd seen as he came through the door a moment ago. There, on a nail, hung a key-chain. The cleanest key had "Jeep" stamped on it.

"Score!"

"You ready to blow this popsicle stand?"

"Like Bruce Willis, dude. Come on."

I grabbed the wad of extension cords, throw-ing them over my shoulder. Bart snatched the keys. Ripping out the door we whisked our way to the Jeep and Bart chunked it into neutral. Both of us grunt-ed, groaned and otherwise gasped for breath as we shoved, pushed and strained the Jeep toward the rear of the lab build-ing. Feeling that there was no time to take a breather, Bart tried the keys in the ig-nition for fit. They did. However, he did not attempt to start the vehicle. We could-n't chance that now.

"We are two lucky guys," I said, sweat mingled with the rain rolling down my face.

"Oh, yeah!" heaved Bart, "but we gotta keep moving."

"Just keep moving, keep moving..." I chanted.

"Look Nemo..."

"Dora."

"Whatever. So, I'll take these cords and plug them into one another as I go. You hold the plug end and wait by the outlet inside, but DO NOT plug it in to the outlet. Okay?"

"What? Plug it in?"

"NO! DO NOT..."

"I heard you," Bart grinned, "no plugging in."

"Right. I'll go over to the furthest barrel I can reach—hopefully in the center — and dip the cord in. When I come back..."

"No, listen," interrupted Bart, "You can't immerse the cord. It will need air to spark. The electric field ionizes, stripping electrons from the air molecules..."

"How do you know this stuff, dude?"

"Professor Jenkins at the Homeschool Academy. Besides, most flammable liquids will only ignite in vapor form."

"Okay, dangling right above the liquid then," I said, "Got it! And remember, don't plug it in until I get back."

"You got it, man."

12 BLOWN AWAY

The cords went taut as I passed the third barrel. *Good*, I thought, unscrewing the pour spout on barrel number three and whiffing the contents. It was gasoline all right. *Perfect*. I snatched a stick off the ground and dunked it into the drum an inch and pulled it out. The stick was dry, so I stuck it in two inches and pulled it out. Dry again.

At seven inches I hit liquid. I then measured the stick against the cord. I then let the cord down gingerly into the barrel to about six inches. Hopefully, I had the wires set right above the contents. I had to hope, since I couldn't see inside. I was riveted with fear that I might be blown to bits any minute. So far, so good; I was still in one piece.

I couldn't believe our luck. So far it was holding out. It was amazing that we hadn't been discovered in all this time. I sent up a quick prayer thanking God for the rain and dashed back to the lab. I was nearly through the door when the yard lights flashed on, flooding the compound. In my haste and excitement I had not avoided the security camera over the door.

"Now?" asked Bart. There was a wicked gleam in his eyes.

"Now, I think, would be good."

"Al-righty then." He moved his hand toward the outlet as we crouched on the floor.

"Hey Bart," I said, "pretty good Jim Carrey imitation. I didn't know you had it in you."

"Yeah, well." He was afraid and stalling. "You do know we are maybe a hundred feet from a potentially large blast. That's awfully close, *padnet.*"

"I know, but we've been lucky so far."

"And blessed. God is with us."

"With us is good, with Him — this young — not so good."

"Yeah. Are you sure..."

"Just do it already!" With that I stood to look out the window. The rain had stopped. The flood lights were on. Bart went for the out-let. In that instant — in that matter of seconds — I saw four figures lumbering trance - like across the yard; three quarters of the distance from the barrels to the lab. In the lead was Dezi! They were packing heat — shotguns and rifles.

"Nooooooo!" I screamed, just as the plug sunk in the socket ... just as the spark ignited ... just as the first explosion jolted skyward. It was too late. The blast rocked the side of the building. I turned away right when the window blew inward, scattering beads of tempered glass around the room. Heat rolled over me like a flaming chariot. Visions of Elijah* flashed before me as my hair blew over the top of my head. I ducked as the second explosion hit the building. Bart was already crawling for the back door.

"Bart!" I yelled, "Dezi's out there, Bart. Dezi!"

"What?!"

"Dezi! We have to get him."

"No way, Pete, we *have* to go. Now!"

"But..."

The door crashed open and Dezi staggered in falling to the floor. The door slammed on his leg keeping the entry ajar. The back of his clothing was charred and still smoking. I clamored toward him and cradled him in my arms. "Dezi! Dezi!" I screamed, struggling to turn him over and wrestle his foot through the doorway.

Dezi rolled his eyes open.

"Wha..."

"Dezi, its Peter...Peter and Bart."

Bart was at my side to help. A wretched and lesion-covered hand groped through the crack of the door as I pulled Dezi's leg through.

Bart screamed. I saw a look of shear horror on his face. I turned to the entry as the hand took hold of my collar. Bart jumped to his feet and slammed the full weight of his hefty frame against the door. There was a howl of pain from outside the door, the hand let go of my collar and Bart crashed against the door again. The hand retracted abruptly and Bart shoved the door shut.

"Pe-ter," moaned Dezi preceding a third blast, followed directly by a fourth. Flames brightened the room as the inferno roared outside.

"Come on!" yelled Bart, "I'll help you get him to the Jeep. Better start praying, *pad-net*."

I sent silent petitions up to heaven. Together we dragged Dezi along the floor leaving a wake in the beads of glass as tongues of fire licked the side of the lab. Somehow we wrestled Dezi to the back door and managed to hoist him into the Jeep. He wasn't a large man, but being pretty much out of it, a dead weight. We struggled with haste into the vehicle. I could feel the heat from the flames behind us as Bart turned the key.

"Smokin'!" he yelled as the engine sparked to life. A rapid succession of gun-shots and a cacophony of shouting assaulted my ears as Bart floored the clutch and jammed the shifter into first. I looked back as he applied the gas and released the clutch, lurching us forward in a big bunny-hop that stalled the vehicle. I nearly toppled from the Jeep as another blast tolled in the yard. I saw a very angry-looking, burly thug barreling down on us and another flailing about in the yard engulfed in flames.

Bart restarted the Jeep as bullets sunk into its body. One slammed into the passenger side mirror, shattering it to fragments less than two feet from my head. Two other men, further back, were circling around the inferno toward us firing automatic weapons. A few others shuffled behind them.

"Go, go, go!" I screamed ducking low. The man on our tail, now only a foot behind us, took a dive for the back seat.

Bart, in a desperate rush — "like a cheetah afta meat-ah" — put the pedal-to-the-metal and spun a tread-full of mud into the face our pursuer. The man's last-ditch effort at grasping the Jeep failed and he fell headlong into the marshy ground. Bart crashed the Jeep through the chain-link gate, snapping the lock and ripping the worn hinges away with a grinding screech as bullets continued to fly around us.

"Woo-hoo!" I hooted wildly, thrusting my fist into the air as we rounded a bend.

I felt a sudden searing pain in my left shoulder. I knew I'd been hit by a rifle slug. I looked over and reached my hand to the place where it hurt. I felt the sticky wetness of blood.

"I've been hit," I shouted to Bart.

"Is it bad?"

"I think it went clean through — no bone, but it's bleeding pretty good."

"Ball up your shirt and press it firmly to the wound. That will help stop the bleeding. And hold on!"

With that we went careening down the road at break-neck speed to who-knows-where. The adrenalin was pumping; I was both excited and scared. I pulled my shirt gingerly over my head, balled it up, and pressed it to my wound. That hurt. *Wow!* I thought, *I have a gunshot wound and I don't even live in the hood.*

We bounced wildly from a pothole and I felt a sudden knot in my stomach as I remembered that Bart had only received his driver's license a month ago. My lone thought was: *out of the fire and into the frying pan.* Bart flicked on the headlights.

"Where to?" he asked as the Jeep bumped and bucked down the bayou back roads.

"Out there!" I replied, unconsciously quoting *Star Trek's* Captain Kirk. Dezi

81

stirred and groaned. "I think we need to get to a doctor."

"You going to pass out?"

"No, I'm doing okay. But I think Dezi needs to get to the hospital to see a doctor, *vite vite*."

"And where might that be? Out here, we might get lucky and run into a witch doctor."

"Look," said Bart, "there's a fork in the road." He slowed the Jeep. "Which way?"

"Rr—igh—t." The voice was Dezi's.

"What?" I inquired.

"Go...right?" Dezi responded weakly. KABLAM! There was another huge explosion behind us — it was the lab. A large orange fireball rolled skyward followed by a billowing cloud of black smoke.

"Right, right, go right," I reiterated. "Dezi, you okay?" I shook him gently as Bart slowed.

"He's incoherent," Bart yelled, "How does he know where to go?"

"He knows these parts better than a gator with GPS. Besides you got any better leads?"

"Good point." Bart, ground some gears and we lurched down the road on the right and on into the night. I could see the blazing glow still reflecting brightly in the rearview mirror. That firestorm would be seen for miles and miles — the whole terrain was flat, the highest point no more than fifteen feet above sea level. It wouldn't be long before rescue and firefighting aircraft would converge on the area.

Hopefully the fire wouldn't spread much or do a lot of damage to the forest canopy. I felt bad about that. We needed all the vegetated land we could get to protect us from hurricanes. The land mass of Louisiana is rapidly eroding away; that's why recent hurricanes have caused so much devastation.

☠ ☠ ☠

Over the next few minutes Dezi became steadily more conscious and sat up with some effort. He was still groggy, but when he spoke it was as if he was another person altogether. For the first time since we had known him he talked like...well, like a sane man.

"Thanks for the rescue. Wh...what were you doing out here?"

"We came looking for you," I answered.

"Yeah, but we found a whole lot more than we bargained for," added Bart.

"I'll say," Dezi intoned, "Pure evil, *Diable*!* American hatred and...and vile disregard for life. The plot...did you...?"

"Yeah, we found your message and I hope we've done the right thing — I think we've got it on a jump-drive. There is a risk that the fire..." I volunteered.

"Oh, the fire," he chimed, "Good idea; it will destroy the virus *and* the mosquitoes."

"We didn't intend to set the lab on fire; we only wanted to send up a homing beacon."

"You done good, even if the lab don't burn down." Dezi winced in pain. His back was pretty charred and, while it wasn't a great deal of surface area, it was unsightly none-the-less.

"Does that hurt a lot?" I asked.

"Like dad bum hellfire," he said, "but I'll live. At least it didn't get my handsome face." He smiled then grimaced. "Hey, getting hit by that blast was...it was a good thing — the shock and pain jarred me out of my stupor. I was in a drug-induced zombie state."

"Yeah, we saw it," Bart chimed in, "it was creepy."

I could hear helicopters coming in overhead. I looked up, "Chopper's coming," I said. Unlike the heavy hammock* concealing the compound, the canopy of trees over us now was thin and the chopper's running lights shown on their call letters. "It's the sheriff's department's, along with a fire crew carrying a bucket."

"Yahoo!" hollered Bart, "probably your Dad."

"Most likely, only one deputy's on tonight — probably Danny G. and he's not a hermit' personification so people will leave me alone. Actually, it's something me and your Dad came up with after I helped him with some poachers back in '04. He felt it might keep me safer."

"So you've been out here — ah, there — for how long?"

"Nearly ten years. And, in a way, I am a hermit. At least I've become one. I like most people well enough, but I like being alone with God, too. There's so much less to trip a man up out in the bayous and so much more time to get focused on Jesus. I've leaned on Him and he's sustained me. It's been good."

"I'll bet it has," I said as Bart pulled into the parking lot of Terrebonne General.

"He's been good to us, too," Bart added as he pulled into the ER drive of the six story light gray structure. I helped Dezi from the Jeep and we walked into admissions as Bart went to park the car. I checked Dezi and myself in while Bart made some phone calls. Dezi was admitted right away while I, no longer bleeding and doing quite well, was relegated to the wait-ing room behind other priority patients.

☠ ☠ ☠

Bart showed up around the time I'd picked up a tattered, six-month old copy of *Highlights* magazine. Saved by the bell.

"*Ca va**?" I asked, to inquire about the calls he'd made.

"Good stuff. That *was* your Dad up in the chopper and it looks like the situation is under control. I related the essence of Dezi's message to the sheriff's office and said we'd swing by with the jump-drive later. Details were sketchy, but Dolores said that Dad was in no danger at this time and that several persons had been apprehended. They're on their way in now. He's gotta file the paper work when they get back.

"That's all I know. Oh! And I called our moms and gave them the low-down. Your mom is pretty whacked-out about it all. I didn't tell her about your gunshot 'cuz your dad told me not to. She was wacked-out enough without that bit of info.

"My dad is on his way in from Lake Fields and will meet us at the station as soon as we all get there."

☠ ☠ ☠

An hour later, after the hospital had reached my father for permission to proceed with medical care, I was taken to an examination room while Bart got to read the *Highlights* magazine. A nurse popped in right away and had me remove my shirt and put on one of those flimsy gowns so I

It was getting on to morning; the sun peeking over the hazy horizon when we drove our 'borrowed' Jeep up to the station. We had a lot of story to tell before we could get some much needed shut-eye, but when the opportunity afforded itself, the sleep would be welcomed.

It took us about thirty minutes to fill the authorities in – the authorities meaning our dads and a CIA agent who Skyped in. After that, Bart's dad drove me home and then he and Bart went home themselves. My mom hugged me and cried and I reiterated our adventures yet once again — in condensed form, of course. And she got all wacked-out all over again when she saw the blood and I had to tell her about getting shot. It was 7:40 in the morning when I crawled into bed. I think I went to sleep as soon as my head hit the pillow.

Both Bart and I slept until nearly four-o-clock the next afternoon. Bart called me soon after he was up, but he'd already made several phone calls to fill our friends in on our adventure. He borrowed his dad's Chevy Luv, the "borrowed' Jeep having been compounded for evidence, and came by to pick me up. We then tooled up Little Bayou Black Drive to Arlow's.

14 ARLOW'S

Arlow's, our favorite gathering place, was decorated with old saws, galvanized gas cans, animal traps, and similar items that hung from the knotty barn-board walls. The Wurlitzer Bubbler reproduction jukebox in the corner still played tunes from the 1950's — Sinatra, Elvis, and the Big Bopper as well as a number of BB King singles and assorted Zydeco* classics. The rustic, eclectic setting inspired a homey, down-to-earth mood — perfect for kicking it with friends.

After all we'd been through, it felt good to sit down with the gang. To pizza! Oh, yeah. I'm telling you, never has the 'za — even Arlow's — tasted so good. A Cajun alligator sausage with olives, mushrooms, peppers and onions — my favorite! I took a bite and my tongue danced a two-step — it was like a *fias do-do** in my mouth. The last strains of Beau Soleil's "Reel Cajun" frolicked from the jukebox as I sank my teeth into another bite.

"Ow, ow, ow!" I yelled, melted cheese burning the roof of my mouth, "That is hah-ott!"

"Hot!? What's hotter than my bad self?" said Bart.

"Lotsa stuff," retorted Dallas, "like glaciers, an' sno cones, an' ice cubes, an'..."

"Your just jealous, cowboy," returned Bart.

Carla jumped in, "Hey! You're both hotter than tar paper under a tin roof in August, alright? What you did — I mean that adventure — it makes you heroes."

"Hardly," I retorted, "we stumbled in and..."

Carla shut me up with a quick kiss. "You're a hero in my book," she said looking into my eyes. I turned redder than a Cajun hot pepper. Girls are crazy.

"Awh," Bart intoned, clasping his hands together and batting his eyes, "You're a hero in..." I smacked him across the chest and he recoiled laughing. Everyone else joined in. Carla smacked him again for good measure.

"Hey, hey!" yelled Dallas, standing on a chair, a slice of pizza in his hand. "I'll bet I can stretch this cheese all the way to the ceiling." A string of mozzarella jiggled between the pie on the table and the slice in his hand — already stretched more than three feet.

"A dollar says you can't," challenged Keilah placing her hands on her curvaceous hips.

"Can!" He moved the slice up another foot, "Two dollars anyone?" He said stretching further.

"Woot, woot!" Jake whooped, peeking out from the kitchen towel in hand, "Go cowboy!"

"Go, go, go." Everyone was shouting and the cheese was stretching — over five feet now, less than a foot to go.

Eight inches.

Six.

Five.

Snap!

The string of cheese broke and thwacked against the ceiling then fell in a drizzle onto Dallas' face and chestnut brown Stetson. Everyone roared with laughter; Bart snorted Dr Pepper out his nose and everyone was talking at the same time — a real *gumbo ya-ya**. It was great having the place all to ourselves.

Right then the front door swung open and in stepped two men dressed in black suits and wearing shades. Twisty wires protruded from their ears and disappeared behind their col-lars. Looking this way and that they strode forward in a calculated cadence. Dallas froze — cheese dangling from his hat. All eyes turned toward the two men coming through the door. Our mouths shut with the door. Bart wiped his face on his sleeve.

The doors swung open again and in came Bart's dad and mine, Warden Davis and Sheriff Meyers. Their stern, somber expressions said they were here on official business. All was quiet.

Warden Davis came around to the front, "Hi kids. Bart, Pete, these men are here to see you." He stepped aside.

Reed and I looked at each other, "Men in Black," we said simultaneously.

"Not exactly," said the taller of the two. "We're CIA — Central Intelligence Agency, U.S. Government." He whipped out a wallet, flashed a badge, flipped it shut and returned it to his breast pocket all in one smooth motion.

"Which of you are Peter and Bartholomew?"

I stepped forward, eyes wide, mouth hanging open.

"This is Peter," my dad volunteered, beaming. He came over and put his hand on my left shoulder as the agent extended his hand. I winced and pulled away.

"Oh, sorry Pete," dad said, "forgot about that." I reached out with my right hand and shook the agent's.

"It's a pleasure to meet you young man," he said, "I'm Agent Smith. This is my partner, Agent Hill."

"Pleased to meet you, Mr. Smith. Call me Pete." I put out my hand to the shorter, slightly plump agent. "Mr. Hill," I said shaking his hand.

"Pete," said Agent Hill, nodding.

"That's *my* boy," offered Officer Davis, pointing at Bart.

Bart stepped forward, "I'm Bart."

"Good to meet you, Bart," said Agent Smith.

"Thank you, sir," said Bart putting out his hand.

"Listen boys," said Agent Hill as he in turn shook Bart's hand, "we're here on behalf of the President. He wanted to personally thank you for what you've done for America and her people — what you've done for the world. But, it's impractical for him to be here. I'm sure you understand."

"Ah, sure," replied Bart, "I wouldn't expect him to..."

Smith and Hill nodded simultaneously as they each put a hand to their earpieces and all eyes watched. Smith spoke softly into his cuff, "Affirmative."

"Boys," said Hill, taking an Android smartphone from his breast pocket, "this phone is about to ring and..."

The phone rang, playing Hail to the Chief.

"Whoa!" exclaimed Keilah, "How'd you..."

"CIA," said Hill smirking, as he stabbed the touch screen, "We know everything."

"Almost everything," corrected Smith.

"It's for you," Hill said handing the device to me. I swung it toward my ear.

"It's on speaker," Hill said quickly before I could offer my greeting.

Holding the cell phone out in my palm I answered pensively, "Hello?"

"Yes, hello," said the voice on the cell, "With whom am I speaking?"

"Peter Meyers"

"And is Bart Davis there?"

"Yes, sir," I answered, looking at Bart.

Bart acknowledged his presence with "Hello, Mr. President."

"So you know who this is?" asked the voice from the phone.

"Why, yes, sir. We've heard you on television and the Internet," replied Bart.

"That's great. Fantastic! Boys...ah...men that is, I'm calling to thank you, to thank you for, well, saving America. There's no telling how big of a disaster this could have been. You have been very brave and I thank you."

Carla gave me a wink and I blushed again. Everyone remained in a stunned hush, so the President continued:

"Peter, Bart, I have called personally, not only to thank you, but to seek your support in the security of this matter. I have intentionally drawn no press attention to the incident and I'd like it to stay under wraps for the time being. I'm asking that you help me with that. All of you.

"This former threat against our national security would be best kept quiet for now. Will you all agree to hold this in your confidence?"

We all chimed in with agreement.

"Well then, I also want you to know that the region will be thoroughly sprayed for mosquitoes — using an environ-mentally safe biological defense, mind you. The virus, we believe, has been contained and destroyed, but this is a precaution. We have the CDC and the FDA on that vaccine, just in case. And we'll eventually share what we know with WHO — the World Health Organization.

"As you know, the terrorists have been captured and are being held until trial and, thanks again to you and the contents of that jump-drive, we have quite enough evidence to put them away for a very long time. Incidentally, that jump-drive contained a lot more than you put on it. You did a great job, men."

"I...I don't know what to say," said Bart.

"That's unusual," piped in Dallas, but no one laughed.

"Thank you, Mr. President," I added.

"Smith, Hill," said the President, "I'm ready."

Smith reached into his jacket.

"Is this where we all get deneuralized," asked Reed.

"Ah, what?" said Hill.

"Ah, no," said Smith. "That's a different agency."

Hill smacked him in the arm and they both laughed briefly.

"Ah, no," he said clearing his throat, gain-ing his composure and producing a carved rosewood case from his pocket. He opened it and reached inside. "Go ahead, Mr. President, sir."

"Bartholomew Benjamin Davis and Peter Jackson Meyers," the President con-tinued, "on behalf of the American people and our allies, I, the President of these United States, do hereby award you the Medal of Freedom for your brave and hon-orable service to our country and to the world. You have our thanks. May God bless America."

With some flourish Agent Hill took two med-als from the ornate box. Cheers rang out and applause thundered as agents Smith and Hill placed the medals about our necks. Jake was waving his towel like he was at a Steelers' game near the kitch-en door. Keilah put her fingers between her lips and belted out her famous ear-melting whistle. (Everyone plugged their ears for that.)

"Free pizza for everybody!" yelled Jake above the *ya ya**. A final cheer and our friends gathered again around the phone. Jake shoved his way into the crowd.

"Ah, Mister President, sir, Mr. President, you will hava pizza, no?" he said, "I send you one, kay?"

"Well, I...ah...Sure, why not?" said the Commander-in-Chief, "I never get to have a good slice of all-American pizza."

"Sir," interjected Smith, "pizza is Italian."

"It may have originated in Italy, but pizza is America's favorite food."

"And this pizza here," said Hill, "I'll bet, it's part Cajun, part Italian, and has a French quarter to boot; now that sounds mighty American to me."

Everyone laughed. Bart yelled out, "To America!"

We each raised a slice skyward, "To America!"

"Hello? Hel-lo!" inquired the President from the phone. The room quieted.

"Sorry, Mr. President," said Smith, "a moment of levity."

"That's quite all right," he replied, "It cer-tainly is a moment to celebrate. I wanted to say thanks again before saying my goodbye."

"Yes, sir; you're welcome," said Bart, beaming.

"You're welcome, sir," I said, "Goodbye and thanks very much for the call."

"And the medals," added Bart.

"My pleasure," returned the President, "only keep them to yourselves for a few weeks. And if you ever want to come up to Washington, well, you're my guests. Give my office a call to set it up. Goodbye men."

"Goodbye," chimed the crew.

I gave the phone back to Agent Hill; he stab-bed the end call button and slipped it into his breast pocket.

"Well, boys...ah..." said Agent Smith clearing his throat, "...men, our time here is complete. You have the agency's thanks as well and, by the way, we give tours at Langley, too; so be sure to stop in when you're up near D.C."

"Sure thing!" I exclaimed.

"Goodbye," said Agent Hill, and with that the agents turned on their heels. At the door Hill stopped, turned and called back.

"Say, Mr. Arlow, do you think we could get *two* pizzas to go?"

15 AWESOME

The afternoon's revelry went on for another hour. With pizza on the house everyone ended up, in the words of Dallas, "tighter than a tick." Everyone admired our medals. We recounted bits from our adventure for the umpteenth time and, of course we played the video games. Reed got caught up in a first-person shooter video game and was screaming, "Die, you zombie scum, die!" with every shot. He could be nuts. I'm pretty sure he is. It was good times.

☠ ☠ ☠

As the party wound down and we were about to leave for the hospital and check on Dezi I stepped outside the door exhausted from the hullabaloo. I was resting against the building and daydreaming when Carla slipped out the door and sidled up next to me.

"You're awesome," she said, a gleam in her eyes, as she fingering the medal around my neck. She looked at me, gently pulling me in toward her admiring face. "Do you think I could go with you when you go to D.C.?"

At that moment — that awkward, untimely moment — Dad, Warden Davis and Bart popped through the door, overhearing her words. She dropped the medal and we tried to look casual rather than embarrassed — which we were.

"Funny you should mention that Carla," said Dad, "I've word that Acquire the Fire* will be there in a couple weeks. Davis and I have been talking and we've decided to send you two..." He paused a moment, "...and the gang."

"*Fo' troo*?!" I exclaimed all bug-eyed. Carla's mouth dropped open.

"Why not? It's a great youth event. We'll rent a van and drive you up. And there's a free day when you can visit the White House and CIA headquarters and..."

"But wait, isn't Acquire coming to New Orleans, too?"
"Well, yeah, sure, but this kind of kills two birds with one stone, you see," said Warden Davis, "and, besides..."

"...D.C. is the only venue on the tour having Third Day* in concert, dude!" Bart whooped.

"Awesome!" Carla chimed. And they high-fived.

16 RECOVERY

The hospital had that hospital smell — that ultra-clean antibacterial soap and fresh-washed linens smell. The picture frames and plaques on the lobby walls that honored hospital donors gave the institution a hallowed feel. We asked at the reception desk about Dezi, and the attendant directed us to the burn unit on the fourth floor where a few medical carts and empty gurneys lined the halls.

A man sat in a wheelchair outside one room and a wo-man shuffled down the hall pushing the IV tree to which she was tethered. At the nurse's station a pretty woman in kitty-cat print scrubs sat at a computer terminal typing in data from a stack of charts. A stethoscope hung a-round her neck.

"May I help you?" she asked making eye contact with my dad as he stepped up to the desk.

"We're here to see Desmond Com-eaux," replied my father.

"I'm the attending physician," said a nearby doctor looked up from his paper work, "Oh, hi Sheriff."

"Hi, Jeremiah," replied my dad, "Boys, this is Doctor Roberts. My son Peter and this is Warden Davis and his son Bart."

"Doctor Roberts," acknowledged Warden Davis. We each shook his hand in turn as he spoke.

"I hear you boys are quite the...ah... you've had quite an adventure." He made a zipping motion over his lips.

"You could call it that," said Bart.

"That's cool," said Dr. Roberts, "I'm glad you weren't hurt badly or worse. Anyway, Mr. Comeaux is doing really well. I think we'll be able to release him tomorrow afternoon if he can stay in town. He said to congratulate you again on a job well done. He wants to see you, but he's asleep now. He needs his rest or I'd wake him. You're welcome to see him in the morning."

"That'll be fine," replied my dad, "We'll pop in about ten if that's okay."

"Should be good. Tell you what," said Dr. Roberts, "I'll have my nurse call you. At the station?"

"Yeah, sure," said Dad, "And, you said he could be released *if* he could stay in town?"

"That's right, we don't want him all the way out there in the bayou in case of infection. He needs a hotel or..."

"He can certainly stay with us," my dad volunteered.

"That would be terribly kind of you, Sherriff," replied Dr. Roberts.

"No problem, we'd like to help out."

"Janis," the doctor called to the nurse at the desk, "Will you make a note to have Suzi call the sheriff's office in the morning?"

"Yes, doctor. Nine-o-clock?"

"Yes, thanks Janis," he said.

"Thanks, Jeremiah," replied my father, "see you tomorrow."

"Yeah. Good seeing you. And I'll be sure to have his discharge papers ready for you."

Dad nodded and we turned to leave.

"Oh," called Dr. Roberts catching up to us, "those five, ah...'zombies' you brought in, they're lucid now, and, though it was quite a drug cocktail that had them under, they'll be released into CIA custody in the morning as well. Don't know if that's any use to you, but, well, they're telling quite a story."

"Yeah?" replied my dad.

Dr. Roberts laughed. "Something involving a swamp monster-thing."

"Sounds like the Warden's department."

"Sounds like a wild tale to me," said Warden Davis.

"Sounds like danger to me," said Bart.

"Danger? That's my middle name," I chimed.

Dad and the Davis' all spoke in unison: "*Fo' troo.*"

I smiled. *You think they know me?*

GLOSSARY/ENDNOTES

Chapter One:

- *Cocodrie*: French-Canadian word for "crocodile"

- cypress: a scaly-leaved, cone-bearing evergreen tree that grows in the bayous of Louisiana, related to pine trees

- brackish: of water that is somewhat salty; a mix of fresh and sea water found in areas like the Mississippi Delta and bayous of Louisiana

- bayous: a marshy inlet or outlet of a lake, stream, etc.

- *bos coyo*: the knee-like roots of cypress trees

- Spanish moss: a plant actually related to the pineapple (and not a moss at all) that grows in pendant tufts of grayish green moss-like filaments on trees of the southern U.S. and in the West Indies

- *chênière*: an oak grove (French)

- delta: the sprawling sand bar fingers of a river's mouth

- Cajun: A person of Canadian-French decent, possibly a corruption of Arcadian; the dialect of the Cajuns

- *galerie*: the front pouch (French)

- *mouche à fea*: lighting bugs or fire flies; winged beetles
- which glow at night.

Chapter Two:

- *M'su*: the French-Canadian equivalent of Mr.

- *joir de vivre*: a French phrase that means "the joy of living."

- *chard*: means "hot" (French)

- *Bon Dieu*: "Good God" (male form, French)

- *bon heur*: "good fortune" (male form, French)

- *mon ami or moi ami*: "my friend" (French)

- Houma: is a city of southern Louisiana; its name means "red" and comes from a Native American tribe that once lived in the area. Houma is the county   seat of Terrebonne parish.

- *fo' troo*: (for true) a Cajun expression meaning "really," "sure thing," or "truth"

- Cahoui: Proper Cajun name pronounced "Sha-we" and meaning raccoon.

- *padnat*: is a Cajun expression meaning "buddy"

- duck grass: or "duck weed" is a small flowering plant that
- floats on ponds and sluggish streams and marshes

- magnolias: any group of trees or shrubs with large, fragrant flowers of pink, white or purple.

- Terrebonne Parish refers to the "county" of Terrebonne; in some parts of the country parish is used instead of county. "Terrebonne" comes from the French meaning *terre* for "earth" and *bonne* for "good" (female form); it means "good earth."

- ragged boot: On a map (or from outer space) the state of Louisiana looks like a boot with the toe chewed up.

- De Cade: a lake area southwest of Houma, Louisiana

Chapter Three:

- *levee*: the bank of a river or bayou; French meaning "to raise"

- *cabane*: French for "shack" or "cabin"

- *goujon*: refers to "cat fish" (French-Canadian)

- Voodoo: a mysterious religious practice of African descent based on sorcery (the use of charms, spells, etc.) and superstition.

- *vite vite*: Creole for "quick"; can mean "hurry"

Chapter Four:

- *mojo*: a spell or curse (Creole)

- *tasso*: is a Cajun expression for ham jerky

- *bon ami*: "good friend" (male form, French)

- **Chapter Five:**

- *float'on*: a thick, tangled web of vegetation, logs and such floating on water like a pontoon bridge

- *moi ami*: "my friend" (French)

Chapter Six:

- *galerie*: a screened porch

- *gris-gris*:(pronounced *gree-gree*) Creole term for a charm; it is a small bag, worn about the neck or pinned inside the shirt which contains any number of   items (hair, fur, spices, plants, bones, etc.) believed to have magical powers.

Chapter Seven:

- *maison*: "house" (French)

- *Vieus avec moi*: "come with me" (French)

- *mon cher*: "my dear" (male form, French)

Chapter Twelve:

- Elijah: An important Hebrew prophet who was taken to Heaven in fiery chariot; his story can be found in the Bible, First and Second Kings; his name means "Yahweh is God"

- *diable*: "devil" (French-Canadian)

- hammock: an "island" or grove of trees

Chapter Thirteen:

- *merci*: "thanks" (French)

- *Ca va?*: "How's it going?" (French, truncated phrase)

Chapter Fourteen:

- *Zydeco*: a rollicking Cajun dance music

- *fias do do*: a community dance get-together (Cajun)

- *gumbo ya ya*: a gumbo is a mixed stew; this Cajun expression means "everyone talking at once."

- *ya ya*: short for *gumbo ya ya*

Chapter Sixteen:

- Acquire the Fire: An awesome youth rally experience (see http://www.acquirethefire.com for more information)

- Third Day: A Christian band (see http://thirdday.com/ for more information and to listen to their music)

1 RUMOR HAS IT

W hataya mean?" asked Dallas. My dad, Sheriff James Meyers, drove the rental van down Hwy 59/20 just south of Birmingham, Alabama. A gentle hum from the tires on the pavement came in through the windows, which were cracked to let in an evening breeze—a futile effort to quell the persistent southern heat and humidity. Dad was into fuel economy and only used the AC on rare occasions—like on days when people were known to spontaneously combust, which is extremely uncommon.

"I mean...well...I don't know what I mean," he said looking at us in the rearview mirror. "That's just what the reports are saying."

"You're telling me," I wiped the sweat from my forehead with my T-shirt sleeve, "that now the reported sightings of a 'swamp monster,'" indicating quote marks with my fingers, "are more frequent and..."

"Yes, Pete, it appears so."

☠ ☠ ☠

I know, weird conversation, huh? I can explain. My dad's a parish* sheriff in southern Louisiana. My best friend is Bart Davis; his dad is a game warden. We often work together to solve mysteries. Kinda crazy for a couple of 16 year-olds, huh? However, just now we, along with a group of friends, were on a trip home from Washington D.C. and Langley, Virginia. We'd been up to the capitol to attend Acquire the Fire*—an awesome youth event—and we'd had the opportunity to tour the White House and CIA Headquarters.

We'd been invited by the President (that's right, the head honcho of the United States of America) after Bart and I had uncovered and thwarted a biological terrorism plot [that we called Voodoo Virus*] in the bayous* near our hometown of Houma, Louisiana. This trip had been kind of a reward. Anyway, this new conversation? Well, I think we're about to get involved in another mystery.

☠ ☠ ☠

Anyway, my girlfriend Carla sighed, crossing her arms. I put my arm around her and pulled her closer, away from Reed who was sleeping with his head against the van's window, drool seeping out of the corner of his mouth. Bart's dad, Warden Davis, turned from his captain's chair on the passenger side of my dad, and assured, "I just need to stop in at Honey Island Swamp and see what's up, okay?"

Reed sucked in on his drool with a snort and a twitch. "Ewh!" exclaimed Carla, leaning away from him. I chuckled and, lifting my hand from Carla's shoulder, smacked Reed on the back of his head.

"Aliens!" awoke Reed with a start. Everyone laughed. Reed, even more of a geek than my fiend Bart and I, was known for his obsession with UFOs and other odd non-existing things, like zombies, vampires, ghosts and werewolves. I think he watches way too may reruns of *The X-Files* on Netflix.

"Another nightmare?" asked Keilah, poking him in the back from the seat behind.

"Ah, yeah," Reed answered, rubbing his eyes, "I guess so." Everyone laughed again as Reed looked around furrowing his brow.

"We were talking about the Honey Island Swamp Monster," I offered.

"Oh yeah," said Reed, "they're probably aliens."

"Probably," chimed Beth from the back seat with a wry smile and a roll of her eyes. Everyone laughed again.

"You're crazier than a fox in a hen house," said Dallas in his southern drawl. (His real name was Travis.) He was our newest friend and a recent Louisiana transplant from rural Texas. He was always saying hick stuff like that.

"Look who's talking about monsters, cowboy," retorted Reed.

"T'ain't no such thang, nor little green men, flyboy."

"Might be, ya know."

Dallas guffawed and Dad piped in. "This probably has whole lot more to do with earthlings than extraterrestrials," he said, "and nothing to do with monsters either, in spite of the myths."

"Even though such rumors have been floating around since before the infamous Harlen Ford sighting in 1963*." added Bart's dad, "Besides there's never been any *real* evidence—everything that was said to be 'evidence' turned out to be a hoax."

"But, that's the strange thing about that digital picture a tourist snapped last week," replied my dad. "It was still on the camera; no Photoshop involved."

"The marsh monster was photograph-ed!?" mocked Keilah, "Again? Oh my good-ness! So what? There are lots of supposed pictures and plaster casts of footprints."

"Marsh Monster," Reed pondered, "I like that." I thought of *The Creature from the Black Lagoon* (which I've seen like ten times).

"Doesn't surprise me," said Beth, turning to Keilah next to her. "What? Pictures in comic books?"

"No, seriously," continued Keilah, "they're at the paranormal museum."

"Yeah," I replied, "and fuzzy pictures of ghosts and zombies; and they're all over the Internet, too, but that doesn't mean..."

"That they're real," Keilah cut me off. "I know. That's what I'm saying."

"This one, they tell me, looks pretty convincing," assured Bart's dad. "It was taken with a professional camera, quality zoom lens and all, at 2400 dpi."

"Not even very blurry," added my dad, "even though it was taken from a moving airboat—which *was* full of eye witnesses, by the way. Saw the picture last week be-fore we left. Awfully clear. Looks like a genuine Bigfoot to me—more organic than synthetic. But that doesn't mean it's not a fake.

"Oh, it's a fake," said the warden, "no matter what it looks like. Even though every neck of the woods—or swamp—has its legends, there's never been convincing proof that there's any kind of cryptid in existence."

"Cyptid?" questioned Bart, rubbing his temple.

"From the Greek *krypto* meaning 'to hide.'" Reed instructed, "It's a creature—or plant—whose existence has been suggested, but is unrecognized by scientific consensus, and often regarded as highly unlikely, though it's possible...if it hides."

"Where do you get this stuff?" I exclaimed.

"Wikipedia."

"You are *such* a geek, Reed," said Bart kind of cranky-like. Reed shrugged his shoulders and leaned once again against the door. We'd spent half of last night talking into the wee hours of the morning too hyped up on the concerts and Mtn. Dew to settle down. Bart was probably tired.

"Wikipedia," mumbled Carla laying her head on my shoulder. It'd been a long weekend—too many late nights and early mornings—so I tilted my head to hers and closed my eyes with visions of Krypton— The Man of Steel's (a.k.a. Kal El's, a.k.a. Superman's) home planet. Cryptid, Krypton—they kinda sounded the same.

We were still a couple hours from home, but we had one more overnight stop to make—so we thought. We were planning on a brief stay in New Orleans, followed by a morning of sightseeing before heading home in the late afternoon. None of us got up to NOLA* often and so some rubbernecking was okay by us. There's always so much to see and do. And the food—not to mention the music—is absolutely to die for. But for now, well, it was time for a nap and that's what I did.

2 A CHANGE OF PLANS

Dad's cell phone jingled to the tune of *Dixie* and I awoke just as he said, "Jim Meyers." I listened in, hearing only his side of the conversation. "Yeah, yeah, okay. (pause) Oh really? (pause) Hmm, sounds interesting. (pause) Yeah, sure. Later. (pause) I'll call you when I get there." He hit the *end call* button on the face of his smart-phone with a sigh and looked at Warden Davis. *Now what?* "Looks like they've got a possible 10-65, Bob."

I knew what that meant: a missing person. Not usually a big deal. Sometimes, sure, but most people show up sooner or later—and when they do, more often than not, alive and well. That is unless you're a kid. Missing kids, well, let's just say if you're a kid you don't want to go missing. Stranger danger and all that.

"Yeah?" said Warden Davis.

"Tour guide was a no-show for his shift a couple days in a row."

"What? And I suppose they think he got eaten by the swamp thing?"

"I'll, ah," Dad looked over the car seat, back at eager eyes and ears, "I'll fill you in on the details later." Bart's dad nodded.

This was getting weird. First, a week ago we hear about the rash of sighting incidents. Then someone snaps a picture and sends it to Bart's dad only hours before we leave on our trip. Next my dad hears about a "coincidentally" timely lecture on cryptids slated at the University of New Orleans offered by a renowned expert, Dr. Roberto Thachne.

Why the lecture now? I'm thinking this through, see. *Probably had a lot to do with people's curiosity about the recent sightings. A university has to take an active role in response to such things for marketing reasons, I suppose.* And now a mysterious disappearance. My interest was definitely piqued.

Bart, Reed, Beth and I had all wanted to attend the lecture, but now I was having second thoughts. I was getting more interested in what was actually happening down in the swamp. The others—Carla, Keilah and Dallas—could care less about the pontifications of some pompous professor and wanted to pass on the lecture altogether. "Hey!" exclaimed Dallas, "I've never been down to Honey Island Swamp, could we, like, take one of those airboat tours?"

"Yeah," piped in Keilah, "me neither. Sounds like a great way to kill some time while you guys are at the lecture."

"Well," replied Dad, "I was wondering what you might want to do while we're helping out with the investigation. I think that would be fine. In fact, better yet, I think we could all go after the lecture. What do you think Bob?"

"Why not?" said Warden Davis. "It could be quite educational. Give the kids something to write about for school."

"I think we've still got enough in the kitty for a charter," said Dad. "I got better fuel economy on the trip than I expected." *Probably due to trying to steam us to death by not using the AC.* In fact, the van was beginning to smell like a sauna, which sort of smells like a gym locker the morning after a big game: rather robust.

"Awesome!" interjected Bart, obviously talking about the swamp tour and not writing a paper. Many of our folks—Bart and mine especially—were always on the lookout for 'educational opportunities.' That was part of our everyday life since many of us were home-schooled. It was kind of a plus and a minus, if you know what I mean. Keilah let out a little squeal and tossed her curls about. Dallas groan-ed. He was smart, but he wasn't keen on writing papers either. I mean who is, huh? We were already scheduled to write about the Langley and DC experience. Wasn't that enough torture? At any rate, we all agreed to write a paper in exchange for another adventure. Bribery, that's what I call it.

☠ ☠ ☠

We pulled into New Orleans an hour and twenty minutes later and nearly forty-five minutes after that found a standard grade hotel with vacancies near the university. Finding a room in the Big Easy* can be more difficult than you might think; the city always seems to have some sort of festival going on, so tourists can overtake the available lodging rather quickly. Even though it was late in the summer, this was one of those occasions.

We unloaded our luggage from the van while my dad checked us in. By the time we lugged the lug-gage into the lobby we had assigned rooms so we all crowded into the elevator and rode to the third floor. "Man, I can't wait until tomorrow," said Keilah bouncing on her toes, "it's gunna be sooo cool!"

"I can," Bart yawned. "I'm bushed."

"Figure of speech," said Keilah as we reached our floor and the elevator door dinged opened. "I could use a couple z's myself."

"I'm so tarred I could sleep in the saddle," said Dallas sauntering bow-legged down the hotel corridor.

"I'll settle for a bed," said Bart. In our rooms—a two room, three bed (plus futon) suite for the boys next to an adjoining double queen room for the girls—we unpacked what we needed for the night and got ready for bed. It was 11:42 when we finally hit the lights and the hay.

I dreamed I was at Acquire the Fire right in the middle of the Third Day* concert. The fog wafted (I love the smell of fog juice), the colored lights flashed, beams swung about the arena and the crowd went wild in worship. There was such a sense of God in the place.

The band segued from *God of Wonders* to *Kicking and Screaming* as the woofers thumped so hard you could feel it altering your heartbeat. Then the lights went to midnight blue and a sudden chill filled the air. I noticed that the crowd control security personnel were clothed in black suits. They wore shades and had little swirly ear bud wires running down into the collars of their shirts. They looked exactly like some of the CIA agents I'd met in Langley.

Then, seemingly out of nowhere, zombie hordes began shambling toward me. Panicked, I turned to run, but found myself hemmed in by the crowd. No one else seemed to see the beasts except the crowd control agents who also began to converge upon me. I struggled to disappear into the crowd, but could not. The first zombie reached out and grabbed me. I tried to fight him off as others joined their kind. I was grabbed by the hair and a bloodied open maw moved in toward my neck for the kill. But, instead of biting me, the creature jerked and slumped to the floor. He'd been shot in the head by one of the agents. I looked at the agent and saw white wings on his back.

I awoke and thought of how the dream had come together. I'd been to Acquire the Fire and I'd been to CIA headquarters. I got that. Then I thought back to how just weeks before Bart and I had thwarted a biological terrorism plot that involved zombies and a Voodoo Virus.

Okay, just my thoughts running wild. *But, was God trying to tell me something?* Had I any idea what I was in for, you would have had to drag me kicking and screaming into it. But Jesus had been with us through it all. No, I was safe in His arms and nothing—not even the hosts of hell—could drag me away from Him. I'd go anywhere with Him or for Him.

3 THE BIG EASY

At 9:30 a.m. the bedside alarm went off and we arose in various stages. Bart and Dallas being the early riser types, were up first. Reed and the girls dragged themselves out of bed reluctantly. Me? Well, let's just say I *did* get up. By 10:30 we'd showered, dressed and re-packed, then went down to the lobby and followed the scent of baking Belgian waffles and fresh-brewed coffee to the dining room for a breakfast buffet that was includeed with our short stay. I thought of Dallas when my mind mused *I'm so hungry I could eat a horse.*

The morning news was on the eating area's flat screen as we filled our plates from the assortment of fruit, baked goods, oatmeal, biscuits and gravy, yogurt, toast and other fare. The weather report called for a decent late summer day. We made chit chat while we ate, otherwise not paying a lot of attention to the usual news of a big city crime and culture.

Just as Bart was filling a new plate with thirds the newscaster said: "This just in, the Honey Island Swamp Tours*..." Our attention was caught up by the report. Bart stopped mid-dollop in filling the Belgian waffle iron. "...have been suspended. Owner Jeb Plouet said that the recent disappearance of a local man caused the parish sheriff to call for a temporary closure of the popular tourist attraction while an investigation is underway. Here's Gina Boyer live on location at Honey Island Swamp Tours. Gina." Her image came on the screen and after a short pause she began.

"Yes, Mike. I'm here at Honey Island Swamp with Jeb Plouet. Jeb, anything to this swamp monster?" The camera zoomed out and panned for a two-shot.

"No, Gina," said the salty looking Cajun* man, "I been runnin' dis here operation for pert near t'irty years and I ain't never seen such a beast. Don't mean it don't exist, mind you. Dat's part of da mystery dat brings folk out here. We all keep our eyes peel' dough."

"What about the disappearance of tour guide Hap Deveaux?" said Gina. "He lives out in the swamp doesn't he?"

"Yup, lived out here goin' on twelve year. One a our guides he was...is. Hasn't showed up for work for two day. I went out

135

dere to his place myself. Not hide nor hair of him. Boat's still docked, too."

"Any signs of foul play?"

"I didn't see none, and police ain't said anyt'ing neither."

"So how will this closure affect business?"

"On da one hand dis ain't really da big tourist season, so, normally, it wouldn't affect us all dat much. On da other hand dere's a boon in interest due to the rash of sightin's, so folk is wantin' to come out, 'specially since da weather is nice an' all. So, yeah, it's affectin' da bonus business we could have had had da cops not closed us down. Government meddlin' is what it is. A fella can't..." Gina turned to the camera as she brought the mic back to her mouth and the shot zoomed in on her.

"Thank you, Jeb. That's Jeb Plouet, operator of the Honey Island Swamp Tours, who's business has been suspended while the parish sheriff investigates the disappearance of, Hap Deveaux, a local man and tour guide. I'm Gina Boyer for Channel Four News. Back to you, Mike." The studio shot showed anchor Mike Metcaff at the news desk.

"Just a moment, Gina," said the anchor. "Have you spoken with local authorities about the disappearance?" Gina's image appeared in a box over his shoulder and then it zoomed out to fill the screen.

"I did attempt to speak with Sergeant Frank Rubart of the Saint Tammany Parish Sheriff's Department, but he declined to comment." The screen went to a divided shot with the studio on the left and the field shot on the right. "He simply stated that an investigation is underway."

"Thank you, Gina. The screen filled with the studio shot. "In other news..." he blathered on about a local bar fight. The waffle iron dinged and Bart looked down to see that the opened device held a half-cooked waffle—gooey on the top side.

"I guess that shoots our swamp tour," said Dallas.

"Not necessarily," said my dad. "I'm pretty sure I can still get us a charter. I'll speak with Sargent Rubart and, if there's no perceived danger, I can take you kids out with me." We finished our breakfast, went back up to our rooms for our bags, checked out and loaded into the van while Dad made a phone call to the local Cop Shop. Hanging up, he said, "Looks like we're good to go. There's no expected threat, and they're about wrapping up what they can concerning the missing persons investigation."

☠ ☠ ☠

New Orleans, or 'Nahlins' as some of the locals say, is the biggest city in Louisiana, but *not* the state's capitol. You've probably heard of it in regards to hurricanes though; a few years back it was hit by a whopper called Katrina. The city is still recovering, but looking good in most areas. Since the lecture was at 1 p.m. we still had some time to gallivant around the city a bit and take in the sights. We would be heading out to Honey Island Swamp after attending the lecture; we had a 4:30 appointment for our private charter.

"Hey," said Keilah, thumbing the screen on her iPod Touch, "guess what Keilah's listening to." She began crooning a few bars from the song blasting into her skull through the earbuds jammed in her auditory canals. "God, I've fallen to my knees, I'm..."

"*Complete*, by Kutless," said Beth.

"Correct," said Keilah, she again thumbed her iPod and sang, "This too shall pass, oh. But it always comes knocking..."

"*Leap of Faith*, Sanctus Real," said Bart. One for Beth, one for Bart.

"Okay," said Keilah searching for another song. "What about this?" She pushed play and warbled, "Just a small town girl..."

Dallas jumped in, "Journey, cool. Our worship band did that song in church last Sunday. *Don't Stop Believing*."

"In church!?" asked Beth.

"Yup, listen to the lyrics, dude. Ah, dudess. It's about lonely, searching people. The sermon was about finding something to believe in." *How progressive*, I thought.

☠ ☠ ☠

We swung by the university and, after getting directions at Administration, we tooled into the lot adjacent to the biology building to make sure we knew where it was before heading downtown.

"Can we stop by Café du Monde for some beignets?" asked Carla.

"Aren't you full from breakfast," I questioned.

"Never too full for beignets," she answered. It never ceases to amaze me how that girl can be so thin and eat so much.

"What's a bin-yay?" drawled Dallas.

"Dude! You've never had a beignet?" Carla looked shocked. "It's only the most delicious pastry in the world. It's a French-Acadian thing. You have *got* to try some."

"Pastry?" he said, curiosity and appetite piqued, "I'm game."

"Might as well," Dad piped in. "I was going to swing us by Jackson Square anyway. It's right across the street."

"Then can I check out the Faulkner House Bookstore?" asked Bart. He liked to read, and the used book store was a great place to catch some classics for a reasonable price. The book store use to be the house where author William Faulkner* lived and wrote.

"If you can make it snappy," said Bart's dad. "We know how you and book stores are."

The city's French Quarter was alive with street musicians—drummers pounding out syncopated staccato riffs on pickle buckets, sax players belting out the blues, jazz trumpeters doing their best to wail like Satchmo*, and small bands or duos playing everything from energetic Folk and Country to lively Dixieland and Zydeco* tunes—all with their tip jars prominently before them, bananas hanging on the rims. (I don't know why and I've never asked.)

There were street musicians and living statues, artists showing and selling paintings and jewelry, fortune tellers and panhandlers. A few ladies strolled the streets sporting frilly, pastel-colored para-sols*, but most people looked like every day touristy types. The lingering scents of steaming gumbo, boiled crawfish, panfrying pralines*, and freshly baked baguettes* wafted from restaurants that seemed to line every street. In fact each new block seemed come with its own café, bar and t-shirt shop. Lather, rinse and repeat.

Twenty-seven minutes later we had made it into the Big Easy and found a parking space near Pirate's Alley just south of Royal Rue* a block from the book store and just two from Jackson Square. Bart ducked into Faulkner's as we strolled into Jackson Square in front of the majestic, white-spired New Orleans Cathedral.

More street performers, artists and fortune tellers dotted the courtyard and we took time to watch and listen (to all but the soothsayers). When Bart rejoined us he had copies of Kate Chopin's *Bayou Folk and A Night in Acadie* and Mike Tidwell's *Bayou Farewell* under his arm and a tattered copy of Tennessee Williams' *Cat on a Hot Tin Roof* in his hand which he held out to me.

"This is for you, *padnet**. I know how you like the drama stuff. It was in the discount bin."

"Thanks, Bart," I said taking the script and tucking it into the back pocket of my jeans. "I've got the guts to die," I began, "What I want to know is, have you got the guts to live?"

"Huh?" said Carla.

"That's from *Cat on a Hot Tin Roof*," I said, "the play Bart just gave me."

"Oh," she rolled her eyes, "okay then." We wandered a few steps down Decatur to

Café du Monde. The place, as to be expected, was busy and we stood in line for a seat.

"We've got less than two hours before the lecture kids," warned Warden Davis. "It's going to take thirty-five minutes to get back across town. We're going to have to eat and run, *if* we get in."

"We can hit the take-away counter," suggested my dad.

"Let's do it," said Carla. "I'm starving." We snaked our way past the line of tourists and up to the take-away counter line (which was much shorter) and within minutes had our white paper bags of piping hot pastries. Our dads each grabbed a cup of chicory joe to go.

"Mmm, mmm," said Dallas through a muffled mouth of beignet, powdered sugar smudged over his face and dribbled down the front of his western shirt.

"I told you they were yummy," said Carla. We ate on our way back to the van and got inside. We'd saved some time by using the take-out so, with an hour to spare, Dad drove us through the Garden District—home of many Anne Rice Vampires.

☠ ☠ ☠

In contrast to the French Quarter, the Garden District, with its Spanish moss*-strewn Live Oak* lined streets (pothole infested streets, mind you) was quiet and reserved. *How could these people in two to four million dollar homes put up with their streets in such disrepair?* Here flower gardens and sprawling antebellum* mansions where everywhere. The perfumes of blooming flowers and fresh cut grass filled the air and contributed to a sense of relaxation.

"Wow, are these plantation homes?" inquired Dallas. Truly, this cowpoke hadn't been out of Texas much.

"No," said Beth, "actually this multi-acre site *was* once a handful of sprawling plantations, but in the late 1800s parcels were sold off until, eventually, these antebellum mansions began to crowd in actually overtaking the gardens. It's now known more for its architecture."

"Wikipedia, right?" said Reed.

"Actually, I learned that from a travel guide."

"Actually," said Keilah, "you're a stickler for facts, actually." Beth gave Keilah a look and stuck out her tongue as Dad crept the van up to a stunning white mansion with a towering turret surrounded by a wrought iron fence.

"Beth is right though," interjected Bart's dad. "There are Victorian styles, Greek and Gothic..."

"I think we ought to head out," said Warden Davis. "Time's running short."

"*Fo troo**," answered my dad.

"What's that place?" I asked pointing at the white mansion.

"That," answered Bart's dad, "is the Davis House. And yes, my ancestors lived there. It was sold in 1955 during the war and later, in 1965, donated to the Women's Guild of the New Orleans Opera Association. The City later took over ownership and management of the place. They continued to lease it to the opera for thirty years operating under the Davis Playhouse name.

"And Pete, you may wish to know that they *did* produced shows there until last year when the City decided they could lease it for more money, raised their rent by a thousand dollars and, in essence, evicted them. It's said the place is haunted, too. Ironically, nobody has rented it since the opera moved out, until recently."

"Cool. Haunted." You guessed it; that was Reed talking with a glazed look in his eyes.

"A haunted opera house," I said, as the van moved on along the bone-jarring streets. "Original."

4 CRYPTOLOGY 101

O ur group filed into the brightly lit lecture hall that seated over five hundred. It was mostly full. Many of the attendees appeared to be students dressed in sneakers, T-shirts and jeans, but there were also a number of older people, some dressed in suits and dresses, seated mostly at the back of the auditorium. Someone had set up a video camera behind the seating area and a screen near the podium was lit up from a video projecttor mounting to the ceiling.

We found seats three-quarters of the way from the front where we could sit together and sat down. The students spoke quietly amongst themselves, clicked open notebooks and shuffled papers for several minutes while others streamed in and found seats. The rich aroma of Starbucks lattes and mochas tantalized my nose. At precisely 1 p.m. a balding and bespectacled, chunky man rose from the front row and spoke into the podium microphone (it did *not* squeal nor did he tap it like in the movies).

"Students and esteemed guests, thank you for joining us today. For those who don't know me, I'm Professor Higgins, biology chair here at University of New Orleans. Today's lecture on cryptology will be given by visiting professor Dr. Roberto Thachne from the University of South Florida in Tampa. He's asked that I leave further introduction to him. My students will take notes and hand them in at the conclusion of the lecture. And, yes, they will count toward your grade."

Dr. Roberto Thachne met the department head at the podium, shook hands, and Professor Higgins took his seat in the front row as the visiting professor began his lecture.

"It is my pleasure to address you this afternoon as I hope it is yours," began Thachne clearing his throat. "I received my double Bachelors in history and biology from Cornell University, my Masters in biology from Yale and my Ph.D. in zoology from The Florida Institute of Technology.

"I might add that my dissertation on today's subject broke new ground and rocked the world of biology." It was clear this guy was full of himself. He reminded me of that puffed up villain in the movie, *Star Trek: Into Darkness*.

"Cryptology, or Cryptozoology as it is more accurately labeled, is the study of cryptids—those plants and animals that science has yet to discover, but have, none-the-less, been discovered by non-scientists, that is the lay public. They are 'the hidden ones' which comes from the Greek kryptos, meaning 'to hide'."

Yeah, yeah, been there, done that.

"I am the world's foremost authority on this science—though some in the science community don't see it as such—and I am dedicating my life to the discovery and documentation of these hidden creatures." A few hands went up around the room.

"You will hold your questions until the end of the lecture," snapped Dr. Thachne as hands slunk back down. "I'm sure I will answer most of them in the course of my discourse and I will not have you distracting me from my flow."

Bart rolled his eyes, "Wow!" he whispered. "He really thinks he's something."

"Now, the question of evidence, I'm sure, is foremost on your mind," continued Thachne, "but I will get to that. Be assured that, if there was not significant substantiation, I would be, as they say, just 'barking up the wrong tree,' but I am not." He pulled a small clicker device from his pocket and pointed it at the projector. An image of a hairy beast standing on two feet appeared on the screen.

"This," he said, now pointing the device at the screen and circling a laser pointer around the creature, "is the famed Sasquatch or Big Foot. This and other similar animals have been sighted in the Northwest United States and Southern Canada. A similar creature has been seen in the Himalayas and is known as Yeti or more colloquially as 'the abominable snowman;' no authenticated photograph exists." He advanced the slide.

"And this is the Loch Ness Monster, known as Nessy, sighted repeatedly in the Loch Ness of the Scottish Highlands. Also, this photo has not been authenticated. There *are* mysterious creatures on earth, of course, but here I segue from land-based cryptids to more water-based creatures. Here in Louisiana and the Florida Everglades you have..." He again advanced to the next slide. "... the swamp thing, the Honey Island Swamp Monster, the Creature of the Black Lagoon or whatever.

"This is the only known photograph of the Honey Island creature taken by a deer hunter in the area. Also not authenticated. And, of course, you have the 1960s sightings by Harlan Ford. The creature has been described as bipedal, seven or so feet tall, with gray hair and yellow or red eyes, and accompanied by a disgusting smell..." *Sounds like Bart.*

"Footprints supposedly left by the creature have four webbed toes."

He advanced the slide. "This is a photograph of a supposed plaster cast of that footprint taken by Ford." He advanced the slide. "As you know, there has been a significant rise in the number of sightings lately and that is why I am here." So far, nothing new. My own thoughts began to wander and I looked around the room. I wasn't the only one. Several students seemed bored and were doodling, tapping pens and passing notes. My mind drifted to our upcoming Honey Island Swamp excursion. I wondered what I would see. *Would I see the swamp monster?* Dr. Thachne droned on:

"Cryptids are solitary creatures and do not wish to be found. They are not afraid of humans, they simply wish to be left alone and, when threatened, can be quite dangerous. In the case of the Honey Island bigfoot, I believe its habitat may be threatened. As the coastal land mass disappears and civilization continues to encroach upon these beings they are reacting.

"We talk about *the* thing when, perhaps, there are many *things*. We may be invading an entire species or tribe. It is our duty—our responsibility—to pull back and let them be. Now, you may be thinking: Why am *I* invading their space? The answer is that science also has the responsibility to know. I am a scientist—a biologist—and I seek knowledge. Knowledge is the greatest treasure we have." A hand shot up, but the speaker ignored it. "It is essential..."

The hand-raiser waved his arm in the air and said, "Excuse me." The professor looked sternly at the student, but continued. "It is *essential* that we document this..."

"Excuse me, sir, why is knowledge ...?"

"I asked that I not be interrupted!" Thachne's face grew redder with every word he spoke. "What *you* have to say is irrelevant to the lecture. *I* am speaking here—I am the teacher and you are the pupil. Do you understand? Or are you stupid?" Wow! Talk about megalomaniacs. A hush came over the room. Thachne cleared his throat, shuffled his notes and finally continued. "Documentation is essential so that we understand our world and our place in it. There is nothing more valuable than knowledge and pursuit of knowledge is transcendent.

"Now, the existence of cryptids *is* factual. Numerous eye-witness reports verify this. Just because no one has been able to collect reliable physical evidence does not discount what is obvious. People have encountered these creatures and, even under hypnosis or monitored by polygraph, the truth is confirmed.

"So, since these creatures exist and wish to be left alone it is essential that we— and I mean professional scientists alone— cautiously and carefully explore their presence. You will note the reports of several 'ape-like' creatures that attacked a cabin in the Pacific Northwest by raining boulders down upon it. These creatures felt threatened. The same is true for the Honey Island Swamp Monster.

"The recent disappearance of this tour guide is a warning. Stay away. Let the professionals handle it. We will let you know what we find."

Blah, blah, blah. The lecture went on to de-scribe the creature as a being capable of thought, possibly a cross between mammal and reptile and most likely living in families. With that he launched into a sermon about protecting one's young and how that was instinctive. He closed with another warning to remain out of the swamps—until he declared it safe—and ended on time without taking questions. *Figures.*

The room emptied to a dull roar of book gathering and idle chit-chat. "What a jerk," I whispered to Carla. My father caught the comment.

"What have I told you about judging others?"

"Sorry, dad."

"Do not speak ill of others," he said. "It only degrades *your* character." I looked sheepish as we returned to the car. *Sheesh!* The guy *was* a jerk. He seemed to care more about these creatures—*if* they even existed—or knowledge, than about people. I doubted he cared about anything, really, except himself. He was like some maniacal dictator—a drug dealer, a terrorist, a murderer. As far as I was concerned, these types of people were the scum of the earth, feeding off others without regard to how they hurt others. I didn't see any reason why such people deserved our respect.

5 DOWN ON THE BAYOU

D o you think we'll see that marsh monster thing?" asked Keilah. "Bigfoot," interjected Reed.

"Whatever," replied Keilah with a flip of her wrist.

"Probably not," said Warden Davis. "It's mostly been seen close to dusk."

We crossed the I-10 Lake Pontchar-train cause-way (it's a bridge of sorts, only a few feet above the water and a creepy fourteen miles long) and turned toward the marshy expanse known as Honey Island Swamp. Located southeast of New Orleans, it's flanked on the north by I-90, on the south by Lake Borgne, on the east by the Pearl River and on the west by the West Pearl River.

"This is a lake?" questioned Dallas.

"Not really," answered Warden Davis. "It's really just a brackish estuary. It is, however, one of the largest wetlands in the world and covers an area of 630 square miles. The average depth is only about twelve to fourteen feet."

"It's like Texas big, dude," Dallas observed. We turned south toward Slidell.

* * *

The twisty-turny gravel road, led up to a large, mostly empty gravel parking lot. A small, weathering bungalow-type building with two rockers on the porch sat off to the side of the lot. A sheriff truck and a beat up Chevy half-ton were the only other vehicles in sight. The carved wooden sign on the building read *Honey Island Swamp Tours*. Another sign sporting a picture of an alligator read *Trespassers Will Be Delicious*.

The rhododendrons were in bloom— bright pink and red clusters against the deep browns and muted greens of the surrounding vegetation. Their fragrant perfume mixed with the pungent, earthy smells of the nearby swamp. Various rustic bird houses hung about the place.

Dad parked the van in the nearest non-handicap parking space and we piled out into the sunny-breezy weather. *Twee, twee, twee* called a bird. *Chur, chur, chur* answered another. The doors of the white, red lettered Saint Tammany Parish sheriff's truck opened and two officers stepped out sauntering our way.

"Afternoon," said my dad, walking toward them extending his hand, "I'm..."

"Yes, Sheriff Meyers," said a rather lean officer, extending his own hand. "We've been expecting you. Pleased to meet yer acquaintance. I'm Frank Rubart and this is Brock Eastbrook."

"Officer Rubart, officer Eastbrook."

"Call me Frank," said the lean man. "And he goes by B.D. as in beady-eyed." The other man didn't respond except to touch the brim of his hat. I suppose he was used to the remark.

"As long as we're on a first name basis, I'm Jim and the kids are..."

"Pleased to meet y'all," he said, tipping his Smo-key Bear hat. "Yer tour guide can take y'all out to the Deveaux place. We've got it marked off with police tape. Yer free to explore the usual tour route, too—plenty of wildlife out there. And let us know if y'all see anything suspicious."

"Sure will," answered my dad "Thanks Frank."

"Jim," he answered, "y'all have a good time. Oh, he's my card; call my cell if ya need to."

Dad took the card, "Thanks Frank."

☠ ☠ ☠

We moved into the tour-gift shop-café building, skirting past a lizard sunning itself on the railing, and met the man from the TV, none other than Jeb Plouet, standing behind the counter of the gift shop, snack bar and tour registration desk. The place was well stocked with plasticized alligator heads, souvenir visors and T-shirts, plush-toy alligators, rubber snakes, key chains, postcards, quick energy food and drinks and more. There were a few aquariums that held baby alligators and turtles near the door by a window.

Jeb looked thinner than he had on the tube, but was, none-the-less, a portly man dressed in baggy overalls, a rather large beige T-shirt and a wide-brimmed floppy tan hat. He smiled a toothy grin and stepped toward us. "Afternoon," he said, "ya must be my charter."

"That would be us," said Bart's dad.

"Well, we'd best git started den," Jeb said. Like most Cajuns he couldn't pronounce the *th* sound, so it came out like a *d*. "Daylight's a-burning. Normally, I'd charge ya twenty buck a head, but dis one on da house, beings as ya got a law officer wit ya. Might help us find ol' Hal. He's my best friend in da world. Why he even... well, dat's a big story. Anyways, come on." He turned and sauntered out the front door over which hung a sign that read:

HONEY ISLAND SWAMP TOURS

We followed. Outside the man indicated the camera hung around my neck, "Ya want ya picture taken?" He smiled, "Prove ya was here and gives us a record should ya go missin'." He grinned his toothy grin. I handed him my camera and we posed for a photograph in front of the carved sign that hung from the porch, then walked toward the boat ramp. Beyond a rustic wooden queue, covered in weathered canvas, was a dock and beyond that a dilapidated building that opened into the water—a shed for boat stowage I imagined.

Moored to the dock was a flat aluminum boat with bench seats running down the center which faced out to the sides; at the stern was a huge Yamaha out-board motor. Jeb put one foot in the vessel and kept the other on the wharf. He assisted each of us onboard while he laid a few ground rules.

"Have a seat anywhere ya like, folks," said Jeb. "The coast guard requires dat I go over a few t'ings afore we git head out. Stay seated while da boat's in motion; please keep ya body parts inside da railing at all times lesson ya want to lose a finger to a gator; dere are lifejackets under ya seat should ya need dem. We'll be underway as soon as ya situated. Tank ya for joining us today at Honey Island Swamp

Tours where adventure awaits—and so do hungry alligators."

It was a well-practiced spiel—and sounded like one. Bart leaned over and told me he wondered if the remaining pitch would be as dull as this or if it would be more like the one-liners that peppered the Jungle Cruise at Walt Disney World. I half expected him to say, "Dis here is da wildest ride in da wilderness!" (which actually comes from the pre-ride at Big Thunder Mt. Railroad).

Speaking of Disney World, I wished Will was with us. He wasn't. His family had planned their trip to the Magic Kingdom a year ago and there was no way he was going to miss it for our trip. Even though we'd had a blast, so far, I envied him. I hadn't been over to ol' WDW for five years.

When we were all seated Jeb started the engine. A black puff of oily gas exhaust blew over us, its nasty smell momentarily masking the nice floral scents of blooming flowers mixed with pine, and swamp. The water looked like strong coffee that had been well creamed as Jeb gingerly pulled away from the dock. "Folks, dis a wildlife management area regulated by state hunting and fishing regulations—including alligator coming up in September.

"We have turtles, alligators, great blue herons, egrets, wood ducks, teal, horned owls, deer, wild hogs, frogs and a wide variety of snakes—some venomous—out here. Below the surface dere are crab, shrimp, crawfish and sport fish—a lot of catfish and white perch. Da catfish are a commercial fish so dey're caught year 'round, the other species are regulated by season."

Jeb gunned the engine, did a quick cookie and we were buzzing into open water. The breeze was quite chilly. Within a couple of minutes he slowed the vessel for a marked *No Wake Zone*. Along the shoreline attractive homes dotted the wooded rises. Stilted shacks also stood on the water's edge, each sporting a dock. Some were in sad disrepair—never repaired or rebuilt since the Katrina storm surge wiped them out—others were quite nice. Several had stacks of crab traps standing next to them.

"Yup, people live out here year 'round in these camps, making a living at shimpin', crabbin' an' such," said Jeb now that the engine was idled down. "Others come down seasonally or on da weekends to fish and trap. Lots of nutria out here, too. Years ago seven came over from Vietnam and now da population runs close to twenty million. Dey kin have up to four litter a year and dey'll eat anything. Da game department pays five bucks a tail fer 'um.

"As ya kin see Katrina did a lot of damage here. Dere was a fifteen foot storm surge and if you look at dat dere house you can see da water line stain halfway up da side. Da water's a tad high right now, too. If it gits any higher I'm gunna hafta buy my chickens hip boots." He gunned the engine again and steered the vessel into a side channel, where he slowed once again to a crawl.

"A friend of mine operates anudder tour outfit. He fell outta his boat once and got a leg bit off by a gator. I called him in the hospital as soon as I got the news. 'Jeb,' he said, 'a gator bit off my leg.' I asked, 'Which one.' He said, 'I don't know, all dem gators be lookin' da same to me.'" I thought that was funny, but it only made Bart nervous; I could tell by the way he looked at me.

"Seriously, dis is a recreation area and people *do* waterski and swim out here as well as hunt and fish. I grew up here and did plenty of dat sort of t'ing, even dough, now as an adult, da idea makes my skin crawl—considerin' the snakes an' gators that make dis dere home."

"But dese bayas be disappearing. Evera year a chunk of sou'dern Louisiana equal to da landmass of da island of Manhattan is lost to da sea."

"Wait a minute," I said. "I thought that was a football field a year."

"Oh, no, no, no. Dat's per day, son—a football field evera day." I was dumb-founded. I lived here and had no idea. Our tour was fascinating. Bart and I had spent lots of time out in the bayous near home, but never had we marveled like this. Sure there was the usual flora and fauna—magnolias and man-groves, gum trees, cedar, cypress and live oaks laden with gray Spanish moss, red leaf maple, Cher-okee rose, duck grass, ele-phant ear and all kinds of animals. Oh! And bugs—*lots* of bugs.

We learned that the tannic acid in the water was what gave the second-growth *bos coya* their knobby knees; the first growth had been logged off. (We also learned that they were related to the red-woods of California and that they could live for nearly 2,000 years.) The pond lilies were in bloom—opened up to the after-noon sun with their yellow flowers.

There were also plenty of snakes. We saw water moccasin, diamond backs, cot-ton mouths, rat snakes and more, all sun-ning them-selves, entwined on branches just off the water's surface on up to ten feet or so. (Like Indiana Jones, I hate snakes.) We did see turtles and alligators, as well as all kinds of birds, too, including a large horned owl.

6 HAP'S PLACE

Da Ocola Indians* lived along dese here banks for t'ousands of years. Oh, look over dere," Jeb said, gesturing. "You see dat dere purple flower? Dat's da Louisiana Iris also known as da *flue de luce**, which is da NOLA symbol and da Saints insignia. Da t'ree points dat stick up, dey represent da trinity. You recognize it? An' look, you can see a gator head over in dat algae. She's probably a seven-footer. If you can only see da head, you can still judge its length. Da distance from da eyes to da end of da snout in inches generally correlates to its body length in feet." That was new to me; handy information.

Twenty minutes later we pulled up next to Hap's camp where his boat was still moored. The place was quiet. Yellow plastic police tape warned *Do Not Cross,* but we did. (After all Dad was a cop.) Jeb stayed in the boat. "Don't touch anything," my dad instructed, "this might be a crime scene."

Bart and I knew the drill. Been there, done that. Anything might be evidence.

"No touchy," I said in my best David Spade imitation.

"*The Emperor's New Groove*," Bart said, recognizing my quote. I smiled and nodded. The rustic building stood on stilts above the waterline. Unpainted and weathered, it looked like it had seen better days. It wasn't much bigger than my living room back home. Stepping inside, we spread out and stood about gawking as our dads poked around. Though a bit unkempt, it didn't have that ransacked look you see in movies when bad guys are looking for something. You know, drawers spilled out, mattresses cut open, overturned furniture, stuff like that.

It just looked lived in by a bachelor; dishes piled on the counter, garbage not taken out, clothes on the floor, bed unmade. *Bart's room*, I thought. The malodor was a bit pungent. *Yeah, definitely Bart's room.* A ceiling fan/light hung on over the sofa-bed and a hunting magazine lay on the nightstand next to it. Yeah, these places had electricity, but not plumbing. The bed appeared to have been slept in. "Looks like he might have been reading," said my dad, mostly to himself.

"Hmm," replied Bart's dad, still in deep thought. I wandered to the kitchen area that wasn't much more than a counter. I knew it was a kitchen area because it had a microwave, fridge/freezer and hotplate. There was no sink. The trash receptacle was near full—TV-dinner boxes and a two-liter soda bottle were on top—with a few roaches crawling around. It appeared that he last ate a dinner of Salisbury steak (a.k.a. mystery meat), peas, mashed potatoes and brownie washed down with Mtn. Dew. *Not into nutrition or gourmet cuisine, I guess.*

"Check this out," Beth was kneeling next to the left of the door jam.

"Whoa," exclaimed Reed, standing beside to her. All of us turned, looked and walked across the small room in their direction. Bart's dad, swung into full game warden mode.

"Don't touch it!" he said like the kid at the end of *Time Bandits*, knelling down and gazing at that the footprint on the floor.

"What is it?" I asked the question I'm sure we all had.

"What does it look like?" said Reed. "It's a footprint. A bare, large, muddy footprint of a four-toed swamp monster!" You could feel the air sucked from the room as everyone took a gasp.

"That," said Bart's dad, "is what you call jumping to conclusions." He whipped a small digital camera from his vest pocket (game wardens wore vests with lots of pockets) and snapped several photographs. "This is likely a hoax, a plant; could be anything. Yeah, it's a print alright—might not be what it appears to be though." He bent closer and pointed at the side of the print. "Hair here. I need to get a forensic kit out here. You've got one at the office, don't you Jim?"

"Sure, but that's a couple hour's drive."

"Right. I'll call the sheriff and see if they've got one." He flipped his phone open, took the sergeant's card from his pocket and dialed. After a pause, while it rang through, he spoke with the officer and arranged for a kit to be picked up at the tour dock. He hung up with a snap, "All set."

"Good. Let's skedaddle back and snag that puppy, Bob. We've got an..." It was then we heard *it*. Whatever it was it sounded...it sounded...it was unearthly and hideous, primal and guttural—like no sound I'd ever heard before and I'd heard bobcat and boar, coyote and bear. I'd even heard Wookie, taun-tuan and sand people—in *Star Wars*—and this was *way* worse.

"Yikes!" said Reed. Warden Davis popped to his feet. Dad put his hand on his gun and the two of them spun to the door.

"Who says 'yikes'?" asked Beth.

"Reed says 'yikes,'" answered Keilah.

"I say 'yikes' and 'let's git outta here,'" said Dallas. Our dads were on the porch looking every-which-way.

"You see anything?" Dad said to Jeb. The guide shook his head no.

"Nothing," answered Bart's dad. "Which way did the sound come from?" Jeb shrugged.

"No idea. Didn't notice," the warden hollered back toward where we stood in the doorway. "You kids have any idea which direction that sound came from?"

"East," I said. (I notice these things.) They strode to the edge of the porch railing on the east side and looked out into the darkening distance.

"See anything?" Dad looked back and forth at Warden Davis and Jeb.

"Nope," said Jeb, "but while dis ain't da first time I heard dat sound, I never heared it afore las' mont'. No idea what it is eder."

"Let's get the kids out of here," said Bart's dad, "and come back with that kit."

"Sounds like a plan. Come on kids, into the boat."

"But..." I said.

"No buts about it. This could be dangerous."

"Danger is my middle name," I tapped my chest.

"Peter, this is *not* the time to joke around." *Man, I love my pops, but he seems*

166

*kind of cranky today. Does he have to ride
me so, in front of my friends? So I'm not
perfect. Who is?*

"Come on now. In the boat," ordered
my dad. Within minutes we were underway and took a recon spin down an eastern running channel before giving up and
tooling back toward tour headquarters.
Our dads, sitting close in the back of the
boat, talked with one another in as hushed tones as possible. Once back, Jeb pulled up to the dock, moored the boat, helped us out and walked us back to our van.
"I hope da tour has been helpful," he said
and then pointed over toward the boat
launch. "Sherriff, if you're actually going
back out dere, ya can use our air-boat
over dere. It's faster."

"That would be great," said Warden
Davis. (That's what he used back in
Houma.)

"I'll git da keys fer ya," and Jeb
wandered into the tour shack as we stood
around the vehicle making chit chat.

"I'll call Dolores and let her know of our
plan," said Dad as he stepped away from
us, taking the radio from his belt and calling into his dispatcher-office manager.

"That sound we heard out there,"
said Keilah, "it was spooky."

"And those tracks," said Reed, "I want
to see the thing that made it."

"No, you don't," said Beth smiling. "It would probably suck you up to the mother ship, do a rectal exam, take your brain out through a straw, implant a chip in your nasal cavity, and take DNA samples from your spine with a super-charged Hoover." Everyone laughed as Reed turned a ghostly grayish white.

"On second thought," he said. (Told you he watched too many *X-Files*.)

Jeb returned momentarily. "Here," he said, "an' be careful. I'm goin' home, if ya need anyting' here's my number." Dad took the piece of paper he held out and Jeb looked us over. "All accounted for den?" We nodded. "Any fingers missin'?" We shook our heads. "Den it was a good tour." He chuckled and sauntered off toward a beat up Chevy truck that looked like it had seen better days. We got in the van, Dad started the engine and we tooled up the drive, Jeb right behind us.

7 MISSING

We'd taken a hotel room at a quaint graying roadside motel in Slidell and ordered in pizza from the gas station-convenience store-pizzeria down on the corner. Our dads were out to Hap's place with the borrowed airboat and a forensic kit. The hotel room was pretty quiet except for the sound of an occasional car passing by on the adjacent road outside, the pizza was cold and no one felt like talking. Our dads were running late. My cell phone rang and I answered. "Oh, Mom, it's you. We haven't heard from Dad yet."

"I know." She sounded like she had seen a ghost—or a swamp monster.

"What is it? Is it about Dad?" There was silence. "What is it?"

"I..I just got off the phone with Dolores," Her voice quavered. "There's no contact with your father. No radio..." she trailed off.

"He hasn't checked in?"

"Dolores can't reach him through either dispatch radio or by cell. There's no answer. Bob isn't answering either. It's been over an hour since they last talked."

"They said they'd be back about 'dark-thirty,'" I said. "Maybe they're on their way and can't hear over the airboat's fan."

"It's well past dark and they'd be docked within twenty minutes. Dolores has dispatched a local search..."

"They need a rescue!?" My dad could be in danger, maybe even...dead. I swallowed hard. Yeah, my dad was a cop; he put his life on the line every day. It was something I had learned to accept. Mostly.

"Peter, don't worry, it's..."

"Why not? *You* are." Moms!

"Just hang in there. I'll keep you posted if I hear anything. You...you going to be okay?" I could hear the distress in her voice.

"What do you think?" I'd get through it, sure, but I felt pretty upset. I could feel the visceral tension welling up inside me.

"You kids hang in there. It's going to be all right."

"Sure, Mom." I thought of all kinds of things I wanted to say and ask, but I didn't need to give her any more anguish. "Love you."

"I love you, too." I hung up and looked at Bart.

"Our dads are missing."

Beth gasped and pulled her hands to her mouth. "I figured that," said Bart hanging his head. "Question is, what are we gonna do about it?"

"Oh, no, no, no, no," interjected Reed. "You are *not* going out there! I mean, you're not thinking of that...*are* you?"

"I am. I don't expect you guys to come; that wouldn't be good. You shouldn't. You won't, but...well, Bart and I *have* to."

"No, you don't," said Beth. "This is best left to the authorities."

"Our dads *are* the authorities and..."

"You *can't* go out there," said Keilah. "It's foolish."

"Look, it's not like we've never been out on a bayou in the middle of the night. We *did* undercover that Voodoo Virus thing," I assured.

"And you were shot, Pete!" said Carla. "You could have been killed."

"But I wasn't."

"What about *this* time?"

"Well," I couldn't help myself but quote *Star Trek's* Worf, "'today is a good day to die.'" She gave me a seething glare.

"Look, it's what we do, okay. Now let's get over it and get to formulating a plan." Bart and I were going out and there was no doubt about it—no debating the matter further—and everyone knew it. (We were pretty pig headed—especially Bart; he smelled like one, too.) What we *did* debate is the best course of action. Getting out there, what to take, what we could do, what we'd find. "We need some boom sticks," I said, thinking of what I'd heard about from *The Grey*—a movie I'd never seen due to its R rating.

"Where on earth are you," said Bart, "a sixteen year-old, going to get shotgun shells —especially this time of night?"

"Ah, yeah, right." My mind whirled. "I suppose C-4 is out of the question, too?"

Carla chuckled, "You are such a pyro!"

"Ya know," said Reed, draping his arm over my shoulder, "I used to be an adventurer like you, then I took an arrow in the knee." We were so ill-equipped. (Absolutely nothing explosive.)

☠ ☠ ☠

"Tony Stark!" I said out of the blue.

"What?" asked Beth.

"Iron Man," answered Bart.

"Yeah," said Beth, "I got *that*."

"He's got a movie idea," said Bart.

"And?" said Beth.

"Iron Man three," I said, "when Tony didn't have a suit he could use he went shopping at the hardware store."

"Oh, yeah," said Keilah, "he bought stuff he could make weapons out of."

"Correct-a-mundo!" I said and followed up with a string of ideas. A minute later it was decided: we needed to get a taxi to a Home Depot for supplies. Carla went to work with the phone book she'd found in the hotel room's nightstand to find both. We decided we could borrow a tour boat when we got to Honey Island Swamp.

Carla insisted in the end that she would go with us, though I tried in vain to dissuade her. She said I wasn't going to go without her and that was that, so live with it. Reed was assigned our home base communications man—he had the only other cell phone among us, besides mine. Now for the details.

"How much money do we have?" I asked. "I've got about twenty-four fifty." Everyone dug into their wallets, pockets and/or purses and withdrew their cash and began counting while I took the hotel notepad and pen from the nightstand and wrote my sum at the top.

"I have fourteen dollars and seventy cents," said Beth.

"I have twelve thirty-five," added Carla. I wrote the amounts down in a column below my original entry.

"Fifteen bucks," said Dallas.

"Twenty-four seventy-two," said Reed.

"Two o' two," said Keilah, sheepishly. "I bought a few T-shirts at the event." Bart was still counting.

"And Bart?" I questioned.

"A hundred forty-seven forty-eight, and some change. One forty eight, fifty...four." All eyes were on him. After a moment he looked up and said, "What?"

"Dude! You've been putting fast-food away like Bill Murray eating breakfast in *Groundhog's Day*," I said. "And you *still* have more money than I started with."

"I came prepaid."

"I'll say," I said. "That's six weeks allowance for me."

"I've been helping the Carreire's with their net mending business."

"Kin I get a job with 'um?" asked Dallas.

"Maybe next year," answered Bart. "We're done for the season."

"Okay," I began totaling, "lessee."

"Two hundred thirty-nine eighty-three," Beth blurted.

"What?" Keilah asked. "You, like, added that in your head?"

"I'm good at math."

"She's right," I said. "Two hundred thirty-nine eighty-three on the nose. We've got about two hundred and forty bucks."

"Oh wait," said Dallas removing his Stetson. He flipped it over and withdrew narrowly folded and sweat-stained a hundred dollar bill from the band inside his sou'wester. Unfolding it he handed it to me. "Ma ropin' money."

"You're what?" asked Carla.

"Ma winnin's from rodeoin.' I put it there cuz I weren't packin' ma wallet. Can't ride a horse with a spur in yer saddle."

"Yeah, okay," I said, "we have about three hundred forty bucks. Now what?"

"Well, said Carla, "we're gonna need flashlights and batteries." I wrote that down. "How about some rope?"

"Rope," asked Bart, "what for?"

Dallas spoke up, "Rope is good for lassos, towin', tyin', climbin', bindin', trippin', hangin', hitchin' up yer pants, an'..."

"We *git* the idear, cowboy," interrupted Reed. "You know ropes." I wrote down rope and waited for more *idears*. None came.

"Anything else?" Silence.

"Ah, flares?" asked Keilah, "For signaling." I wrote it down.

"Say, Pete," said Bart, "I think you just need inspiration. You get to the hardware store and it will come to you." *What do you get from a hardware store that will help you save your dad from who-knows-what out in a swamp?* I guess I would have to improvise.

☠ ☠ ☠

My cell phone rang again and I fell up-on it like I was trying to snatch a twenty dollar bill from a fire before it burned. "Mom? Dad?"

"It's your mom. I'm just checking up on you. See how you're doing before bed."

"Heard anything?"

"Nothing new. I called Dolores. She said the local sheriff team has come back in." I could tell from Mom's voice she was trying to be stoic. "They found..." I heard faint sobs on the other end of the connection. Then there was that question I couldn't ask. I couldn't ask if dad was dead, so I just sat there, listening.

"Peter, they found the boat and the forensic kit. They found...muddy footprints and...blood." She began to sob bitterly. I sat there in shock. If she was here she would come over to the bed, compose herself, sit down beside me and wrap her arm around my shoulders where we'd be a comfort to one another. But she wasn't here; I wasn't there. We were both alone in this. "It doesn't mean anything, it could be nothing." *Yeah, right.* "You going to be okay?" *Okay? Okay with my dad missing, possibly dead? Like, nooo.*

"You'll tell me if you hear anything?" I said, and then thought better of it; I didn't want her calling to find me gone. "Better yet, I'll call *you* tomorrow. Don't want to wake the whole room."

"I haven't decided if I need to come out there yet. For now I'm going to monitor the situation through Dolores. They'll resume the search tomorrow morning. As long as your safe and sound, honey."

"Okay, Mom, we are. I better go. We're pretty bushed," I said, not wanting to out and out lie, saying we were going to bed when we weren't. And truthfully, we were feeling pretty wiped out. "I love you, Mom."

"I love you, honey."

"Goodnight," I said and hung up. I shook off the sadness in my heart by calling upon a memory verse: *"Why so downcast, oh my soul; put your trust in God.**" I sent up a quick prayer, then struck a dramatic pose for quoting Shakespeare.

"'To woe the slings and arrows of outrageous fortune...to take arms against the sea of troubles, and by opposing them, end them...'"

"There he goes with *Hamlet* again," whispered Carla to Bart.

"I know, he's weird like that," he answered back.

"To task, my friends!" said I. *Said I? Maybe I am a nutcase.* I called the cab company.

8 PUTTING THE PLAN TOGETHER

Half-hour later Bart, Carla and I arrived at Lowe's (no Home Depot in town) an hour before closing with no real idea what we wanted beyond a couple of flashlights and flares...and some rope. We began systematically wandering the vast isles of hardware and home improvement supplies.

"Duct tape!" said Bart. "We need duct tape."

"What do we need duct tape for?" asked Carla.

"I prefer gaff tape," I said.

"What's gaff tape?" she asked.

"It's like duct tape only it's a theater or film tech's best friend," I answered. "Comes in matte black and comes off clean without residue."

Carla shook her head "Oh, cool. So, why do we need it?"

"I dunno," said Bart, "but either one can come in handy with over 1001 uses."

"Yeah, nice. What else?"

"How about a chainsaw?" I asked thinking about how they were used as weapons in various zombie and horror movies. "No, too grizzly."

"And too expensive," added Carla.

"Look here," said Bart, approaching an entire wall of hardware and wire of every size and tinsel strength. "We could use some wire for trip lines with those screw eyes between two trees."

"Hmm, not bad," I said. "Grab a roll of thin wire and a pack of eyes." We moved on and found ourselves in plumbing.

"What are we gonna do with stuff like this?" asked Carla. "Build a toilet?"

"I need some PVC pipe, some quick cement, a few couplings..."

"For what?"

"A potato cannon, of course," I said.

"Pota...a what?" she asked.

"It shoots stuff," I explained. "Not just potatoes, but anything you can stuff in the barrel. It's powered by any flammable gas like hairspray, WD-40, butane, etc."

"Oh, yeah, pyro stuff. Got it." I chose a coupling, two sizes of pipe, a can of cement and an end cap from the display.

"We have to get an electronic click igniter—like for a barbeque—and some flammable aerosol."

Bart got an idea. "Hey, how about some of this smaller PVC for blowguns?"

"What? Like, *you* know how to make poison darts" I said, shooting down his idea. We bee-lined to the outdoor aisle and found the barbeque replacement parts section, picking up a sparker unit and an Aim n' Flame lighter, then went back to hardware for a couple of awls the right size to bore holes in the PVC pipe for a filling valve and the igniter. While in the section I grabbed a cheap hammer, hatchet, pliers, a small wire cutter and screw driver—all but the hatchet came in a kit and they were pink (Carla liked that).

"Flares," said Carla, "don't forget flares." On the way to the small automotive section for road flares, we passed an aisle loaded with things like butane torches, small bottles of propane and canned butane. *A pyros dream aisle.* We picked up a couple of each then rounded out the shopping spree with a couple coils of nylon rope, a bag of shop rags, three flashlights, a twelve pack of flares, a brick of batteries, a twelve by sixteen foot tarp and a five gallon can of paint thinner. We passed on the duct tape. Forty minutes later we checked out to the raised eye-brows of the clerk.

☠ ☠ ☠

Two hours later, give or take a few minutes, Bart, Carla and I were on our way from Lowes to Honey Island Swamp armed

with a cab trunk full of hardware. I had
originally tried to ditch Carla by telling her
we would go the hardware store and swing
back by for her. But, you know, she's as
smart as she is pretty and wouldn't let us
out of her sight. Besides, the Lowes was
on the way.

The cab driver rolled his eyes at us but
asked no questions. I guess cash fare was
cash fare. On the way I assembled the potato cannon with the windows rolled down
to alleviate the toxic fumes from the plumber's cement.

We arrived at the tour location, paid
the driver sixty-bucks, leaving the whole of
$9.74 left among us. It was around 12:30
p.m. and all was quiet. It was dark except
for a single mercury vapor street light illuminating the dock an eerie green-yellow.
A gentle breeze blew in off the water. The
*mouche a fea** flitted in the distance. The
cab driver pulled up to the dock as we instructed and sat wringing his hands and
looking around like he was nervous while
we unloaded. Finally, we waved him off. I
think he was glad to get out of there.

"Bart, pick a boat and see if everything's in order with the outboard. Carla
and I will get batteries into these lanterns
and get organized. When you're done...oh,
don't start anything until we're ready...
when you're done come on back and we'll
get loaded."

"Sho nuff," he said and took off down the dock. I called Reed and let him know we'd arrived at position A and that we were okay while Carla went rummaging through our collection of plastic bags, pulling out heavy duty flashlights. I soon joined her at the task and found the blister pack of batteries, but couldn't for the life of me get it open.

Carla picked up one of the lanterns and opened the battery chamber. I rummaged again and found the box knife we'd bought. It was in a blister pack. *How are you supposed to get a box knife out of a blister pack without a box knife?*

"I need a knife or something," I whispered. Carla dug into the pocket of her jeans and pulled out a pocket knife. I smiled. *Gotta love a girl who carries a knife—or else*, I mused. I pulled the blade open and tore into the blister packs, handing batteries to Carla who arranged them in the cavities of the lanterns. She tested her work with her hand over the lens and flipped the light back off. We finished that project just as Bart jogged up the dock.

"No gas, no gas tanks," he said, huffing.

"You're kidding me!"

"Nope. Probably take them out of the boats at night so that no one can take off with them."

"Ya think?" I said.

"Ya think to look in the boathouse over there?" said Carla. Man, did I mention she was bright? Bart trotted off toward the boat house and traipsed down the gangplank.

I turned back to Carla, "I'm glad you came along."

"You'd have thought of it," she replied nonchalantly as she removed the two coils of rope from our bags and draped them over her neck and shoulders. I dug into our wares again and removed the hatchet and secured it in my belt. She bent down and fished out a couple of the flares and the pink-handled hammer from the girlie tool kit. She ripped open the package of flares and placed them on the ground, took the hammer and began beating them.

"What are you doing!?" I cried. She stopped and looked up with a smile.

"My brother, Josiah, always did this to his Piccolo Pete's on the Fourth of July. It makes them explosive. Mom, hates it when he does it. Anyway, I figure these will work the same way."

"Wow, great idea, but don't do them all, we might need some for signaling."

"Gotcha." She went back to pummeling flares.

Bart was back, "I need some bolt-cutters; it's locked."

"Don't have any," I said, reaching to my belt. "Here, take this hatchet and chop through the door if you have to."

"Got it." And bam, he was jogging back down the dock again. *Pretty good shape for a chunky guy.* Meanwhile Carla loaded the flares back into the bags, putting the beat up ones in one bag and the unaltered ones in another. *Man, why didn't I think of that idea.* They looked like sticks of dynamite. Now, maybe they would function like them. *What a woman!*

Bart was back again carrying two gas tanks, hatchet in his belt. "They're going to need a new door," he huffed and headed off to the boat. Carla and I gathered up our supplies and followed.

9 OFF AND RUNNING

After hooking up the gas lines to the tanks and pumping the primer Bart gave the outboard's starter cord a yank and the engine sputtered to life with a plume of acrid exhaust. Carla and I stowed the gear on board and sat. Soon we were under-way. Bart stood near the stern at the wheel of the boat as he gingerly trolled us out into the watercourse. "You remember the way?" I asked.

"Like duh," Bart replied. "Have you ever known me to get lost?"

"Only in thought," said Carla as Bart gunned the throttle and the chilly air and spray whipped over us. *At least it keeps the mosquitoes away.* We tugged on our jackets. Carla clicked on one of the heavy duty flashlights and aimed it over the bow. The outboard thrummed and whined as the boat cut through the murky water. The light shone eerily ahead, illuminating only a few yards of the water-way forward of the boat. I thought of how sometimes the path of life before us only showed the next few steps and did not light God's whole plan. *Thy word is a lamp unto my feet and a light unto my path** I quoted from the Psalms to myself. What lay ahead, I had no idea. I guess I would know when I got there—maybe. I hoped.

I wasn't particularly keen on bayous at night. The last time we were out in the marshes and swamps we ran into terrorists and zombies, but even without such dangers there were alligators and snakes. Did I mention I hate snakes? Honestly, bayous are creepy places—especially at night. Dark gray tentacles of Spanish moss swayed eerily from the scrubby trees, the moon—a sliver of silver in the brooding sky—gave little illumination, but still carved haunting shadows across the murky water.

The three of us were alone in new territory and people had gone missing. Two of the three were my dad and Bart's dad—trained law enforcement personnel. What were three kids going to do? We too could turn up missing. We could die.

Bart swung our vessel—not ours really—east, down a narrow channel overhung with cypress toward Hap's place. The trees formed an arched canopy that cut out even more moonlight. He throttled back the outboard to maneuver more carefully through the creepy labyrinth.

Labyrinth, that made me think of David Bowie* (rest his soul). Talk about creepy.

"It's just up ahead," said Bart, yelling above the chug of the engine, "around a couple of bends." I didn't doubt him, but Carla snorted. Bart had a sixth sense about navigation and could remember how to get anywhere he'd ever been before.

"And you know this, how?" she asked.

"Trust him," I said, "he knows." Two turns later, there it stood, leaning like a wounded soldier, proud and brave, but injured none-the-less: Hap's camp, stilted and weathered, silhouetted against the shadowy *bos coya** that surrounded it. Bart smirked at Carla and throttled back some more, easing the boat up to the wharf next to the airboat our dads had borrowed. I jumped up and made my way to the gunnel near the bow, grabbed the tie line and secured it to the dock.

After he cut the engine, Bart did the same in the stern. We sat there in silence, listening for a minute. There was the gentle lapping of the water, the hum of mosquitoes, the croak of frogs, the groaning of the shack and the flap of the police tape in the breeze—nothing out of the ordinary (aside from the police tape, that is).

Out of the blue Bart rattled off, "Did you guys know that the words listen and silent have the same letters only in a different order?"

"Well, that's interesting, Bart," I said, picking up a flashlight. "Let's have a look around." Side by side Bart and I, followed by Carla, crept out of the boat and gingerly ascended the stairs to the *gallerie**. The three of us stopped in unison outside the door that moaned on its hinges, ajar. No light came from the crack and I pressed my hand against the door, swinging it open with a creak and shining my light inside.

Searching the room with the beam, my sight fell upon the forensic kit sitting on the bed toppled to one side, contents spilling out. Carla's light joined mine and scanned the room and we stepped further inside after Carla looked behind the door with trepidation. Bart walked over to 'kitchen' counter. Roaches scuttled away from the light.

The place was pretty much the same as we had left it only hours before except for the kit and a few more muddy, four-toed footprints—some were scuffed as if something was dragged through them. I knelt down for a closer examination. "They're still moist and fresh," I whispered and pointed to one that had been smeared. Bart swung his light around the nearby floor and stopped the beam on another partial print.

"Look here," he said. "That looks like a boot print."

"*Fo troo*," I replied. "See how it's scuffed across the floor?"

"Uh, huh," said Bart.

"Probably a scuffle."

"Scuff, scuffle, makes sense," said Carla.

"Not good," intoned Bart, ignoring her smart remark.

"There are others," I said, thinking the prints might have come from our dad's shoes. I stood and scanned the room a-gain. Nothing. I went to the bed.

"Well," said Carla, "we know they were here and we know the monster returned. There may have been a scuffle and now they're not here."

Bart put his hands on his hips and said, "The question then is: Where did they go?"

"It doesn't look like there are any more clues," I said, gathering up the lab-field equipment from the bed and stuffed it back into the kit. Bart turned back to the door and took a step. I heard a tinkling noise from where his foot stepped and shone my light down at his feet and gasp-ed. There on the floor, rolling to a stop, was the spent casing from a police issue Glock*—my dad's sidearm!

Well, it might not actually be police issue and it may or may not be my dad's; it would take a ballistics expert to confirm that. However, the Glock was, after all, the sidearm of choice for sixty-five percent of U.S. law enforcement officers. I bent down and picked it up, looked at it and stuffed it into the pocket of my jeans. Probably not the best crime scene etiquette. I scanned for more casings. There were none.

"Time to move on," instructed Bart. I nodded and we went back outside and did a once-over of the *gallerie* and dock. I took out my phone to report back to Reed. It showed just two bars. Reception was dropping off. *Dead zone*, I thought, then wished I hadn't. I dialed and he picked up.

"Hey, Reed," I said.

"Call me Redeye," he said. "That's my...ode name."

"Okay, 'Redeye'," I glanced at the others, rolling my eyes. "This is The Rock." That had just dawned on me since my name meant 'rock' in Hebrew. Besides that's what they use to call Dwayne Johnson, the wrestler, turned movie action figure. *Yeah, that's me: The Rock.* "We're at point B. It's confirmed, our dads have been here. We found the kit and airboat just as was reported. We also found fresh prints and possible signs of a scuffle.

"Someone fired a round—there was a casing on the floor. Could be Dad's gun; don't know. We're moving on now, but I don't know where."

"You're kind...break...up," he said. "What's tha...you said about..ooting?"

Shooting.

"Dad, I think, shot his gun. No idea at what. Anyway, I've only got two bars out here. Reception could get worse."

"Two what?"

"Bars."

"Roger tha..." *Roger?*

"Okay, I'll call back if and when I can. Roger that?"

"Ca...back, okay?" said the staticy voice on the other end of the failing connection.

"If I can."

"Yeah."

"Over."

I hung up after returning an *over.* "Let's go."

Back in the boat, Bart gave the starter cord a yank and brought the outboard back online as Carla and I untied the lines. Soon we were back out on the channel heading further east at a slow crawl with Carla aiming a light over the bow.

"We're not going to sneak up on anyone this way," I yelled above the motor.

"Did you want to swim, then?" he asked.

"Didn't bring my Speedo," I said. Carla chuckled. I didn't wear a Speedo, I had trunks. "I'm just sayin'..."

"When I find an interesting place to trawl into, we can get out and do some exploration on foot, okay?"

"Interesting?" inquired Carla.

"He means 'with potential,' like as in something that might be worth looking into."

"Like?"

"I don't know. Lights, other people, a space ship, perhaps." I smirked.

"Ha ha." She shivered from the cold air and spray, so I scooted closer and wrapped my arms around her as Bart ruddered southeast up an even thinner channel. Clusters of duck grass encroached upon the sides of the boat and Bart slowed. I yawned and snuggled in closer to Carla, laying my head on her shoulder.

"We'd best keep our eyes peeled, *pad-net*," said Bart. He was right; if we were going to find our fathers I had best be a-lert. (America needs more lerts. They also need round tuits, but that's another joke.) I lifted my head and scanned the marsh-land around us. Patches of earth and piles of downed limbs rose up from the levee— or water's edge—along with the musky smell of decaying vegetation.

In the sunshine these branches would sport many a sunning snake. Being reptiles they are cold-blooded and need to warm themselves in order to raise their body temperature. *I wonder where snakes go in the night?* I shuddered then began to nod off.

☠ ☠ ☠

"Pete, Pete," said Bart awaking me. I rubbed the sleep from my eyes.

"Sup?"

"He's found an 'interesting' spot to dock," said Carla.

"Yeah?" I said, looking around. Bart had cut the outboard down to a crawl and was moving toward the bank through a thicket of duck grass and lilies. "What is it?"

"Nothing really," he said, "just Honey Island. At least I think it is. It's an island anyway. I've been around it once now and there's a boat pulled into a lagoon about quarter a mile back."

"You see anyone? Or they see you?"

"No, I didn't. I don't think we were seen, or heard. No signs of a camp. Just a yacht anchored in the lagoon."

"A yacht?"

"Might be a private research vessel, but it looks like a yacht. Maybe a forty-footer and nice as best I could tell."

"That *does* sound interesting. We gonna check it out?"

"That's the plan."

We gathered our gear—plastic sacks full of hardware—as Bart beached the boat. I scuttled out and helped Carla to shore. She looked like a bandito with coils of rope over each shoulder like a pair of bullet sashes. Bart handed us the parcels and jumped out as well. I took out my phone. One bar. Probably couldn't get reception that was decent enough for a call, but a text might get through. I quickly texted Reed...ah, Redeye:

```
huny isld
found yacht
nothing nown yet
confirm by txt
the rock
```

Hopefully he'd text back. I'd check later.

10 MARSH MONSTER

We set out on foot along the marshy shore of the island. Not wanting to risk being seen, we didn't use the flashlights. It was easy enough to follow the waterline in pale glow of the crescent moon, but the lack of light did slow us down a bit. Marshland can look quite solid when it isn't, so careful steps are in order. Bart took the lead (carrying the paint thinner) and I in the rear behind Carla, each of us lugging a plastic sack of assorted stuff we hoped would be useful.

"I wish we had backpacks," whispered Carla. "This sack is heavy and it's cutting into my hand. I have to switch hands every few minutes."

"I can carry it for you," I volunteered.

"I can pull my own weight, Pete."
Snippy.

"Oh, I know, I know, but I don't mind, really, helping you." I do *try* to be a good boyfriend.

"I'll be okay. Thanks."

Truth be told, my own sack was cutting into my hand and I had to switch frequently, as well. It wasn't the best of circumstances, but it would have to do.

About fifteen minutes later I could see the yacht bobbing offshore and we hunkered down behind a stand of cypress to form our next plan of action.

"Look," I said, "we have no idea what we're walking into. It could be nothing, it could be some serious trouble. Carla, I want you to hang back be-hind us, out of sight, so in case we're seen and we do run into trouble, you can phone Reed and relay what's happening—hopefully he can be reached...*if* we need to."

"What?"

"You heard me, here's my phone. It's on vibrate. It's safer, and we need a back-up."

"I don't want to become separated..."

"I know, but it's the best plan. Let's stash some gear here." I sat my sack down behind a cypress and the others did the same.

"So, what's the plan, Stan?" asked Bart. "I mean, the Rock."

"We climb aboard the yacht and take a look around, I guess."

"How are we gonna get out there?"

"Oh, yeah," said Carla, "I'm not swimming with gators."

"You're staying behind remember," I said. "And gators aren't out at night, I think."

"You think?" said Bart. "Well, I'm not swimming either."

"Then, I guess we travel inland," I said picking up my sack. "Get your gear."

"I want a code name, too" said Carla. Okay, all my friends were nuts. As they say, 'birds of a feather flock together'.

"Okay, how 'bout Gator Girl?" said Bart.

"How about M?" she asked.

"You know," I said, "she died in the last Bond movie."

"Uh, okay, I'll go with Gator Girl then."

"Bart?" I supposed he wanted a code name, too.

"Call me" he said, thinking, "...uh...the Black Knight."

"You mean the Dark Knight as in Batman?" asked Carla.

"No, I was thinking the knight in *Monty Python and the Holy Grail* who keeps on standing guard as all his appendages are cut off."

"It's only a flesh wound," I quoted.

"That's the one," he said.

"Okay then, Black Knight, Gator Girl, let's go."

Carla took hold of my arm and felt what little muscle I had, "Okay," she said, giggling, "Rock."

"You should see my peck pop," I grinned. "Come on, follow me." I took off toward the boat and turned inland. We crept along slowly and cautiously keeping to what timber we could. After a short time Bart stopped dead in his tracks. "What?" I asked in a whisper.

"My eyes are playing tricks on me, *padnet*. Look!" He gestured with his free arm. "Over there." I nearly wet my pants when I saw what he saw. There in the distance, not twenty yards from us, hunched a greenish-brown figure with glowing green eyes backlit with an eerie blue glow.

"Is that, is that..." I said.

"What you think it is?" Bart nodded. Carla came up to us from the rear. Bart gave her the universal *shhh* sign and, seeing what we saw, she gasped. The slicked down, hairy creature lumbered back and forth like it was guarding a nest. I signaled a retreat and we fell back behind some shrubbery. *Ni!* I thought. After some discussion we decided to circle south and see what we could from the rear, not wishing to encounter the creature outright.

☠ ☠ ☠

Ten minutes later, there he was again! *Why had it moved along with us? Could it be another crea-ture?* I was baffled. I gestured we continue to circle and we moved on.

"Is that thing," asked Bart, "heading us off?"

"Beats me," I said, "or maybe there're two of them."

"What's that glow behind them?" asked Carla.

"Search me," answered Bart. "Mother ship?"

"I think we need to get back there," said Carla. "See what they're guarding."

"Yeah," I said, "let's keep moving." And we did. Another ten minutes and there was *another* creature. I was really wondering what was going on. *Was this a secret UFO landing site? Or were these really swamp monsters guarding their nursery?*

I noticed the breeze coming at us from the creature's direction, "You smell anything?"

"No, why?" said Bart. "You let one rip?"

"If I did you'd be dead right now," I retaliated. "Aren't these swamp things supposed to smell awful?"

"That's what they say," said Carla.

"Well," I said, "the wind is coming from his direction and I don't smell anything. Do either of you?"

"Not really," said Carla while Bart shook his head.

"Weird," I said. "Anyway, what are we going to do?"

"We're going to have to take one out, if we're going to get past," said Bart. "But we have to do it without alerting the others."

"*Fo troo*," I said. "How we gonna do that?"

"You're the genius," he said.

"Thanks, yeah, leave it to ol' Peter."

"The Rock," interjected Carla.

"Okay, what's in our utility belt, Batman?"

"Black Knight. And you know as well as I do, Rock. Bat gun, bat flares, bat torch, bat..."

"I know, I know, okay? Let me think." I thought. *Well, lessee, there was the ol' Rambo rush—the run and gun. That wouldn't work; too noisy. The Katniss Everdeen hornet nest maneuver from Hunger Games. Probably not, I hate bees. Best thing to do is draw it away from its post and sneak behind. But how? The ol' rock in the brush? Nah. Think, think.* I thought and thought for a good five minutes before I came up with what I hoped was a reasonable plan. Hopefully, this thing was dumb enough to fall for it.

"Okay, I think I have something."

"What movie is it from?" asked Bart.

"Ha ha," I said.

"Well, they've always worked for you before," said Bart.

"I guess this is sort of based on a premise from many a Western, if that helps. You know how the cowboys always stick their hat on a stick and raise it up over a boulder to draw fire?"

"Yeah, but, Dallas ain't here an' we got no hat," said Carla in a southern drawl, putting her thumbs in her waistband and standing bow-legged.

"That's not the point," I said. "What we have to do is draw him out then sneak behind him. We need a diversion, so here's what we're going to do. Bart, I'm going to twist a screw-eye into this tree. I'm going to tie some of this nylon rope to the loop. You are going to do the same thing, screw-eye, tied off line, tight..."

"Taut," corrected Carla, removing the rope from over her shoulder.

"Taut. Tied off to that tree way over there. You see it?"

"Uh huh."

"Carla. Meanwhile you gather some limbs, tree limbs, two legs, two arms. Then I'll wire together a dummy using the tarp for a covering. We rig up a second line and use it like a pulley to which we attach the dummy and pull it across the clearing like its walking. The swamp thing is either going to try to scare it off, attack it, or run off and hide. Understand?"

"No," said Carla.

"It's like a decoy," explained Bart.

"Just gather the limbs, and keep it quiet." I instructed and she set off. I rum-

maged through our gear and fished out
the package of screw-eyes, the tarp and
the nylon rope. I tied the end of the cord
onto a screw-eye, handed the cord and
another eye to Bart along with the pliers.
"You might need these to twist the eye into
the tree."

"What about you?"

"I'll use the screw driver for leverage.
Now go." He hit the dirt and crawled a-
cross the open space using the tall grass
as cover, letting out the line as he went as
I set to work boring the screw-eye into the
tree beside me. The creature continued to
pace back and forth in the distance. After
a minute or so I was done with the screw
eye task and I emptied the bag of rags into
one of our sacks and began gathering
moss, stuffing it into the bag. That would
be the dummy's head.

Carla arrived back with four gnarled
sticks—two about six inches around and
four feet long, and two about three inches
around and three feet long. I took out the
wire cutters and wire and fastened the
bunch together into a really thin-looking
scarecrow, attached the head at the top,
running the wire through it and making a
loop. Carla and I gingerly opened the tarp
and shaped it like a hood around the
figure.

"Knife," I whispered, and she pulled it
from the pocket of her jeans, handing it to

me. Bart returned, crawling across the ground. When he stood up, his front was covered with mud. I cut the tarp up the middle from the bottom to the top and a-cross each side about a foot underneath each of the 'arms' and cut pieces of cord to tie them to the sticks, thus forming sleeves and pant legs, and tied a cord below the head to form a neck. *Blue Man**, I thought. "Ready for another trip, Bart?"

"Sure," he answered, "I need some more mud." I attached the dummy decoy to the remainder of the line and handed an end to Bart.

"Here, this one goes through the screw-eye, but don't tie it off, bring the end back. And take this other coil of rope in case you need to tie it to the other to make it long-er."

"Will do," he said, lying back down on the ground. While he was gone I wired a flashlight onto the dummy's arm while Carla loaded the trash and supplies back into the sacks. Five minutes or so later Bart came crawling back and handed me the second line.

"I had to tie them together," he said. "What now?"

"You guys go on ahead in that direc-tion," I indicated to my right, the dummy on our left. "I'll switch on the dummy's flashlight and follow you, pulling the line. The dummy should move across the open space. We'll see what happens. If the creature moves out toward the dummy, start circling in toward that eerie light. I'll meet up with you in a few." They nodded and set off. I counted to one hundred before switching on the dummy light, crouched low and took off after them, looking back over my shoulder.

The dummy lurched along the line with a slight bobbing motion in sync with each of my steps in the opposite direction. Immediately I—or rather the dummy—had the creature's attention. It stopped in its tracks and observed for a moment before rushing to a nearby stump and picking up what looked like a rifle. *Ha! Human*, I thought to myself, *Knew it*. Now it was bounding through the brush toward the decoy. *Perfect. I'm a genius.*

Behind me I heard the words, "Hold it right there, buddy." The male voice was too far back from me to be addressed at me so I kept on. The 'monster' was talking to the dummy. *Dummy.* I didn't bother looking back; I was running out of line and just then there was a snag—the line wouldn't pull. I yanked and looked back. The dummy was bobbing against a tree. Time to hightail it out of there. I dropped the line and set off in a duck walk, knees burning with the effort.

I found the others with some searching, all the while noting the movements of the man dressed like a yeti. He examined the apparatus and ran back to his stump where he brought something up to his mouth. We were too far away to hear, but I was pretty sure he was using a radio to make a perimeter breach report.

"Follow the light," I said, "*vite, vite*.*"

☠ ☠ ☠

Minutes later we stealthily approached the blue glow, which grew brighter as we drew closer. The chugging sound of generators grew louder, too. It was soon clear that the lights did *not* come from a space ship or some netherworld nursery, but were, in fact, an array of halogen flood lamps illuminating a dig—an archeological research site, perhaps? *But why the sentry of costumed goons then?* We approached with caution staying hidden in the overgrowth and came to another low-lying clump of duck grass where we stopped to observe and converse.

There was a small backhoe at work removing mud from a hole already the size of a backyard shed in volume and depth. A pump exhumed water from the hole, expelling it into a ditch some yards away. Nearby was erected a rather elaborate tent and a man, dressed in dungarees and hip boots, bustled about the area.

"What do you make of that?" I asked the others.

"An excavation?" asked Bart in return, shrugging his shoulders. Carla just shrugged.

"Let's think about this," I said, "Speculations?"

"Exhuming a body?" said Carla.

"Gas or oil mining?" said Bart. That was a big operation down in Louisiana. *Too big and too small*, I thought then gestured for more ideas.

"Treasure hunting?" suggested Bart. "Ah, building...?"

"That's it!" I exclaimed in hushed tones. "They—whoever they are—are looking for pirate treasure!"

11 PIRATES!

"We have to get down there!" I said.
"You're kidding me," said Carla.
"They're..."

"But its treasure," said Bart.

"And they're probably just as violent as Black Beard," Carla finished.

"Maybe," I said. "So we don't get caught. We go in for a looksee and then get out. Okay?"

Pirates? I'd never met a real pirate. It's said that pirates frequented the waters of the lower Mississippi back in the seventeenth to nineteenth centuries. Among them was the infamous buccaneer Jean Lafitte who bartered with the Americans for pardon in exchange for information regarding the attacks of the British Navy. He even fought along-side the states during The War of 1812* and helped win the war in 1815. He was never heard from again, though it is thought that he survived, married and settled in the Bahamas to raise a family. He and his brother had operated a smuggling outfit out of a warehouse down at English Turn (less than forty-five miles from where we sat).

Many have speculated that he buried treasure in these parts and many have looked for it to no avail. *Probably a myth like the swamp monster.* But that didn't keep people from looking. That *had* to be it, it was the perfect site—navigable by the surrounding lakes and rivers; an easy route from one to the other—especially back then.

"Okay," said Carla, "let's say that's it. So why the disguised swamp thugs?"

"Duh," said Bart. "Secrecy, to scare people away."

"But people search for treasure in these parts all the time," said Carla. "No one thinks anything about it."

"Unless..." I interjected with finger in the air, "they were sure they had a good find. You'd protect that."

"Yeah, yeah!" said Bart way too loudly in his excitement.

Shhh! scolded Carla.

"Sorry."

"And," I continued, "if anyone got too close..." I drew my finger across my throat in a slicing motion.

Bart swallowed hard, "Oh no," he said.

I was thinking the same. *Our dads!* It was at that point that one of the costumed swamp goons, minus the head portion (meaning no mask to hide the quite human head), emerged from the tent and began shouting and gesturing 'come on.' That's when the other men dropped what they were doing and went into the tent.

"Uh oh," said Carla. "I think I know what that might mean."

"And I think you're right," I said. "They're on to us."

"And they're going to come looking for us," added Bart.

"Yup," I said as the small army emerged from the canvas shelter toting weapons and scattered in pairs in various directions. "Time to fall back, team."

"Wait," said Bart, "isn't that…isn't…?"

"It's Thachne!" exclaimed Carla quietly.

"No," I said raising my eyebrows, my voice evident with disbelief.

"It *is*," said Bart. My mind raced, trying to piece this puzzle together. We not only needed a plan, but we needed to get away and then we needed to get back into this 'dig' and find out what was going on, find out where our fathers were, hopefully rescue them, and then get off the island and back home. *Could they be in the tent?* Yeah, that's what I was thinking: *Piece of cake, sure.*

"Hold on a moment," I said, pulling out my phone, keeping it low and shrouded in my jacket. I checked for reception. Only one bar and no text from Reed. I knew that a person couldn't text a 911 call and calling them was not an option without better reception. I noted the time, 3:14 in the morning, and cautiously closed the device, slipped it back into my pocket and looked at the others who were looking back at me, hope written on their faces. "Nothing," I said. "We're on our own." I then reiterated our entire situation and my thoughts to Bart and Carla as they silently listened.

"I agree," said Bart, when I'd finished. "We *do* need to explore the camp, or, um, dig, but we have to do it when the opportunity presents itself and that isn't now. It's too dangerous. We need fall back and wait for things to cool down."

"I couldn't agree more," I said softly. "Hide the gear; cover it up," I added. "Especially that paint thinner—hide it good." We went about doing just that. The big things went behind a log and we covered them up with grass and moss. The other items were nestled in their sacks and snuggled down into tufts of duck grass before we came back together. Although we were never far from one another at any point.

"Remember where this is," I said quietly when our heads where so close together I could smell the hints of pizza on the others breaths. "Make mental notes of our position." My stomach rumbled—it had been hours since we ate. *Or was it just nerves?* I could hear rustling in the brush off to our right. "Come on, quietly." I turned left in my squatting position and went prone in the muck, crawling with my elbows, as the others followed suit.

☠ ☠ ☠

Now we were all well caked in an icky-smelling swamp grime, but no one complained. We were, after all, alive and free. There's something to be said about that, don't you think? Yeah, life can be scary, perilous, a pain and full of hard-ships, but it also has its simple joys. *Thank you Jesus*, I prayed, *keep our dads safe—and Hap, too.* Had I not even thought to pray for them until now? I'm afraid I'm not the Christian I often think I am. I would have to work on that.

I led our group back toward the island's shore and toward our boat, making sure to keep to the cover of vegetation. When we arrived, it was just as I'd feared: Our vessel had been discovered and was now guarded by one of the goons —this one not costumed as a marsh monster. I stopped in my vantage point not twenty yards from where he stood and motioned Bart and Carla up beside me. "You see that?" I whispered.

"I do," said Bart. "Not good."

"Expected though," I commented.

"What are we going to do?" asked Carla. "How are we going to get off the island?"

"We'll find a way," Bart assured, "but we have other matters to consider first." We were running out of time. It was now close to four in the morning and the sun would be cracking over the horizon in a-nother hour and a half—give or take. We had to get a plan in motion.

"Nothing we can do here," I said. "Back the way we came. Let's see if our stuff is safe and see if we can come up with a plan. We'll have about an hour to do it, whatever it is. Sun'll be up before long."

12 ENDANGERED SPECIES

W e made our way through the marsh back to our stash and found it undisturbed. The night was alive with the sound of music—the music of the night. *Cool. Two stage music-al references in one thought.* But the music was all pretty creepy-like. Frogs croaked, mosquitoes buzzed, owls hooted, wild boar snorted and gators groaned in the shad-ows. It was enough to set ones nerves on edge. Running into the tusk of a hunting pig or into the jaws of a hungry gator was not something I wanted to do.

At one time alligators were an endan-gered species, but they have come back and, though heavily regulated, the hunt-ing of gator is once again allow-ed. They were endangered because they were hunt-ed and killed relentlessly for the hide (and the meat's pretty tasty, too). That's how I felt—hunted for my skin and meat. If we were caught *we* would be endangered. Maybe even 'extinct,' if you get my drift.

Down here, in southern Louisiana, the land is flat as a pancake; there are no mountains, there are no caves. The best one can do for cover is find a low place behind some foliage and hunker down... and hope, you aren't found. And, quite frankly, you didn't just want to climb into any old hidey-hole for fear of gators and spiders and, heaven forbid, snakes. Plus there were cougars and bears and all manner of other natural threats. But, that's what we had to do.

With as much stealth as possible we searched for someplace to take cover near where we'd left our goods. Fortunate for us each pair of goons made plenty of noise traveling through the brush and we were able to avoid them, though their activity had died down considerable and backhoe man was back to work as was pump guy.

At last we found our stash, gathered it up and located a reasonable place to hide. It was low and tangled with vines, twisted with gnarls of dead wood and laden with tall fern. However, it was quite damp. We lay there on our backs, huddled together behind the pile of woodland debris and spoke in soft tones. The stars were out (as were the mosquitoes), showing through a thin canopy of trees against an ever lightening sky. We'd seen it go from near black to dark purple.

"You know," said Carla, "I prefer to sleep in my bed."

"Well," I said, "we won't be doing any sleeping tonight."

"You know what I mean," she responded.

"Sure, now what are we going to do?"

"I have no idea," said Bart. "I'm just the brawn; you're the brains."

"Oi! And what am I?" asked Carla. "Chopped liver?"

"No, but, no offense, you smell like it," I said.

"It's called *parfum' de swamp*," she retorted. "You like?"

"Where did that expression, 'like chopped liver,' come from?" asked Bart.

"I believe it was a Jewish or Yiddish* phrase used to express exasperation," said Carla. "Meaning 'I never get the lime-light' because liver was, like a side dish. Now who's the brains?"

"Yeah," I said, "we're all going to be chopped liver, if we can't figure out how to get out of this—and soon. We *have* to see what's in that tent and what's in that pit."

"And?" asked Bart.

"And I think I have a plan," I said. Carla sighed and I spoke quickly. "Indiana Jones did it in *Raiders of the Lost Ark*, though it's not original in the movie, Bond's done it, too, but I digress, the point is we sneak up on a guard, incapacitate them, and steal their outfit in order to infiltrate the nest." I took a breath and finished my thought, "We need a swamp monster costume."

"Those dudes are toting guns," reminded Bart.

"I am aware of that," I said. "Stealth is in order, okay."

"So, why do I get the sinking feeling, that *I* am the stealth?" asked Bart.

"Because you are," I said.

"What am I going to do? Bonk one of them on the back of the head with a rock? What if I kill it, uh, him? I don't think I want that on my conscience. What makes you think...?"

"Stop rattling," said Carla. "Use your Vulcan nerve pinch, Tuvak*."

"Just because I'm black doesn't make me Tuvak..."

"I was talking about the pointy ears."

"Why not Spock then?"

"You got me there."

"Okay, you two," I said, "quit bickering. Listen, the plumber's cement we bought, its ether based. You just have to swab it out on one of the rags and hold it over his nose."

"What if it sticks to his face?" asked Bart. "And what makes you think I can get that close and overpower him? They've got AK-47s, dude!"

"Look, you've got twenty pounds on me, Bart. Besides you're part Houma Indian, You've got more sneak."

"You guys are *so* racist," he said with a smirk. "Let the minority do the dirty work. Okay, but only because you're such a wimp."

"I knew you'd understand," I said pulling the container of plumber's cement from the bag while Carla got a rag. "Now get cracking, *padnet*." Bart took the items and traipsed off. I took out my phone and checked for a text from Reed. No such luck and still only one bar.

I sent Reed another text, with our location and situation asking him to send in help, hoping it would go through. Texts have a way of getting through even with lower reception when calls won't, though sometimes it takes time. I would endeavor to send one every half hour.

I was worried. Sure Bart was strong, but goons where dangerous—trained in the martial arts and stuff. *Right?* That was probably more movie theatrics than real life. I thought back to our visit to CIA headquarters. We'd seen their training facilities and program. *Did Thanche have a training pro-gram? Did he hire professsionals?* I regretted that I'd sent Bart on this mission. He was my friend; *I* should have gone. *Was this even going to work?*

13 TAKE DOWN

In the distance we watched as Bart crept up be-hind one of the goons. He went slowly and un-detected. At last he crouched into position, ready to spring, and waited for the guy to make his pass back in front of him. Timing and stealth would be everything. "You think he can pull it off?" whispered Carla.

"Hey, it's Bart we're talking about. Sure." But I wasn't all that sure myself. We watched and waited while the man turned and started back across his post drawing closer to where Bart lay in wait. Just a few steps more and it should happen. I readied myself to run in with assistance should it be needed. Exactly how I might be able to help, I didn't know.

And then it happened: Bart sprang from the brush and threw his massive arms around the goon. One arm went all the way over the man's throat. Bart's other hand held the rag and he smashed it a-gainst the goon's nose and mouth, holding it there with all he was worth as the goon thrashed about wildly. Bart wrapped his legs around the man and they fell to the ground.

A minute later the thrashing stopped and they lay there entangled on the earth. I rose from my crouched position and made a dead run as best I could through the brush toward the pair, with Carla on my heels. Bart was just crawling out from under the subdued guard when we arrived.

"I did it!" Bart exclaimed quietly panting for air, "I did it!"

I bent down and removed of the hood and shirt of the monster costume. I noticed several empty cans of energy drink lying in the mud. *The goon must have been trying to stay awake on his post.* "You sure did, buddy," I said, working quickly. "I knew you would. Can you give me a hand?" Bart went to work on the guy's pants and foot coverings. Carla pulled off his webbed gloves.

"Here," said Carla, handing Bart a rag and what was left of our rope, "bind and gag."

"Looks like this is going to fit me best," I said, examining the footwear that was something akin to a green-brown knee-high stocking with a hard four-toed sole attached. "Ingenious."

"Well, put it on," said Carla, handing me the gloves and pants. I laid them next to me on top of a nearby stump and, after taking off my jacket, pulled the costume shirt over my head.

"Pants next," I said. "You might want to turn away if you don't want to see my boxers."

"They're Sponge Bob Square Pants," teased Bart. (Truth be told they were *Iron Man* boxers. Okay?) Carla turned away without comment and I slipped out of my shoes and jeans then pulled on the monster trousers. I put my own clothes into one of the sacks. Soon I had on the footwear and gloves.

"Aren't you kinda short for a stormtrooper?" asked Carla when she'd turned around. *Haha.* She was starting to pick up my movie quoting vibe. Bart laughed.

"Laugh it up fuzz ball," I said with a Han Solo smirk. "Now, here's the plan. I'm going to walk into the camp like I belong and walk directly into the tent to see if our dads are in there. Things could go one of three ways: One, ol' Thachne will be in there and I'll have to have an excuse for the interruption to get me back out. Two, Thachne won't be in there and it will be a piece of cake. Or three, someone will question me, find out I'm not one of them and I'll be captured."

"Take the AK-47," said Carla. "That will serve as a deterrent."

"I am *not* shooting any one," I said.

"I didn't say you would. It's just a prop. The guard would have it on him and you can threaten with it, if need be." Bart handed me the semi-automatic weapon.

"Makes sense, but the thought chills me."

"Think of it like an acting gig," said Bart. "Improvise." *I could do that.*

"Okay, here goes." I started off, but Carla caught my arm and pulled me into an embrace, planting a kiss on my mouth.

"Good luck," she said. I set off feeling energized.

☠ ☠ ☠

I hurried into the camp with as much bravado as I could muster, holding the AK-47 across my chest. *Hope I look confident.* No one took a second look as I approached the tent. *Here goes.* Pulling aside the flap, I ducked inside. Nervous sweat dripped down the inside of my costume. There was a Persian rug on top of a tarp floor, the room apportioned like those to which nomadic sheiks might be accustomed, only more modern. The spicy scent of bayberry drifted from an incense burner which sat upon a table at which Thachne worked—a set of books and charts before him. He looked up from his work. "Yes?" *Come on Peter, think!*

"Sir," I began in my deepest voice, still thinking on my feet and trying to find my 'motivation' (that's an actor's term), "uh, there's a...a perimeter breach. Intruder alert." I noted that no one else was in the room. *No dads here.*

"What happen to 'hey, boss'? Perimeter breach? What kind of talk is that? Who are you?" *Uh, oh. Cover blown. Run!* I turned and ran from the tent. I kept running. Thachne came out after me yelling, "Stop that man!" I ran for all I was worth, veering away from my friends to keep them safe, though close enough to yell to them my last bit of direction before angling away.

"Run. Hide, Split up. Leave the gear." They immediately ran in the opposite direction as the pit workers dropped what they were doing and came after us in pursuit. Fortunately, in their single-minded effort to catch us, the pursuing men didn't pass near our stash. Shots rang out behind me and I leapt over a log and hit the dirt face first. Or, as it were, hit the mud face first, skidding to a stop in the muck and mire. When I rolled over I was greeted by the sight of two AK-47 barrels pointed at my face.

14 OF MONSTERS AND MEN

I was bound, and tossed like a fresh catch of shrimp, into the hold of the yacht. Flailing down the stairs, I heard the hatch door lock behind me as I fell into a heap on the floor, moaning in pain as my ribcage hit the bottom step with a dull thud. *Great! Now what?*

"Welcome to paradise," said a voice in the dark. "What you in for?" *Wait, I know that voice!*

"Who said that?" I asked.

"Pete, Pete, is that *you*?" This second voice I certainly knew; it was my dad.

"Dad!" I cried, dragging myself toward the voice.

"Peter! What are you doing here?"

"Do you have to ask?"

"Came to rescue the old man, huh? You shouldn't have, you know that."

"Is Bart with you?" asked the other man whom I now knew was Bart's dad.

"Yes, and no," I answered. "He came out with me, but I think he got away with Carla."

"You brought Carla on this?!" Dad's voice was emphatic, even angry.

"She insisted, I tried to..."

"You just don't know when to... Peter Jackson Myers! For crying out loud! This is dangerous!" He used my full name and we all know what that means.

"I can tell." *Oops.*

"Don't be smart with me, young man," he said curtly.

"Sorry, Dad, but you know I *had* to," I said sheepishly, pulling myself to a sitting position.

"You don't *have* to do anything; you *choose* to. And I don't know what's with you, Peter."

"I guess he takes after the old man," said Warden Davis.

"You keep ou..." began Dad, but halted. "I, I guess you're right. Peter, I'm sorry. I know you mean well. It's just that..."

"I know, Dad. I'm just glad you're a-live."

"I suppose you have a plan...," he stated, "had a plan."

"I did, sort of." Bart's dad coughed in the dark. "And Warden Davis, I'm sure that Bart and Carla are okay."

"Let's hope so," he said. "So, tell us what's going on. I'm sure you've found out something."

"As a matter of fact, I *do* know a little. Did you see the hole they're digging?"

"What hole?" asked Dad. "All we know is that Dr. Thachne is up to something and that he has a fake Swamp Monster out here."

"Not *a* fake monster," I said, "an army of them. He's using them to keep people away."

"From what?" asked Warden Davis.

"I don't know, except that he's excavating something. We think he might be treasure hunting." My father, or maybe it was Warden Davis, *hmmmed.* My eyes were adjusting to the gloom now; that plus the thin glow of morning light now creeping in from a portal over our heads aided my sight ever so slightly. I couldn't make out much, but I could tell we were being held in the ship's galley*. A small door led from the room—*probably to the sleeping quarters or berths as they are called.* "How long have you been here?" I asked, not having much else to say.

"We were captured at Hal's camp," said Dad, "sometime before eleven, I'd say. We've been in here since—roughly six or seven hours—I would guess, now that the sun's coming up."

"Haven't had a wink of shuteye," said Warden Davis.

"Have they come back to check on you, give you a bathroom break or anything?"

"That would be no," answered Warden Davis. "We'd hoped that was what was happening when they threw you in here."

"And I could use a restroom," said my dad.

"You could pee in their sink," I suggested with a grin.

"Can't get up," he said.

"Tied to something, then?"

"Yes, son, plus they broke my leg."

"Oh, Dad! No!" I said, clambering over to him in the growing light.

"It's okay, Pete," he said. "It's not a compound fracture."

I am not one prone to swear, but an inglorious name came to mind. *Let no unwholesome thing come from your mouth**, said the scriptures, which also came to mind, so I bit my tongue. "Warden Davis, are *you* okay?

"I'm a tad hungry," he answered, "but otherwise I'm fit as a fiddle. I don't think they meant to harm your father. They would have killed us if they meant harm. They're just a little rough."

"A little!?" I was furious.

"What about Hap Deveaux?" asked Bart's dad. "Have you seen him?"

"No," I answered. "None of us knows what he looks like, but we haven't seen any other prisoners either."

"Uh, Peter," said my dad, "can I ask you a question?"

"Sure, Dad."

"What's with the Halloween costume?"

"Oh, ah, this little thing? I was auditioning for a position on the goon squad."

"Peter?" Dad said, drawing it out.

"Bart knocked out one of Thachne's men, and I traipsed into his camp..."

"A disguise?"

"It didn't work," I said.

"I'd say it works rather well," Bart's dad mused. "Sort of slimming."

"You think so?"

"A little blue boa to offset the eyes and, well..." Bart's dad laughed instead of finishing his sentence.

"Yeah, well, we have to get out of here," I said. "What are our assets?"

"What do you mean?" asked Dad. "They took our guns and radios, we're tied up and I can't really walk all that well."

"These things I know," I said, looking around the room which was growing lighter by the minute. "We're in the galley. There might be knives in a drawer or cupboard—at least some food."

"Did you miss the 'we're tied up' part?" Warden Davis was just like his son (or vice versa). I struggled to get my feet under me and stood—which was difficult with my hands and feet bound—hopped over to the counter and peered in the sink. Nothing there. I scanned the counter. Again, nothing. I turned around, facing away from the counter and tried with my roped hands to pull open a drawer, but it wouldn't budge.

"Try lifting up," suggested Bart's dad. "They're like those in a travel trailer, with a lip." I was about to do that when I heard footfalls on the deck above. Quickly, I crumpled to the floor and slid my body away as quietly as I could. The hatch flew open and in crashed Bart and Carla. Behind them, silhouetted by the rising sun, stood other figures. Two of them parted, leaving a third outlined in shadow.

"Are there any more river rats I should know about?" It was Thachne. After hearing that... that...crook drone on about marsh monsters, I'd know the voice anywhere. I knew something else, too: Bart was about to mouth off.

"I wouldn't tell you if there was and I'm not saying there isn't." *Sure enough.*

"Well, they're going to have to be a lot more clever than the lot of you."

"Bart, don't say anything," reprimanded his father.

"Oh, I'll get what I want out of you," threatened Thachne. "My little operation is too precious to have anything go wrong. But

I don't really have the time just now to converse."

"And what operation would that be?" asked my dad.

"Wouldn't you like to know?"

"Actually, I would."

"Well, I'm not telling you, mister policeman. And when I figure out what to do with you...hmm, perhaps a mysterious drowning, a gator feast? Anyway, you won't be around to report anything. Until then, I must get back to my little project. *Adieu**." He turned to go. "Tie them up!" he said to the goons with him and they came down the steps and commenced binding my friends.

"Wait, wait," I yelled up the steps after Thachne. "My father needs medical assistance and we need to use a restroom."

"Good luck with that," he laughed maniacally and disappeared as the two thugs continued tying up my friends. Finally they left, the door slammed shut and the lock was secured. The footfalls fell away and the boat stopped swaying.

"Carla, Bart, are you okay?" I asked.

"Nice of you to ask," said Carla. "A few bumps and bruises and I'm covered in mud, but other than that..."

"I'm fine," added Bart.

"So what happened?" I said wanting to know what they'd accomplished and how they'd been captured.

"You know," said Carla, "running, being captured, tied up, thrown in the cooler. Ever had that happen to you?" (As a matter of fact I had.)

"Been there, done that," said Bart.

"Did you get behind enemy lines, first?"

"No," said Bart. "We were hunted like wild dogs."

"How about our stash?" I asked.

"What stash?" asked my dad, in a way that said he was afraid to ask.

"Just a few things," I answered.

"Like what? Don't say explosives?"

"Might be," I stammered.

"Peter Jackson Meyers" There he went again with the full name.

"Just some flares and paint thinner."

"And a potato cannon," interjected Bart.

"A potato cannon?" questioned Warden Davis, "What were you planning to do with that?"

"Haven't actually decided that," I said. "Carla, do have your knife?"

"No, they took it from me."

"Drat! Okay, back to the drawer," I sighed, struggling again to my feet. And then an anger welled up in me as I thought about those thugs searching my girl. "Did they...did they..."

"No, they didn't touch me," she said, "just had me empty my pockets." I breathed out a sigh of relief, but I was still hopping mad as I hopped over to the drawers. At last I worked one open—lifting up as was suggested. I then turned around and looked inside.

"See anything?" asked my dad.

"Lessee, butter knives, forks, spoons... nope, nothing useful." I hopped sideways, spinning back around in the process, to another drawer, opened it, spun again and peered within. "Can opener, large spoons, spatula..."

"Cool it with the running commentary," chided Bart. "Just find something useful, like a knife."

"So what if we get a knife?" said Carla. "So we get out of our bonds, that door up there, it's solid steel and locked tight."

"Look for a blowtorch," said Bart. I rolled my eyes and moved to the third and final drawer. It was what is commonly called a junk drawer and contained nothing but a flashlight, batteries, a roll of string, a hammer, a box of toothpicks... but there I go again with a running commentary. *Wait! What's that?* I turned away from the drawer and rummaged through it, tossing assorted items on the floor until I felt what I was looking for. There it was, in my hand: a pair of wire-cutters.

15 THROUGH THE LOOKING GLASS

Half hour later we had managed to chomp through each other's bonds with the wire cutting tool. By the time we were done my hand was cramped and so was my brain. We hadn't yet settled on how we might escape from our floating prison. We tossed out ideas, ate what food we found and used the restroom. Yeah, we found out that the little door off the galley led down a hallway. The hall also led to another locked steel door at the other end. It had berths along its length and, *thank the Lord*, a bathroom.

A lot to accomplish in a half hour, yes, but we were desperate in more ways than one. Now, we just sat there. I got up to pace the floor. I think better on my feet. It was then that the light hit me. It was the shaft of light beaming in from the portal, but it also gave me an idea. "We can crawl out the window!" I exclaimed.

"I don't think so," said Bart's dad. "It's too small." I walked over and eyed the opening.

"I might be able to do it," I said pulling on the release handle. The window unsealed with the sucking sound of rubber and I climbed atop the dining table to gaze out, squinting in the low sun. I pulled my head back in. "Other than being over water, this should be as easy as pie."

Carla piped in with, "I've had your pie; it ain't that good."

"What are you going to do, if you can get out?" asked Bart.

"I'll go for the blow torch and come back to cut you out."

"You've got a blow torch?" my dad asked, raising his eyebrows.

"Sure," I said, "doesn't everyone?"

"That is if they haven't found our stuff," added Carla.

"You actually have an acetylene cutting torch?" asked Bart's dad.

"No a blow torch and paint thinner," said Bart.

"That's probably not going to work," said Bart's dad. "It doesn't burn hot enough."

"Oh," was all I could muster.

"What else might you have?" asked my father. I reeled through our list of articles, thinking as I did about how one of them might solve our problem. Little came to mind.

"What kind of lock is on the door?" I asked of Bart and Carla who'd seen it in the light.

"A small padlock," said Carla.

"Probably quarter inch thick hasp," added Bart. "Our best bet is probably the hatchet. Maybe."

"Maybe, I can get the hinges off with the screw driver," I said.

"Sounds like a plan," said my dad, "*if* you can get through the window, *if* you get to your stash and *if* you get back here without being caught. That's a lot of ifs and I don't like it."

"We don't have a better plan," I said. "I *have* to try."

"I know you do, son."

"Well then," I said, climbing once again to the portal, "here I go." I stuck my arms out the round little window and pulled myself up, twisting and turning my shoulders, trying to get one through.

"Or not," said Bart. I dropped back from the window, panting.

"Help me up," I said. "I'll try feet first."

"I don't think it will work," said Carla. "Let *me* try."

"No way," I said. "I'm not letting..."

"There you go, pampering me again," she said. "I am perfectly able..."

"I know, I know," I said. "I'm sorry, but let me try again first."

Bart and his dad hoisted me up and I slid my feet out the opening and wriggled while they shoved, but my hips just wouldn't go through and they pulled me back inside. I was drenched in sweat. "Okay then..."

"I don't think it's a good idea for Carla..." began my dad.

"Mr. Meyers," Carla cut him off, "with all due respect, I have already saved these boy's bacon thrice. I can do it again."

"Saved our bacon!?" I said.

"My knife to open the blister-packs, the idea to..."

"Okay, okay," I relented.

"I like bacon," said Bart. We all looked at him for a moment. *Looks like it,* I thought, but kept my mouth shut.

"Let's do this," said Carla. Bart's dad shrugged his shoulders and hoisted her up to the window feet first. Her hips passed through with some effort, but they did. She got hung up at her chest for a moment, but then let out her breath and wriggled through one side at a time. Now she was dangling out the window, Bart and his dad holding her forearms that were bent at the elbows. I stuck my head out between their arms and looked at her hanging over the water.

"Hey, Gator Girl," I called down, "watch out for alligators." Her eyes went wide and she glanced around, frantically. She looked back at me with fury on her face.

"Let go," she called back up. Her arms disappeared through the opening and a second later she splashed down. I poked my head out and saw her thrashing madly for the shore. All of a sudden I felt really queasy and worried. I watched her scramble onto the bank, glad there were no alligators around. She turned back and waved, then slogged off into the brush. I pulled my head back inside.

"Brave girl you've got there," said my dad.

"Looks like a keeper," added Bart's dad with a wink. Dad gave him a semi-shocked look and Bart's dad responded to it: "What?"

"You're right, it won't be long before he's hitched," sighed Dad. I blushed and ran to the toilet to throw up. I told you I was feeling queasy.

16 ARMED AND DANGEROUS

We spent some time looking about the space for weaponry. Wisely the bad guys didn't leave any official ones lying around. We did, however, come up with the following: a fire extinguisher, a box of shotgun shells, sheets off the berths, some olive oil and... get this...a sack of potatoes. I now had a plan and we went to work. When our plan was ready we sat down to further ponder our 'sitch' and worry about Carla.

☠ ☠ ☠

Oh, by the way, I also found a cribbage* board and a deck of cards in the cubby over the table and, now as prepared for conflict as we could be, given our assets, we set about playing pairs to pass the time. I was starting to worry. I mean, worry more.

Dad and I were lagging behind, and with the Davis team nearing the finish line, a skunk looked quite possible, though it was now their deal and we would count first. "I'll play through, *padnet*; it ain't over until the fat lady sings."

☠ ☠ ☠

We were sunk. Warden Davis had a pair of tens that put them over the line.

"UGH!" *One measly point!* So close to victory, but there were more important matters at hand, we heard footsteps on the deck above! And we froze.

17 CARLA TO THE RESCUE

The rustling of the lock put my nerves on edge. Instantly we were on our feet, cards scattering across the table as we quietly went to our posts and gathered our equipment. Dad poured the olive oil on the steps where we'd removed the non-skid marine carpet. Warden Davis picked up a sheet and stood on one side of the hatch; Bart did the same at the other side. I had my trusty fire extinguisher at the ready.

The shotgun shells, with the shot removed, but the powder left intact and stuffed with toilet paper, had been screwed into the light sockets ready for the throw of the switch manned by my father. (That was something I'd seen in the James Bond film *Sky-fall*, albeit a modification—they'd use shrapnel in baggies.) The sack of potatoes? Well, that lay in the corner as we lay in wait. After a moment the fumbling at the lock stopped.

Tang, tang, tang. Metal against metal. My heart leapt inside my chest. *Was that Carla?* Again*, tang, tang, tang.* Bart grabbed a spoon and tapped back. The tapping was returned from the other side. *It had to be Carla.* We all relaxed, but stayed at our posts, quietly listening to a sound—ever so faint—that must have been the work of a screwdriver at the hinges of the small door. I glanced at the clock on the wall, Half past nine. It had taken Carla more than an hour to get back. I watched the clock tick around its face as the work continued from the other side. Ten minutes, twelve, fifteen.

"What's taking her so long?" I said. "She should have those screws loose by now."

"You're the only one I know who's got a screw loose," said Bart. *Haha.*

"Peter, I doubt she's adept with a screwdriver," said my dad. "Give her some time. It's not likely an easy task."

"You might be surprised," I said, cocking my head,"Carla's pretty handy." Seventeen minutes later the tapping began again.

"Now what?" said Bart.

"Probably time to knock the door down," suggested Warden Davis, "and hope she's standing aside."

Bart pounded the door twice with his fist and yelled in his loudest voice: "STAND BACK!"

His dad laid the sheets down on the slippery steps and Bart took a step back himself and barreled into the hatch.

BOOM! The door shook and a crack appeared on the seam to the left. He stepped back and threw himself once again at the door. BOOM! The sound echoed across the swamp and I thought how it carried and how it would probably be heard by Thachne and his goons. The gap widened and Bart rubbed his shoulder. He readied for another run, but his father pushed him aside.

"My turn," he said and took a run at the hatch.

BOOM! The door flew open to the right.

"I loosened that for you," said Bart. We scrambled up the steps, Warden Davis first, pushing the door aside.

"Good to see you," said the warden from on deck. Bart and I helped my dad up the steps. At the top I grabbed Carla and gave her a bear hug, but she barely hugged back. She was pale and sweaty. *Probably over exertion in the hot sun.*

"So, what's going on out there?" asked Dad, always the cop.

"They're busy...in the dig," she answered with a ragged cadence of speech, "but not...not with the...heavy equipment.

They're down in…in the hole with shovels and picks. I…I climbed a tree so I could see…" She swayed and caught herself on my arm and I took hold of her. She was cold and clammy.

"What's wrong?" asked Bart's dad.

"Snake…" she said under her breath, "Snake bite."

"Oh, no," I said, laying her down on the deck.

"Didn't…see it in the…tree. Too late."

"Let me see," said the warden. She showed us the back of her arm. About six inches up from her left wrist were two bloodied puncture wounds in the fabric. Warden Davis swung into action, whipping off his belt he wrapped it around her upper arm and cinched it down. "How long ago?" he asked, pulling up her sleeve.

"Half hour…maybe less."

"First aid kit. Bart, have a look a-round." Bart took off toward the upper deck to search in the cabin while his dad took off his shirt, bundled it and put it under Carla's head. Dad took off his outer uniform shirt and did the same. "What did it look like?"

Carla closed her eyes and answered, "Diamond-back or…cottonmouth" and then she turned her head and vomited on the deck, fortunately not in my lap.

"Okay," said Warden Davis, "we need to get her to a doctor. Peter, I want you to find the keys to this bucket. When Bart gets back I'll have him take you kids in. You can use the ship's radio to call ahead for EMTs."

My mind raced as I stood. Yes, I had to see Carla to a hospital. But shouldn't we all just get out of there and call in the authorities? "There's no reason any of us should stay," I said. "Dad needs a doctor, too. And we can radio the coast guard to take care of these..."

"You're right, Peter," said my dad. "Bob, take Carla down below deck and get her in one of the berths, I'll drive us in." Bart returned with a first aid kit and handed it to his dad.

"Come on," I said, taking Bart by the arm. "We need to find the keys and get this boat out of here."

"I don't need no stinkin' keys," he said, as his dad lifted Carla from the deck.

"You told me in Cocodrie*, that you didn't know..."

"Googled it since then. Grand Theft Yacht. Let's go." We ran toward the cabin to get underway as Warden Davis and Carla disappeared below deck. Dad kept watch and it was a good thing, not five minutes later several men barreled from the tree line toting AK-47s. Dad saw them and hobbled as quickly as he could to the line and, untying it from the stern railing, tossed it into the water. They leveled their guns and Dad hit the deck as shots rang out.

A lot began happening at that moment. Bart was under the dash at the helm yanking on wires, I was seated in the captain's chair praying for Carla, but jumped from the seat at the report of gunfire and spun to the window just as the men broke into a run across the beach. Bart jumped as well and bonked his head.

"Keep working! *Vite vite!*" I shouted to him. I ran to the cabin door. "Dad!"

"GET DOWN!" he yelled. "Get us out of here." Warden Davis emerged from the hatch as more shots rang out. Dad crawled across the deck toward the anchor line, stood and worked the winch as the warden ducked back into the hold. He must have hit the light switch because several explosions rumbled from below me.

The men on the beach hesitated for a moment, probably thinking they were being shot at. The engine roared to life. A shot hit dad in the shoulder and the impact knocked him over the rail and into the water, but he'd gotten the anchor up. The yacht began pulling off the sand.

"DAD!" I screamed and took a running leap over the side without thinking a second thought. Shots were directed at me as a dove. Not having any idea how deep the water was I flattened out for a belly flop. It was going to hurt, but far less than breaking my neck. The men continued firing at the boat as it pulled away, picking up speed rapidly, and I swam for my dad who lay on his back in the water. Reaching him I felt with my feet for the bottom and found it. Blood seeped from the wound in his shoulder and mingled with the bayou forming a spreading pool on the surface.

"Dad, dad," I whispered.

"I'm okay, son," he managed, "but you shouldn't have..."

"I'm here, Dad," I said cutting him off, dragging him for shore. When I got there the yacht was well underway down the bayou and I looked up to the sight of AK-47s in my face.

Again.

18 KILLER INSTINCTS

It wasn't looking good for us, I'll tell you that. Frankly, I was feeling pretty scared. On a good note our fathers were alive and so was Carla. None of us were dead...yet, and Bart was headed for help. On the other hand, dad had a broken leg and a gunshot wound; Carla had been bitten by a venomous snake and once again some of us were in captivity. My father and I were bound back to back in Thachne's tent and the treasure hunter stood over us cursing.

"You're crazy, man!" I screamed with vehemence. "You shot my dad!"

"Oh, you haven't seen anything yet, boy! And you are *not* going to spoil my party!"

"And what party is that?" my father hissed.

"It's none of your business," Thachne snapped. "We've found what we're looking for and in a matter of minutes we'll be long gone."

"Treasure," I said, "this is all about some stinking treasure."

"You are a smart boy," retorted our captor. "Too smart for your britches, but you figured it out too late. My men are pulling your boat around now. We'll have Lafitte's—I mean *my*—treasure out of here in no time."

"Jean Lafitte?"

"It ain't the guy from the Capt. Crunch box kid."

"But how? After all these years?"

"I found his map in an old warehouse wall down by English Turn, but that doesn't matter. You are going to die."

"What have you done with Hap Deveaux," asked Dad.

"Why, so thoughtful of you to ask," answered Thachne. "He's been my guide. Do you think I could have navigated these bayous without someone who knew these parts?"

"You kidnapped him?" questioned my dad.

Thachne laughed, "Of course not. I simply offered him a job that paid well. Funny what a little money will do and now I have plenty to buy what I need—even people. Of course, I never paid him and had to, ah, dispose of him." He laughed, "I think the gator found him tasty—Cajuns are kinda spicy."

"You are one sick man," my dad said.

"And *you* are a dead man," Thachne retaliated. A goon poked his head into the tent.

"Boss, we've got the last chest unburied, but we need your help getting it to the boat."

"I hired *you* for the muscle, lunk head!"

"I'm sorry, boss, it's too heavy for the three of us."

Thachne swore. *Who needed to go to R rated movies?* "You just can't get good help these days." The villain took a cigar out of his vest pocket, bit off the end, spit and lit the other end, puffing clouds of foul smoke into the air. "You know," he said through puffs, "I'm going to enjoy watching you die." He took a drag off the cigar, blew a stream of foulness into the air and turned back to his goon, "Shoot these two."

"My gun's back at the boat, boss."

"Idiot!" yelled Thachne, throwing his hands in the air. "Okay, we'll drag the loot to the boat, but then you come back here and waste these meddlers. I have grown tired of them. Come on!" They turned to leave.

"You're not going to get away with this Thachne," chided my father.

"Oh," said the pirate, turning back, "I think I am. Mexico really isn't all that far

away. *Au revoir.** Or should I say *adios* *?"
The men left laughing.

I didn't want to die. Sure, I was looking forward to heaven—no matter how good this life was, heaven was ultimately better. And though I longed to be in eternal fellowship with my creator (which was hard to focus on in this earthly life), I believed I was here for a purpose. I didn't want my dad to die either because I would miss him. Yeah, he rode me sometimes about my perceived shortcomings and placed restrictions on my life, but I loved him. He really did have my best interest in mind.

Mark Twain once said, 'When I was a boy of fourteen, my father was so ignorant I could hardly stand to have the old man around. But when I got to be twenty-one, I was astonished at how much the old man had learned in seven years.' I didn't see my dad as stupid by any means, but, at sixteen, I was growing to appreciate his wisdom and love more than ever.

I had to get us out of this jam.

19 BEST BET

That was my second death threat this year. I don't know, I don't think it was something I was going to get used to. Sweat dripped down my back. The sun had to be nearly full mast in the sky. I don't know if I was sweating because of the rising heat or because of my nerves. Since my palms were clammy, I determined it was my nerves. *Yeah, definitely my nerves.* I had to think fast, but my mind was a jumble of terror. Synapses were firing left and right in my brain. Our situation was serious and I knew it. We were trapped. We were scheduled for execution. We hadn't found Hap and he'd been murdered. The treasure was about to be taken away and these pirates were going to get away Scot-free. *Scot-free. What did that mean, anyway?*

My mind raced through the mega-catalogue of movies stored in the recesses of its gray matter hard drive: *Star Wars, James Bond, Indiana Jones, The Avengers,*

Jaws, Crocodile Dundee, RED and *RED 2, The Hunt for Red October, The Princess Bride* (of course) and a host of other films —westerns, sci-fi's, spy movies, even rom-coms. I wasn't getting anything. *Where was inspiration when you needed it? Spies!* Again, I thought back to our tour of CIA headquarters. *Had I gleaned anything useful from what they told us and what we saw?*

Rule number one: Don't get caught. *Well, so much for that.* Disavow who you are. *Was that Mission Impossible or CIA? Both.* Take in everything. Remember the details. *Okay, okay! What else?* Be creative. Think outside the box. *That was me.* Weapons training, hand to hand combat. Martial arts. Codes, encryption and ciphers. Languages. Poisons and drugs. Escape techniques. Knowing how to lie. Explosives. *Oh, yeah!* Evasive maneuvers. Computers and communications. Disguises and playing a part. *I can do that.* Clandestine operations. Agent acquisitions. Improvisation. Surveillance. Flying an airplane and parachuting from one. Rope climbing... *This isn't getting me anywhere, brain!*

"Peter," Dad shook my wrists, "got anything?

"I'm getting a jumble, Dad."

"We have to hurry, son."

"I know, I know," I whined, having self-doubts.

"I know you can do it, just think!" He struggled at the ropes between us.

"I am, Dad, I'm thinking too much." *That's it!* The key was the ropes. *Knife. Fire. A shard of glass.* That had worked before. My eyes searched the tent. There were beer bottles, but I had no way to reach them. We were tied to a tent pole in the center of the pavilion. I looked down at the plush carpet on the floor. And then it came to me. In my mind's eye I saw a room with a Persian rug, tapestries on the wall, a large fireplace and two men sitting back to back in chairs at the center of the room.

"Dad! Dad!" I said. "Relax your hands. This might hurt some."

"What are you going do?"

"Just follow my instructions."

"Okay, son. I believe in you." I had a good dad. Sure he could be tough on me. But he believed in me.

"Dad, I think I might want to be a CIA agent someday."

"I think you'd be good at that. Now, let's do this."

'There are some times in life when you fall down and you don't feel like you have the strength to get back up. Do you think you have hope?' The words of Nick Vuji-cic*, the speaker at Acquire the Fire, came back to me. *'I just want you to know: It's not the end. Are you gonna finish? Are you gonna finish strong?'* He had no arms or

legs, yet with Christ in his life, he had it in him to finish strong. I could do this; I had it in me.

☠ ☠ ☠

I didn't know if my new plan would work any better than the last. It was just an idea. I mean, just because it works in the movies doesn't mean it will in real life. You knew that, right? Well, I know that, too, but, hey, I figure anything's worth a shot (especially when you haven't got a better idea). This was our best bet and it came from another of my favorite films: *Indiana Jones and the Last Crusade* (yeah, I liked Dr. Jones). It would be followed, I hoped, by another little surprise based on the movie *Tangled*, Disney's telling of *Rapunzel*.

Since we were back to back we worked at each other's bonds like Sean Connery (my favorite "Bond, James Bond" by the way) and Harrison Ford in the Nazi mansion. It's hard to work at what you can't see, let me tell you, but there was no alternative. *Jesus, make this work*, I prayed.

20 TREASURE!

Working as fast as I could I wedged my thumb under Dad's bonds and pulled with all I had, cinching up the other coils around his wrist while making the loop under which I had my thumb as large as possible.

"Tuck your thumb into your palm," I instructed. When I felt him move the thumb into position I pulled the loop down toward the digit. "Now, keeping your thumb as close to your palm as possible, bring it up through the loop."

My father did as I instructed.

"Now curl your fingers into your palm." When I felt him do so I worked the rope over each of his knuckles until the loop cleared his hand. "Okay," I said, "it's all yours. Twist the loop and alternate back and forth, looping over your fist until the rope comes free."

Within a minute the rope fell slack from his hand and he worked it off the other. He brought his hands out in front of him and untied the bonds from his feet then turned and untied me.

"Well, so much for part A," he said. "That worked quite well, son, though I thought you were going to sever my hand. It's still numb and tingling."

"Yeah, well, now comes the hard part." We rose from where we'd been seated and grabbed some of the heavier books and stood on each side of the tent flap waiting for our elected would-be executioner to return. When he came through the door we would bash his head in with the tomes like Rapunzel did to Flynn with her frying pan, but after five minutes we figured he wasn't coming back and decided to just hightail it out of there. We dropped the books and I poked my head out the opening.

"The coast is clear," I said. "Can you get along?"

"I'll make it. Where are we going?"

"Back to the stash. Grab those beer bottles and put them in that knapsack." I said, pointing. We worked together and gathered the containers from the trash receptacle next to Thachne's desk and left. I helped Dad hobble along and, although he didn't complain, I saw the pain on his face with each step. At last we arrived at the stash. I gave my father the potato cannon as he picked up a limb to use as a crutch.

"Uh, son," he said, "I do believe we left the potatoes back on the yacht."

"We don't need potatoes," I said. "Besides, what good would they do? We're using Molotov cocktails, hence the beer bottles."

"I wondered what you wanted with those. I thought you were recycling." I smirked and handed him the remainder of the rags and the Aim n Flame, instructing him to stuff them in his pockets.

I grabbed some of the beat up flares as well as the butane, stuffed them in my back pockets and picked up the five-gallon drum of paint thinner, "You're on your own the rest of the way. I can't help you and carry this at the same time. Can you make it?"

"I will." My dad was such a trooper; I was learning to appreciate him more by the minute. Another ten minutes and we were back at the tree line looking across the shore at the tour boat.

Thachne and four thugs were shuttling buckets of doubloons from a broken trunk on the beach to the boat and dumping them onto the deck. A second rotting sea chest lay on the deck, opened, with gold and jewelry spilling over its lip. Other larger articles of gold lay about the deck.

I noticed the trunk on the shore—split open as it was—nearly empty. The men must have dropped it because, even

though they must have been working on
the transfer for a good ten minutes,
Thachne was still swearing and chewing
them out as they work-ed. Their guns
were slung over their backs as the carried
the booty. I looked at my dad; sweat poured from his face and his shirt was stained
with perspiration at the pits, back and
chest and with blood at his shoulder. New
anger welled in me.

"We have to work fast," I whispered.
"Are you okay?" He nodded. "You hold the
bottles and I'll pour. When they're full, you
stuff rags in the necks while I load the gas
chamber with butane." He picked up a bottle and I screwed the lid off the thinner;
hefting the container to pouring position I
filled the first bottle. My dad sat it down,
wedging it into a clump of grass so it would
stay upright and picked up another bottle.
When we finished the last bottle I took it
from him and tried it in the cannons muz-
zle. It slipped too easily. There was no resistance which meant the gas wouldn't
pressurize in the chamber behind the bottle and would leak out as fast as I could
fill it. "How many rags do we have?" I asked.

Dad removed the wad from his pocket
and counted, "Seven."

"Give me three." He did and began
stuffing a rag into the neck of one of the
six bottles we'd filled. I handed him the
Aim n Flame and took the bottle from him

wrapping it in another rag. I wedged it into the barrel. It made snug fit and I began filling the chamber with butane.

"Pete, what if the charge shatters the bottle?"

"There's going to be an explosion."

"I know that, you'll get burned."

"Let's just hope the bottle doesn't shatter then."

"Let me do the shooting, son."

"But you've never shot one of these. I have the experience, Dad. I can shoot a spud through a tire swing from twenty yards."

"But..."

"It's not impossible. I used to bullseye womp rats in my T-16 back home," I said.

"You aren't Luke Skywalker."

"But the force is strong with this one. I gotta do this, Dad."

"I know. Looks like they've finished up. Better hurry." I took aim and prayed. I had three shots and I knew there was a risk. I had to make the first shot count; it might be my only one. *Jesus, protect us.* I steadied the barrel, realigned my aim and, letting out my breath slowly, squeezed the igniter button. WHOSH! The gas ignited and propelled the bottle from the barrel with a pop, the charred rag that had cradled the bottle fell at our feet. The projectile arched over the swampy beach to the horrified stares of the men standing in the boat sixty or so feet away. I didn't even look to see if I was on target.

"Another one!" I yelled and Dad bent over for another bottle and, wrapping it in a rag in one swift motion, handed it to me. I looked back at the boat while stuffing the bottle in the barrel. I saw that my shot had hit the backside of the bow. I re-chargeed the chamber. The water behind the boat was aflame. *It just impacted on the surface*, I thought. The men were scrambling for cover and their weapons. Again I took aim as Dad lit the rag fuse and they leveled their guns. I squeezed the ignition.

WHOOSH! The second shot was off and Dad handed me another cocktail which I shoved in the barrel. I looked up while re-charging the chamber for our third and final shot and saw that the bomb had smash-ed into the center of the boat's wooden seating benches. Flame spread rapidly across the inner hull as the men—one with his pant leg on fire—dove from the boat. In the water now Thachne ordered his goons to splash water into the boat.

"Get the fire out you lunk heads!" he screamed hysterically over and over. I knew that it wouldn't work, you didn't put out a flaming liquid with water.

Dad lit the rag and I fired my third shot. It alighted on the canvas roof which burst into flame, burning chunks dropping into the boat. The men stopped their frantic, inept effort to douse the conflagration and made for the shore.

KABOOM! The boat's gas tank ignited in a thunderous combination of black cloud and fireball that rolled sky-ward. The concussion knocked the men off their feet and they bit dirt—mud actually. I took another bottle and the final rag and stuffed them into the cannon.

"I know I haven't got a fuse but..."

"You can still add fuel to the fire," said Dad, completing my sentence. "I know, but I have a better idea." He removed the bottle from the barrel and put the rag inside its neck.

"Here," he said, handing me the bottle and the Aim n Flame, "Charge onto the beach and lob this at the men. Don't worry, their guns are wet now and they're distracted. Go, then run back here as fast as you can."

I ran with all I was worth toward the men. "Get that boy!" yelled Thachne and, when the men began to pull themselves from the mire, I lit the Aim n Flame and touched off the rag, lobbing the bottle toward them. It fell to the beach but didn't shatter. I turned and hightailed it back to the trees as the bottle exploded behind me. I looked back and the goons were on my heels. I reach into my back pocket for a flare, ripped off the cap and stuck it to the starter and tossed it over my shoulder. I don't think it did any-thing a normal flare wouldn't do. I didn't look back to find out. When I arrived back at the tree line, my father had just finished emptying the re-mainder of the paint thinner in a swath across the forest edge.

"Give me some fire," he said and I toss-ed him the lighter. He clicked it on, shoved me behind him and lit the ground on fire. "Come on," he said, pulling me be-hind him into the woods. He and I staggered along side by side, Dad grimacing with each step.

Flup, flup, flup, flup, flup, flup, flup. I heard the sound, but didn't see the source, but I knew what it was—a chop-per. We stopped running. "STAY WHERE YOU ARE. PUT DOWN YOUR WEAPONS." The amplified voice was broadcast from the helicopter pilot. A moment later I heard a strafing of machine gun fire. Dad pulled me to the right and we began an arch back towards the shore. Arriving again at the tree line we took cover and surveyed the situation.

Thachne and his goons lay face down in the sandy mire and duck grass. The chopper sat on the beach, rotors slowing, a Coast Guard SWAT team, guns drawn, surrounding the thugs. We walked onto the beach.

"THAT YOU, MEYER'S?" came the voice from the chopper's speaker. Dad waved as we walked toward the group of captives and captors. We were rescued! I sent up a prayer of thanks.

☠ ☠ ☠

The fuel burned up and the fires died down. Only the wooden seats of the aluminum hulled boat still smoldered when a flotilla of boats rounded the bend in the island—a small Coast Guard cutter, a Saint Tammany Parish police boat and a yacht—lit brightly by the climbing sun above the treetops in the east. They pulled up to shore where Dad was speaking with the rescue crew from the chopper. Bart's dad stood on the yacht's deck with a rifle held across his chest and waved to Dad who waved back.

When the boat beached Bart came out from the wheelhouse, waved, bounded down the ladder and sprang over the bow. When he reached me we hugged. Not some sissy hug, mind you, but that manly back pounding guys give one another after a touch-down. *Ouch!* My ribs hurt from the tumble down the boat's stairs and the belly flop into the water.

"You are one sight for sore eyes," he said.

"You ain't too bad looking yourself," I teased.

"What happened here?"

"Whasamattayou?" I said gangster-like. "Wa's it look like? We blowed up da bad guys," I laughed.

"You have all the fun," he mused.

"Come, look at this," I said, shoving him toward the tour boat laden with gold glittering in the sunlight. I couldn't believe it! There it was, like Aladdin in the cave of wonders. Except this was the boat of wonders. Gold everywhere! It was like *Pirates of the Caribbean* only without Johnny Depp.

"Whoa!" exclaimed Bart.

"Yeah, Lafitte's treasure."

"No?!"

"*Fo troo,*" I answered, thinking of what Gandalf said in *Lord of the Rings*: 'All that glitters is not gold.'

21 HOUMA AGAIN, NATURALLY

I t took the rest of the day to fill in the authorities back at Slidell City Hall, pick up Carla from the hospital where Dad was patched up and get our friends from the hotel. Reed *had* received our text and contacted the St. Tammany Sheriff about the same time that Warden Davis was radioing in to the Coast Guard from the yacht. Reed, Dallas, Keilah and Beth were all relieved to see us and after much ribbing about Batman a.k.a. the Black Knight, Gator Girl, The Rock and Redeye; lots of hugging; and the reiteration of our adventure, the warden fueled up the van while we got to-go at the Popeye's next to the service station. We set off toward Houma as we chowed down our spicy chicken and jambalaya.

☠ ☠ ☠

An hour later Bart's dad drove the van west on 182 into Houma and down West

Park to Barrow and turned south. We passed the Cajun Café Dance Hall, sided and roofed with corrugated tin and painted with an alligator enjoying a cocktail. It looked like a *fais do do** was in progress as the parking lot was full and I could hear the faint sounds of a lively Zydeco band wafting out the back door. Man, even though I was wiped out, it made me want to two-step!

"Dudes," said Keilah, "the Scarlett Scoop. I could *so* use some ice cream right now." The nearly square, purple art-deco building was on our right surrounded by its wrought-iron fence.

"Oh yeah, oh yeah" sang Bart, dancing Gangam style as best he could in his seat.

"Ice cream it is," said Bart's dad. He put on the blinker and turned at the light and drove around the block, coming in the back side. We clambered out of the van (Dad crutching) and stepped into the small establishment, nearly filling the dining space, and were hit by the intoxicating a-roma of freshly waffled waffle cones. The walls were covered with a simulated old-fashioned newsprint and the ceiling, hung with period-looking lighting globes, repli-cated the old saloons of the 1800s.

A stained glass window spelled out *Scarlett Scoop* over the ice cream cases that wrapped around the walls in an L-shape, taking up half the interior. Colorful bags of old time candy hanging from hooks decorated the place. We wandered across the beautifully tiled floor up to the glass cases and were greeted warmly by the teenage boy behind them. The place was cool in more ways than one. Some ice cream was going to make it even cooler.

"Ladies first," said Dallas, tipping his Stetson and gesturing the girls toward the counter.

"Such a gentleman," said Keilah sidling up to the ice cream cases. "I'll have two scoops of Creole cream cheese in a cake cone." I think Dallas blushed, but I couldn't tell for·sure; it could have been sunburn. And yeah, I noticed the alliteration. *So clever.*

"A triple cone for me," said Beth. "Death by chocolate, peanut butter cup and pralines and cream on top, please."

Carla ordered a scoop of red velvet cake on top of a scoop of birthday cake topped with sprinx in a cup. Such a party animal, huh? Bart got his usual, mango sorbet topped with gummy worms in a cup.

"I'll...ah, I'll try an Oil Spill," said Reed. "Oh, wait. Maybe the Lagniappe Pop Rouge. No, no, the Oil Spill."

"Make up your mind, flyboy," said Dallas. "It took less time for the Alamo to be taken."

"Gregory Corso said 'If you have a choice between two things and can't decide, take both.' In a waffle cone, please."

"Who's Gregory Corso?" asked Bart.

"An American poet," answered Beth.

"*You* read poetry?" asked Keilah.

"Are you kidding me," said Reed, receiving his ice cream. "I saw the quote on the Internet."

"Figures," said Keilah.

I ordered a double Spiderman in a waffle cone and our dad's got chocolate sodas. After we all got our frozen confections we each took a seat in one of the red and white striped cushioned chairs at one of the white marble-topped parlor tables to savor our well-earned desserts. Dallas? Oh, yeah, he got a scoop of vanilla.

"What a week!" exclaimed Reed.

"You kin say that again," said Dallas and Reed did.

"I don't suppose they'll be any medals this time," said Bart.

"You've got doubloons! Who needs medals?" said Dallas.

"I don't think we'll get to keep those," said Bart.

"I wouldn't be so sure," interjected Dad. "According to Supreme Court rulings just last year, what can't be legitimately claimed by a government entity, well, its 'finders keepers.' You may be some very rich kids."

My eyes popped, "You're kidding me! I can replace my boat that got blown up in our Voodoo Virus caper!"

"We'll see about that," said Dad, "but, I'm telling you this: the bulk of it will go to your college funds. Right Bob?"

"You ain't just whistlin' Dixie, Jim." Warden Davis turned toward Bart and I, "Just remember boys, *'Where you're treasure is, there will be your heart also.'*"

Yeah, I thought, *the desire for treasure can really mess you up.* I wanted only to store up my treasure in heaven. "Oh well," I said with a sigh, "I'm just glad we're all back safe and sound, I've got rehearsals starting this week."

"What are you in Pete?" asked Reed.

"Phantom of the Opera."

"The Andrew Lloyd Webber musical?" questioned Beth. "You can't sing."

"That's for sure," said Bart. "He sounds like a wheezing weasel when he warbles in worship." Everyone chuckled.

"Haha," I snorted. "No, it's the non-musical version—a play. I'm playing Raoul. No singing required."

"Well, then I *migh*t come and see you," said Carla. "You promise, no singing?"

"Cross my heart," I said.

Carla cleared her throat, "And, ahem, who's playing Christine? Hmmm?" she raised an eyebrow. *Ooo, jealousy.* I hoped

268

there wouldn't be any kissing in the show and I'm sure she did, too.

"Uh, Mary Murray."

"Oh, she's cute," said Bart, ribbing me with his elbow and giving me a wink. *Ouch!* Carla seethed and glared and pouted and crossed her arms with a harrumph. *Nice.*

"It's at the Le Petite?" inquired Beth, changing the subject for which I was grateful. "When's it open?"

I nodded. That was the community playhouse in town, which was formerly the original Court House. "Right after school starts."

"Wow," said Reed, "that's kind of like a co-inky-dink."

"A what?" asked Keilah, wiping ice cream from her face.

"He means a coincidence," said Beth.

"Huh?" Dallas lifted his Stetson and scratched his head.

"I mean, like, that haunted antebellum that's the opera-theater we saw in New Orleans. The Davis house."

"How many times I gotta tell you?" Beth turned to Reed between licks. "There are no such things as ghosts."

"Says you," said Reed. "Might be." Beth rolled her eyes.

"There weren't no Marsh Monster," said Dallas, "now was there?"

"Might still be," mumbled Reed.

"Thing is," said my dad, "and I hate to tell you this, you know, but the city finally found some renters and..." he paused, "... they swear the place is haunted. Something is trying to drive them out and they want out of their lease."

"Cool," said Reed, "the Davis Playhouse Phantom.

"Sounds like," interjected Bart, "something for the, uh, Bayou Boys to investigate."

"Sounds like trouble," said Carla. "I think Gator Girl will opt out this time."

I puffed up my chest. *Ouch.* My ribs still hurt. "I think I'd like..."

"After the play, Sherlock," said Dad, "after the play's over, and..."

"And then The Rock rolls into another case," said Reed in his best announcer voice.

"Hopefully, not so dangerous," added Bart.

"What?!" I exclaimed. "Danger is..."

"Peter Jackson..."

"I know, Dad, I know..."

"I was going to say," he said, "Peter Jackson 'Danger' Meyers." I smiled and Carla kissed me on the cheek. I was so glad she was okay *and* that she'd gone along on our rescue mission. I don't know what I'd do without her. Or my dad. My real treasure was right here with me.

Thank you, Lord.

GLOSSARY/ENDNOTES

Chapter 1

- Parish: What they call counties in Louisiana.

- <u>Voodoo Virus</u>: The first book in the *Bayou Boys Adventures*.

- Bayou: a low laying, slow moving, usually brackish (mix of sea and fresh) body of water.

- Acquire the Fire (see the end of the glossary)

- Harlen Ford sighting of the Honey Island Swamp Monster: http://en.wikipedia.org/wiki/Honey_Island_Swamp_monster

- NOLA: <u>N</u>ew <u>O</u>rleans, <u>L</u>ouisian<u>A</u>

Chapter 2

- The Big Easy: Another name for the city of New Orleans (especially the French Quarter).

- Third Day is a Christian rock band: https://thirdday.com/ (You may also watch their videos on YouTube and look up the other bands I've mentioned on the Internet.)

Chapter 3

- Honey Island Swamp Tours: http://www.honeyislandswamp.com/

- Cajun: A person of French-Canadian decent, possibly a corruption of Arcadian; also the dialect of the Cajuns.

- Satchmo: Nick name of Louis Armstrong, the great American jazz trumpeter: http://en.wikipedia.org/wiki/Louis_Armstrong

- Pralines: A candy confection (pronounced *praw leans*) of Louisiana made from sugar coated pecans.

- *Baguettes*: French bread

- Zydeco is a rollicking French–Cajun music style.

- Parasol: An umbrella (usually frilly).

- William Faulkner: Pulitzer Prize-winning author, http://en.wikipedia.org/wiki/William_Faulkner

- Rue: Street (French).
- *Padnet*: Cajun term for "friend" of "buddy."

- Spanish moss: A gray moss-like plant that hangs in trees and is related to the Pine-apple, even though it looks nothing like it.

- Live Oak: An evergreen oak; there are several related species native to the South.

- Antebellum: Meaning "before the war" and has come to specifically indicating something that existed or was built before the American Civil War.

- *Fo Troo*: Cajun expression meaning "that's for sure."

Chapter 6

- Ocala Indians: These Native Americans lived primarily in Florida, but also settled in the lower areas of Louisiana. (The Houma Indians also settled in the area.) http://www.ocala.com/article /20030101/OCALACOMHIST ORY/101010019

- *Flue de luce*: Literally, "flower of the lily" (French).

Chapter 7

- "Why so downcast, oh my soul, put your trust [hope] in God" Psalm 43:5

Chapter 8

- *Mouche a fea*: lighting bugs or fire flies.

Chapter 9

- "Thy word is a lamp unto my feet and a light unto my path" Psalm 119:105

- David Bowie was a British pop star; he starred (and was totally creepy as the Goblin King) in the movie *Labyrinth*.

- *Bos coya*: the knee-like roots of the cypress trees that grow out of the swamp (Cajun).

- *Gallerie*: The French-Cajun term used for 'porch.'

- Glock: A semi-automatic pistol.

Chapter 10

- *Vite vite*: A Cajun term meaning "quickly."

- Blue Man Group: A theatrical-musical group known for their odd performance, bald heads and blue costume and make-up. http://www.blueman.com/

Chapter 11

- War of 1812: http://en.wikipedia.org/wiki/War_of_1812

Chapter 12

- Yiddish: The High German language of the Jewish people.

- Tuvak: A black Vulcan in the TV series *Star Trek: Voyager*.

Chapter 14

- "Let no unwholesome thing come out of your mouth" Ephesians 4:29

- Galley: The kitchen of a ship of boat.

- *Adieu*: French for "farewell."

Chapter 15

- Cribbage: A card game (also known as Crib) that utilizes a peg board for tracking points.

Chapter 17

- *Cocodrie*: A small town and bayou in southern Louisiana. The name means "crocodile" or "alligator."

Chapter 18

- *Au revoir*: French for "goodbye."

- *Adios*: Spanish for "farewell."

Chapter 19

- Nick Vujicic: See http://www.lifewithoutlimbs.org/ (You may also view his videos on YouTube.)

Chapter 21

- *Fais do do*: Cajun for a dance party.

- "Where your treasure is there will your heart be also" Matthew 6:21

To learn more about an <u>Acquire the Fire</u> youth event near you see: http://www.acquirethefire.com

1 THE PLAY'S THE THING

Deep within the catacombs of the Paris opera house the Phantom sat down upon the throne and wrapped his black cloak around himself while the company roared threats from the wings. A venomous fog rolled from the stage lip as eerie blue-green light bathed the stage. Mary Mur-ray, playing Christine, stood staring, seemingly mesmerized, into a full-length mirror. I burst from the stage right wing, the other members of the cast flowing in behind me.

"Christine!" I said, stopping at my mark boldly holding a prop broadsword before me. Mary turned from the glass—a single rose-colored pin spot shone upon her face from the batten above.

"Raoul!" said Mary.

"Is he...?"

"He's gone," she said, pointing to the set's throne. I looked and the dark cloak hung limp on the seat—the illusion of the phantom's disappearance complete.

"The Opera Ghost?" asked a voice from the crowd. It was Steve Catt, in the role of Erik.

"Gone," she said again softly, "vanished into the bowels of the earth."

"You loved him?" I delivered my line.

"I pitied him," Mary replied, looking into my eyes. I stepped toward her and she stepped toward me, raising her arms. I sheathed my sword and we fell into an embrace, my head bending tenderly toward her face. "I love *you*, Raoul."

"I love you, too, Christine. The phantom...he will not harm you now." I continued in toward what should be a kiss as the lights faded to black and the house curtain dropped. I could hear the thunderous applause coming from behind the drape as we ran from the stage to prepare for our bows.

The curtain call music began as the drape rose. Members of the chorus filed onto the stage and took their bows as the applause continued. The principles were next and finally Mary and I stepped into the limelight—her curtsy, my bow. We took one an-other's hands and bowed again, the audience clap-ping on, standing to their feet. We parted and gestured to up center stage as the Phantom stepped from the shadows, removed his mask, and took his obeisance. We all came back together, clasping hands, and bowed together as a company. The curtain descending once again and we left the stage in smiles.

☿ ☿ ☿

"Well, that's it," said Steve, as we walked toward the dressing rooms.

"Yeah, the final curtain," I said.

"I wish it weren't," he replied. "I love the roar of the crowd..."

"...the smell of the greasepaint," I said completing the famous quote as we walked past the green-room (that's where actors hang out when they're not on stage).

"I'll miss this cast, too," he sighed. "It was like family."

"Always is," I said as I turned the handle on the dressing room door pulling the door open and allowing Steve to enter.

"Hey, Pete, Steve," said Antonio, seeing us in the mirror where he sat pulling chunks of gelatin from his face. The makeup was awesome; it looked just like a hideously deformed burn.

"You were a great Phantom," I said. "Too bad it's over."

"Yeah," he replied as he continued peeling, "it was my first starring role."

"Well, you were great, Tony," said Steve.

"Thanks," he said, turning toward us as we sat down to remove our own makeup. "You guys were really good, too."

"We were, weren't we," said Steve with a smile. "The three caballeros."

"*Aves raras*," I replied in Spanish.

"Aves raras?" questioned Tony, as if right on cue from the Disney movie.

"*Si, señor*," I answered rubbing cold cream into my face. "That means 'strange birds'," I said, finishing the lines from the animated classic.

"Oh," said Tony, "a movie quote."

"So, where you birds flying next?" asked Steve. "Got another gig?"

"Not right away," I said removing the cold cream from my face with a tissue. "I might try out for *Godspell* after I get back from NOLA*."

"Oh, whatcha doing in the Big Easy*?" Steve asked reaching for the makeup remover.

I handed him the jar and took another couple of tissues, wiping my face as I spoke, "Going to check out an O.G."

"An Opera Ghost?" asked Steve.

"Exactly," I answered. "Well, sort of. There's a supposed haunting at the Davis Playhouse."

"You're pulling my leg." He stopped mid-smear as I tossed my tissue in the trash.

"Actually, I'm not," I replied. "I mean I'm sure there's no ghost, but something— or someone—is 'haunting' the place. Just like the Phantom of the Opera."

"That's weird," he replied, "life imitating art."

"Not too original," said Steve.

"No, but Bart and I will get to the bottom of it."

"Gonna excommunicate, then?"

"It's called an exorcism," I said, "if you want to see it like that, but nothing so spooky."

"Yeah, yeah," he said, "that's what I meant."

I threw the last bit of tissue in the trash, "Well, next time guys," I rose to leave.

"Sure, take care Pete."

"You, too, Steve. Tony."

"Laters."

☠ ☠ ☠

"You were great, Peter!" said Bart, meeting me in the lobby and throwing his arm over my shoulder for a quick sideways man-hug.

"Thanks," I replied pulling on my windbreaker and stepping out of the theater's lobby onto the main drag through Houma. Mary Murray's mom honked from her car parked on the side street. Mary waved from the rolled-down window.

"See ya, Pete. Nice job," she yelled as they pulled away. I waved back as my girlfriend, Carla, joined us from the sidewalk handing me a bouquet of six roses, a look of jealousy on her face.

"Thanks, babe," I said. "How'd you like the final show?"

"Nice job," she replied coolly.

"Yeah, well, uh," said Bart. "I'll leave you two lovebirds alone. 'Nice job.'" He winked and headed out down the sidewalk.

"Wanna grab some ice cream?" I asked, turning to Carla and taking her hand just as my mom drove up.

"Nah," she said, "I baked us some pie. It's back at your place."

"Mmm," I said as we walked toward the car. "What kind?"

"Sweet Potato-Pumpkin-Pecan*." Yeah, (I know it sounds weird, but it's a Louis-iana thing, especially in the fall.)

"My fave," I said opening the back door and she ducked in. I followed after. Mom turned from the driver's seat.

"How'd it go, sweetie?" she asked.

"Great," I replied.

"I don't see how you could have gotten any better than when I saw it last week, but I'll bet you knocked them dead."

"He was awesome," said Carla. Mom just kept looking at me smiling.

"Uh, Mom, you wanna get a move on? I hear there's pie waiting."

"Oh, yeah, sure," she said, turning and putting the car in gear. A second later we were rolling to-ward home.

☠ ☠ ☠

The night air was wet and sticky. Mom and Dad, Carla and I sat on the gallery* stuffing pie in our pie holes between gulps of milk and snippets of conversation. The October moon hung low and nearly full in the twinkling sky. The brush twinkled, too; the last of the fireflies were out dancing in the cool air among the foliage.

"Heading up to Na'lins* tomorrow morning after church," said my dad to no one in particular, "Bob and I have a court appearance to make on Monday concerning the Roberto Thachne* case and," he turned to me, "I thought you and Bart could go along and visit the Davis Playhouse."

"Cool," I said, "From one phantom to another."

"Nobody will get shot this time?" asked my mom, sheepishly.

"You never know." *I shouldn't have said that.* Mom was pretty concerned about dad being a cop and putting his life on the line, but she was overly concerned about me, since I was shot during my Voodoo Virus* caper.

"We'll be fine," said Dad, scowling at me.

"You better be," said Carla, "More pie?"

"Don't mind if I do," I said, reaching for the dish.

"That's enough for one night, Peter," said Mom, "It's getting late and time for me to take Carla home." She rose, gathering the dishes. "I'll get my keys and be right back. Come on Jim, help me get these in the dish-washer."

Dad got up. "See you in the morning, son. Carla, great pie. Thanks."

"Goodnight Mr. and Mrs. Meyers. Thanks for letting me come over."

"You had pie," said Dad with a wink, "How could we say no?" Carla laughed as my parents went through the screen door into the house.

After a moment of relaxing cricket sere-nade, Carla, sitting beside me on the porch swing, turned toward me. "You were great in the show, Peter."

"Thanks, babe. And great pie, too."

"Yeah, thanks."

I put my arm around her shoulders and drew her in close for our last few moments together.

2 A HOUSE DIVIDED

B art's dad again filled us in on the history of the Davis House as we rolled through the Garden District of New Orleans: "The Edward A. Davis House was built in 1858. It combines the Greek Revival and the Queen Anne styles of architecture. It was acquired by the Women's Opera Guild of New Orleans in 1955 through the donation of the last owner."

I'd already learned that a few weeks ago when we were in New Orleans before we'd found ourselves in another mystery where we'd come face to face with modern day pirates, buried treasure and a creepy Marsh Monster—I mean, Marsh Monsters.*

Arriving at our destination, we exited the car, squeaked through the wrought iron gate and stood at the base of the steps leading up to the old white house.

"So this place has presumably been haunted since the early nineteen hundreds?" I asked as we stepped up to the porch of the Women's Opera Guild headquarters also once known as the Davis Playhouse.

"That's what they say," said Warden Davis, Bart's dad. "It's even been on *Haunted Mysteries*."

"People are crazy," I said. "Everyone wants a ghost story in New Orleans."

"Good for the tourist business," said Warden Davis. "You know they have all those haunted tours. Factoid: New Orleans is known as the most haunted city in America."

"Well, here we are, *The Ghostbusters*," said Bart.

"I ain't afraid a no ghost," I quoted from the movie's title song, humming a few bars of the catchy tune.

We stepped into the veranda and were met by a salt and pepper bearded man.

"Where yat?*" he asked with the tradit-ional New Orleans greeting, extending his hand, "I'm Dennis Jenkins, but you can call me Sparky, like everyone else." I assumed the name Sparky came from being the house electrician/lighting designer—a traditional nickname for people of that trade in theater. "I was the live-in lighting guy—when this was a theater." *Bingo.*

"Pleased to meet you," said my dad, "I'm Jim Meyers and this is my son, Peter. And this is Warden, I mean, Bob Davis and his son, Bart." We each offered our hand in turn and shook.

"My pleasure," replied Sparky, nodding. "Right this way." He turned to his right and we followed him from the lobby to a large room filled with cubicles—you know, those office thingies. The room had two ornate fireplaces and floor to ceiling windows draped with fine curtains drawn to the side with gold-colored cord. Two large, elaborate chandeliers hung from the intricately carved plaster ceiling. The bland beige cubicles seemed sorely out of place in the beautiful white room. "This is the work room, also once known as the great hall, or the dining hall, depending on when you're talking about."

"I assume," said Bart's dad, "it was originally the great hall and is now the work room, so it must have been the dining room in between?"

"Right you are," said our guide. "It became the dining room when the real dining room became the theater, which is now a board room/lecture hall of sorts."

"Sort of confusing," I said.

"It gets that way," he replied. "I'll show you the rest of the place, if you'll follow me." He set off through the room, angling this way and that through the maze of office partitions. At the back of the room we went through an arch and found ourselves in another smaller room with a bay window. There was a cushioned bench seat wrapped in a u-shape underneath the three windows. Another ornate chandelier hung in the center of the octagonal space. "This is the solarium," he continued as we passed through, "It was originally the sitting room or parlor or solarium and now it still is, I guess, though it also served as the theater's greenroom."

We walked down a short, wide hall past a narrow door in a five foot wall on the right and a short hallway off to the left and turned right into another room. Actually, the hall just got wider. "This is the service area for the kitchen, was and is. In between it was the backstage area. That's the kitchen," he indicated to his left, "was and is. Always has been. In the back there's a pantry. It's mostly storage now." We crossed the hall and walked up four steps. I recognized the space immediately.

"The stage," I said. A single bulb glowed bare in a floor lamp in the center of the stage illuminating the area wrapped in black drapes. The main curtain was drawn at the proscenium and the light gently lit the seating area beyond.

"Right you are," commented Sparky. "It's still an auditorium, but was the original dining room."

"What does the company—the business here—need with an auditorium?" asked Bart.

"It's an animation business called Razzmatazz Studios" said Sparky. "They have staff meetings here and it's where they sweatbox—I believe that's what you call it—their work." He stepped off the stage lip, descending another staircase into the auditorium and walked down the center aisle. I noticed two more fireplaces and two more chandeliers. *Man, this place is ritzy*, I thought. A glass panel—a curtained window—was at the back of the theater at the second story level. We all stopped back in the lobby where we'd started, at the bottom of the grand staircase. "Well," said Sparky, "ready for the upstairs?"

"Lead on," said my father. Sparky started up the stairs and we followed. Dad was still limping a bit in his splint boot from the broken leg the pirates gave him in our last caper.* A showcase of animation cels were framed on the stair-well walls. It was nice work. At the top of the stairs we gathered on the landing where we stood in front of elevator doors. Sparky beckoned and turned left.

"The library," he said. A floor to ceiling book-case lined the entire hall. A few overstuffed arm chairs sat along the opposite wall with an end table between them.

Sparky opened a door at the far end of the reading room and stepped inside.

"This was originally the master bedroom, but served as costuming for the theater, it's now the CEO's office of Razzmatazz." The large walnut desk, the lush furnishings and lavish wall art sort of gave that away. Another fireplace stood against one of the walls. A small wet bar divided the room's formal office space from a sitting area with a sofa, recliner and a seventy inch flat screen TV.

Sparky continued through the room toward two double windows—again floor to ceiling—and hung a left toward another door. "This is the passageway to the second floor of the turret," putting his hand on the knob giving it a tug. It didn't open. "Hmm, locked." Our guide circled around us and went back through the room and out the door. Once again, we followed like sheep.

Back through the library and past the elevator, he pointed to the door in front of us. "Restroom." To our right was a railing. I noticed the lines tied to it. Over the empty space beyond I could see the tops of stage curtains and see the glow of the light below. *Fly loft**, I thought. He turned left and opened another door. "Was another bedroom," he said, going inside. "Once the theater's men's dressing room, now another office. Chief Financial Officer's."

Outside the room again, he crossed the hall and we walked past the fly loft to our right and into another door. "This was the lady's dressing room, before that a bedroom, now—you guessed it—another office. VP of operations." We didn't go inside. "And that concludes our tour. Any questions?"

"Yeah," said Bart, "What's been happening here? I mean, with the ghost— the 'hauntings'?"

"You'll have to ask the Razzmatazz people," he looked at his watch. "They should be here any time now. But, I will say this: The place has always been haunted. At least when it was a theater, or so they say. I've never seen a ghost and I lived here—right in this house—pert near twenty years, but others say they have. We were even on that cable ghost show, ya know. Anyway, the legend is that one of Ed-ward's—Edward Davis'—one of his house-keepers—a young black woman— was beaten to death by his drunk son. Supposedly she haunts the place."

"Ever see *any*thing strange?" I asked.

"Oh, yeah, sure. I guess you could say that, but I think it's all explainable."

"Like what?" asked Bart.

"Oh, flickering lights," he said, "Swing-ing chandeliers, stuff gone missing — misplaced, but mostly just people saying they saw the woman sit-ting in one of the seats. No one will sit there, it's kept open for..." The door below us creaked open. Bart's eyes widened at the sound.

"Anyone here?" cried a voice that echoed through the house.

"Up here," answered Sparky. There were footfalls on the stairs and soon we were met with a young man in an Armani suit ascending the staircase followed by an older, heavy-set and tall man in khaki slacks, a white shirt and a tie, loose at his neck.

"Hi Sparky, solved the mystery yet?" said the man in the Armani.

"No. Still giving the nickel tour, Mr. Barbor," answered our guide as he gestured around the space.

"And our guests," he said breaking onto the landing, "can call me Jonathan. Welcome to Razzmatazz. This," he said gesturing to the man beside him, "is Council Member Bart Burkmann."

"Council Member Burkmann," Dad said. The councilman grunted. "Jonathan. Good to meet you. I'm Jim Meyers, this is my colleague Bob Davis, his son Bart and my son Peter," my dad said indicating each of us in turn and extended his hand. Jonathan reached out and shook it and Dad offered his hand to the other man as did Bart's dad. Bart and I did the same. Burkmann kept his hands at his sides, his face pinched as if he was sucking on green persimmons.

"Well, I hear you boys come well recommended," said Jonathan. "I hope you can help us out." The councilman harrumphed and rolled his eyes. "Yes, well," continued the CEO, "Why don't we step into my office." We walked back through the library and into the Master Suite and Jonathan indicted the seating area. "Have a seat, can I get you anything? I have bottled water, Pepsi, and—"

"No thank you," said Bart's dad speaking for us all, "we're good."

"Then to business," said the CEO sitting on the end of the recliner. "Thing is, we can't continue to work here with this ghost and my good councilmember wants to keep us here—he likes the rent we put into the city's coffers." He chuckled, the council member did not. Clearing his throat, the CEO continued, "It seems, at least, that something or someone doesn't want us here. A ghost, perhaps. Now I don't believe in them, but something doesn't want us around, that much is evident."

"What evidence would that be?" I asked.

"Let's see," Jonathan spoke as he rose to pace the room, "Noises to begin with—you know, moans, creaks..."

"This an old house," said the council-man, speaking at last, "it's bound to have some..."

"Yes, yes," said Jonathan. "What about footfalls on the stairs and upper rooms when they're supposedly unoc-cupied? What about scraping noises? And how do you account for the screams?"

"Screams?" asked Bart.

"Female screams" answered Jonathan turning on his heels and waving the air. "Like someone's dying. And laughter, but that's just the sounds. Things go missing or are moved, rather. Art is found in the waste bin or marked up. And things get broken."

"Have you actually seen anything move or get broken before your eyes?" asked Bart.

"No," he said, "We just find them that way."

"Do the lights still flicker or the chandeliers swing?" Bart continued his line of questioning.

"Oh, yeah, I guess that's moving isn't it?"

"It could be construed that way," said Bart, "Any physical manifestations?"

"What do you mean?" said the CEO, tapping his chin.

"Apparitions, appearances."

"No, nothing like that. I mean, well, except..." He paused.

"What?" I said.

"In one of our finished animations, when we viewed it in the sweatbox...the theater."

"How's that?" asked Bart's dad.

"I can show you," said the CEO. "Come over to my desk." We rose and followed him over to the opulent piece of furniture and he asked us to gather around a very thin, twenty-eight inch flat screen that spanned the surface area.

"Man!" exclaimed Bart, always the tech enthusiast. "That is the thinnest screen I have ever seen!"

"State of the art," said the CEO beaming with pride. "Less than a quarter inch thick. It's the new OLED—Organic Light-Emitting Diode, paper-thin. It's what they've been using in smartphones for a few years, but now they're making screens as big as walls with this stuff." He monkeyed with the mouse and the thing flickered to life. "The blackest blacks, highest contrast ratio, everything."

"Coolio," said Bart, "I've not seen that in the stores."

Jonathan clicked on a file and a playback window opened and began loading a file. "It won't be available to the public until after Christmas, but I've been beta-testing it all year," he said clicking the window to full screen, then again a third of the way along the progress bar at the bottom of the screen. "It appears about here. Watch," he said. The animation was now playing on the screen.

3 UNSCRIPTED

There it is," said the CEO pointing to the screen. "Do you see it?" A wavering trans-parent image of a woman floated over the animation sequence. It had shimmered in and out of focus briefly, then disappeared.

"Can you play that again?" I asked.

"Sure," said Jonathan, clicking back on the progress bar. The video replayed and, right on cue, the image once again appeared, shimmered and dis-appeared. In all the 'manifestation' showed up for five seconds. Something dawned on me.

"Notice anything peculiar?" I said.

"It's peculiar, alright," said Jonathan. "None of our animators put it there."

"No, I mean it doesn't move in the sense of live-action. It's a still photograph. Looks like it might be a black woman from the hair and features, though it's washed out. *Except* that it's been 'animated,' if you will, to appear as though it moves."

"You're right," relied the CEO. "It's very limited animation. A simply warping effect. I recognize it from our effects toolbar."

"What's the time-date stamp on the video?" I questioned.

"Why do you ask?" said Bart.

"Bear with me," I answered. "Just a hunch."

"We finished it in late September;" said the CEO, "the twenty-ninth I believe."

"Let's have a look at it—the file I mean," I said.

"Peter," interjected Dad, "what difference does it make when the video was made?"

"Not when it was *made*," I answered, "when it was last *altered*—assuming, someone opened the file and added the superimposure after the file was completed."

"Superimposure, isn't a word," said Bart.

"You know what I mean—superimposed."

"Or keyed it in," said Jonathan, clicking the file closed. "Okay, yeah." The mouse hovered over the video's icon until the file information appeared in a drop down. The date-time stamp read October fifteenth, 2013. Jonathan let out a whistle.

"Someone last saved this video less than two weeks ago," I said. "Meaning..."

"Someone—or some*thing*—altered the file," added Jonathan.

"So" said Sparky, "the photograph was layered in?"

"That seems to be the idea," said Jonathan as he clicked on another icon. "Let's open the program application." The Final Cut splash page appeared on the screen and began loading. "If I'm right, the application will show a second video layered on the timeline."

"Loaded from a flash drive, I assume," said Bart.

"And," interjected Jonathan continuing to click away, "I'll wager it's a still image with effects applied." The workspace opened and he clicked open a menu and scrolled down, clicking on the original editing file. When it was finished loading the CEO moved the cursor along the timeline and found what we were looking for. Indeed, a single image of a black wo-man with applied effects and fade in and fade out points sat above the animation file. He hovered the cursor over the superimposed image and the source file information appeared. It read: File Not Found. "Well, it's not on the computer," said the CEO. "It was rendered, then removed."

"One mystery solved," said Bart. "Only a human could do that."

"Probably," I said, then added tongue in cheek, "but maybe the ghost was a techie.

But it couldn't have been this ghost; she's been dead for nearly a hundred years. I doubt she would know how to use a computer."

"You're sure about that?" asked Sparky.

"It's logical to assume," I said, "but then again, 'once you eliminate the impossible, whatever remains, no matter how improbable, must be the truth.' Author Canon Doyle wrote that in his Sherlock Holmes novels, however it was quoted in *Star Trek* by Spock."

"Sounds like we have some insight here at least," said Jonathan.

"Good work, Peter," said my dad. "You too, Jonathan."

"So where do you go from here?" said the CEO.

"We keep gathering evidence and information," said Bart, "and form a hypothesis."

"Then we look for a way to blow this thing open," I added.

"Good police work, that is," commented my dad.

Jonathan rose from custom ergonomic desk chair and put his hand on my shoulder, "What more can I do to help you? I have a meeting with a client in thirty minutes, but I'll be free this afternoon."

"Great," I said, "that will give me some time to put together some thoughts and maybe a plan of action. Can you gather your people together for a meeting here this evening?"

"I'll see what I can do," replied the CEO. "It shouldn't be a problem though."

"Okay then," said my dad, "I think we need to get out and grab some lunch."

"Oh! Might I suggest Slim Goodie's Diner?" said Jonathan. "It has a Crawfish *Étouffée** that will send your taste buds into another plane. It's on me, if you wish."

"Mmm," said Bart, "I love a good *étouffée*." No surprise there, I can't think of a food he doesn't like.

"You don't have to do that," said Bart's dad.

"But I want to," said the CEO. "I'll call ahead and tell them you're coming. We often do take-out here and they have my credit card information."

"Well," said my father, "I guess it's Slim's place then. Thank you."

"Yes, thank you," I said, "And I'll bet you that Slim isn't skinny."

The CEO laughed, "You got that right, anyway, my pleasure. It's on Magazine, between Louisiana Avenue and Toledano. It's not far from here. I'll draw you a map." He picked up a pen and drew on a piece of the company's stationary. He handed it to my dad and I saw it over his shoulder; it was the most amazing map I'd ever seen—

true artistry. He'd drawn what must have been the diner's logo (which looked like a fried egg with wings) and a caricature of what had to be Slim with a crawfish in one hand and a spoon in the other along with the route.

"Here's the master key to our offices," he said, sliding it across the desk. "Can I have your cell numbers?"

"Sure," said my dad taking out his smartphone. "What's your number?" The CEO rattled off his number as Dad dialed and it rang through to Jonathan's iPhone. He answered then hung up, storing the number in his address book as Dad did the same for the CEO's number. I called next from my cell and we did the same.

"All good, here?" he asked.

"Good to go," I answered.

"Okay, then," said Jonathan moving toward the door, "you have the run of the place. I'll call you in a couple hours to let you know about that meeting. Enjoy your crawfish."

"Thanks, Jonathan," said Bart's dad. And with a wave of his hand the CEO left the office. Sparky said he was going to bow out of lunch and the council-man grunted that he had a meeting, too. A moment later we heard their footsteps on the stairs—at least I'm pretty sure they were the men's.

☠ ☠ ☠

Slim met us at the door and was extremely hospitable. He was a jolly old Cajun and treated us like we were royalty. The place was a typical old-fashioned diner—small, crowded, simple and a tad on the dingy side. (I was surprised such a place was frequented by a CEO who wore an Armani suit.) There was a sit-down counter facing the kitchen and an 'L' of booths wrapped around the walls that were painted yellow and smattered with dozens of Polaroid photos of guests. The booths were red and other red highlights festooned the cafe. A second room was painted blue with red highlights. The smell was amazing! We were given a seat by one of the front windows painted with the Saints* logo and the words 'Go Saints Go.' While we waited for our food, our group sat there chatting about our case.

"What's the next step Peter?" asked my dad, sipping his aromatic coffee.

"I'll call Reed after we're done here and get his take on ghosts." Bart chuckled and shook his head. "Hey," I said, "It's a starting point. I need to know what to expect and what not to expect."

"And then?" asked Bart's dad.

"We have to observe the phenomenon," I said. "See for ourselves what's going on."

"I must remind you," said my dad, "we only have what's left of the weekend."

"I'd like to get back home by Monday evening," said Bart. "There's a harvest party at the Zumstein's place."

"Oh, yeah," interjected Dad, "Monday's Halloween, isn't it?"

"And it's now Sunday," said Bart's dad. "Do you think we have enough time?"

Our food arrived. The steaming scent of the *étouffée* was intoxicating. Our waitress, in a blue diner-logoed T-shirt poured more coffee into our father's mugs. "More soda?" she asked Bart and me.

"Yes, please," intoned Bart, who'd already consumed two tumblers of Mt. Dew. He seemed to live on the yellow-green fluid. "What's the story behind your tattoo?" he asked, noticing the *flue du luce** just below her sleeve with the number 1,833 emblazoned across its face. "What's the number mean?"

She beamed and spoke in a southern accent, "Thanks fer askin.' One thousand eight hundred an' thirty-three people's what died in Katrina. They're true saints now. Ma nana was one a' them."

"I'm sorry to hear that," said Bart, "but it's really nice that you've honored them that way."

"Thanks," she said. "Nana didn't like tattoos, though," she chuckled, "I hope she's lookin' down with approval."

"She was a Christian?" said Bart.

"Oh, yeah," she smiled. "Taught me good, too. Only I never been so good when I was a kid. I'm tryin' now. Church and all. An' I know that prolly not all them folks that died went to heaven, but I hope so."

"I'm glad to hear that," said Bart. "We're Christians and Jesus has really been our Savior in more ways than one."

"Mine, too. I was doin' crack for so long, but I've been clean fer goin' on two years. I really regret tryin' to find ma peace in the pipe. But, you know what they say: 'No Jesus, No peace; Know Jesus, Know Peace.'"

"*Fo' troo*,*" I said.

"Anyways, thanks for askin'," she re-iterated. "I gotta git t' work. Y'all enjoy."

"Sure, thanks," said Bart. She lifted her coffee pot off the table and moved along.

"You always ask about tattoos?" questioned my dad.

"I try to," said Bart, "I got it from my friend Ed Shonkski. He said that tattoos usually have deep personal meaning and that showing an interest in people and their heartfelt feelings was the surest way to bless them."

"Well, I think you made *her* day," commented Dad.

"Yeah," I said, "every time someone brings it up she recalls her stories of hope and redemption*. Cool."

"And this *étouffée* is cooling, too," said Bart, poking his thumb in the air. "Let's eat." Quickly all of us, except my dad, also gave the thumbs up sign. Dad looked perplexed and slowly did the same.

"You're last," I said, "you get to offer the prayer." Dad smiled and we bowed our heads. He said grace for our meal and we dug in, continuing to converse and propose plans of action. And, let me tell you, *étouffée* had never been better.

4 POLTERGEIST!

"Hey, Reed," I said into my cell phone, "it's Peter. Mind if I pick your brain?"

"Ewh," he replied.

"Not literally, you fool."

"Who you callin' a fool?" Reed laughed.

"Certainly not you, Brainiac. I called for information. Information only you would know, buddy."

"Pick away."

I sat on the bed in a hotel room dad had rented, talking to our resident paranormal expert while Bart was in the can and our dads were out rustling up some grub. *Para* by the way, is Greek for 'alongside.' I learned that in Sunday School when we studied the Holy Spirit or *Parakletos* (translated to mean: one who comes alongside). Yeah, Reed was some-where right alongside normal. He knew all kinds of stuff about ghosts, vampires, werewolves, aliens, and the like. "So," I said, "this Playhouse Phantom seems to make its presence known mainly through stuff like screams, scraping, clomping on the stairs, moaning..."

"Ah," said Reed, "What you have there is a poltergeist."

"A what?"

"Poltergeist. It's German for noisy ghost."

"Okay," I said, "It also moves things."

"Still a poltergeist. Does it manifest itself in any way?"

"Though some people have reported sightings in the past, there are none recently except, well, it seems to have shown up on a video—in an animation."

"Casper?" poked Reed.

"Huh?"

"Casper, the Friendly Ghost. An old cartoon."

"Uh, no. It wasn't intended in the animation. It wasn't there when the studio finished the sequence."

"Hmm, that kinda sounds like a residual which means it lingers and manifests itself in sort of a film loop—doing the same thing over and over again, but this is different, I think. The idea that it was in an animation sequence just made me think of that, but it really has nothing to do with animation. This is highly irregular, except that specters *do* mysteriously show up in photographs from time to time. However..."

"Take a breath, dude," I interjected. "Okay, okay. I'm thinking this could be a demon. What do you think?"

"Possible, but unlikely. You haven't described the character of a demon. They tend to try to influence and/or harm through possession."

"That's what I thought. Demons can be dangerous. In fact, I think they are the only real things we might call ghosts since I don't believe that dead people actually walk around."

"Believe what you will," said Reed.

"Look, I don't mean to poo-poo you're 'belief' in the spirit world, but, you're a Christian, have you considered that spiritualism is forbidden in the Bible and that it says 'to be absent in the body is to be present with the Lord.*'"

"Yeah, yeah, I believe that too, it's just that, well, I guess I never really considered that. I'm just keeping an open mind. There's a lot of stuff we can't explain."

"But we need to explain this and that's why we're here. I was hoping you could help me."

"I'll do what I can," Reed assured.

"Okay, so, assuming this isn't a spirit or demon, what might be going on?"

"Well, most of what you've described could be attributed to an overactive imagination or, perhaps, common noises perceiveed as haunting."

"But there's more than noises," I said.

"People do misplace things and forget they moved them, but you mentioned this video. Did you actually see it yourself?"

"I did," I answered, "but it really wasn't much. Actually it was a single image superimposed onto the timeline—a simple video effect. We've come to the conclusion that it was a human creation. At least that's the hypothesis. At any rate, there have been no...no..."

"Manifestations?"

"Yeah, manifestations—other than that."

"Have you interviewed any eye-witnesses?"

"No, but we'll try. Oh! And there's a docudrama."

"Really?"

"Yeah, that cable ghost show, *Haunted Mysteries*, did a piece on it," I said, hearing the flush from the adjacent room.

"Yeah, I'd watch that. I'll look it up on the Internet."

"Bart and I will, too. Let me know what you think."

"Will do. Anything else you want to know?"

"I think that'll be it for now. Keep cool, but don't freeze."

"Ditto," said Reed, ending our connection as Bart exited the john.

"Sup?" said Bart.

"Reed, says we probably have a poltergeist," I answered. "If it isn't...for crying
out loud, Bart, close the door!"

"What?" he said, flopping down on the
bed next to me.

"Did you have to stink up the whole
hotel?" I said rising and going to close the
bathroom door, "Do *not* go in there!" I said
waving my arm behind me like Jim Carrey
in *Ace Ventura: Pet Detective* and closing the
bathroom door. Bart beamed as the hotel
door opened and our dads walked in.

Bart's dad came up short, then began
fanning the front door, "What kind of road
kill have you two dragged in here?" My
dad tried to ignore the conversation and
sat a bucket of KFC on the end table.

"It was Bart," I said.

"Humbly at your service," Bart bowed
dramatically from his sitting position.

"Son, son, son," said his dad wagging
his head and closing the door, "Someone
light a match." We all laughed, but my
father looked a bit uncomfortable. Bart's
father was so much like his son, always
making jokes. Seems like my dad would be
used to his humor, they spent so much
time together, but then I guess most
adults don't seem to find 'potty humor' all
that funny.

I hate to transition from taking a dump
to eating, but that is, in fact, what we did
next. Bart, characteristically, was first to

the bucket of chicken —selecting a drum-stick and breast. Jonathan had called my dad while they were out. Our meeting with the Razzmatazz Board set for 7:30 p.m. and since it was only 4:24 we said a quick grace and began to chow down.

It was Halloween week on A&E so I clicked on the tube and planted my bum in front of it. As 'fate' would have it the movie playing was *Poltergeist* by Steven Spielberg. Honestly. It had begun airing at 4 p.m.

At first it was just spooky and creepy— a family being haunted by moving objects —but then it got pretty terrorizing, with the kidnapping (possession) of the daughter. Though pretty much PG, as rated, it none-the-less was a real creep-fest. Bart was rather uneasy with the film through-out. "I'm not so sure I want to spend the night in that house," he said three-quarters of the way through the movie.

"Oh, Bart, you're such a ...such a chicken," I said laughingly as a thought crossed my mind. "I guess you are what you eat." His dad chuckled and then quickly composed himself.

"That was, uh," he said, "funny, what you said about what you eat, Peter. I know it wasn't really an insult." When the movie was over we got ready to go and set off for Razzmatazz Studios.

5 ON THE BOARDS

Jonathan Barbor had called a meeting of Razzmatazz Studios Board of Directors as I'd asked him to. Bart and his dad, my dad and I, along with Mr. Lurchman (I mean Councilman Burkmann, though he reminded me of Lurch from the *Addam's Family*) and another council member by the name of Jaynie Harrison joined the assembly. Sparky wasn't in attendance. The CEO filled them in our little progress so far and then sat back in his chair with his hands behind his head with the words, "Any thoughts?"

"This is ridiculous!" exclaimed Harrison. "Ghosts! You just want to back out of your lease agreement, which would be fine with me, but..."

"I assure you we want to stay," said the CEO, "but if this nefarious activity continues we can't."

"That's right," said the man that had been introduced to us as Walt Iwerks*, one of the board members and chief animator, "several of my sequences have been vandalized and police can't come up with any clues. We can't work in this sort of environment and that's all there is to it."

"Then get out," said the councilwoman with dramatic flair, "but be assured, we *will* collect the remaining lease."

"Let's not be hasty councilwoman," said Jonathan coolly. "We're trying to find a solution. That's why the boys are here."

"Boys!" she snorted and Lurch lurched.

"These 'boys' come highly recommended," said Jonathan in our defense. Harrison harrumphed.

Another board member, leaning forward in his chair, piped in, "Jon, why don't we just call a medium in on this? The Quarter is full of them."

"With all due respect," began the CEO, "I think that's just a bunch of mumbo jumbo, and I believe…"

"What? That there's no such thing as ghosts?" said the board member. "Maybe, you haven't seen them like I have, but…"

"Have you seen this one?" asked the CEO, butting in.

"None of us has," the man retorted, "but that doesn't mean…"

"That this is…"

"Gentlemen," said my dad, "let's try to discuss this situation calmly. My son has come up with some ideas. Why don't we hear him out and work on solving the issue at hand. If they don't succeed, then you can try whatever you desire." The room was silent for a moment.

"Okay," Jonathan said at last, "Master Myers, what do you have for us?"

I took a moment to look at each face and began. "Since a lot of these things seem to happen overnight—the moving objects and the like—except for the noises, I suggest we observe a common work day and then stay the night."

"We don't generally work on Sunday and the day is all but spent anyway," said the CEO. "We were planning on short day tomorrow, beings it's Halloween, but I will gladly accommodate you in every way I can. Of, course you may also stay here to-night if you wish."

"We have a hotel room only a few blocks from here," interjected my father. "The boys may stay here if they wish, but I think my old back would just as soon sleep in a bed. *If* you don't think there is any danger—even though my son seems to find it."

"Has anything happened today— anything haunting?" asked Bart.

"Not that I know of and there hasn't been anything violent in the past so it should be safe," said the CEO. "Either way, you have the key. Make yourselves at home."

"Then I don't think we need to stay to-night," I said. "Let's wait and see what—if anything—happens tomorrow."

"Fine," said my dad and the meeting adjourned. At the door we were met by Lurch.

"I'd be careful," he said in a deep, booming voice, looking down at me with a furrowed bushy uni-brow, eyes locking on mine. He turned slowly on his heels and walked out. Yeah, total creep factor.

"You rang?" I whispered to Bart as we exited Razzmatazz. It was quarter to nine when we got in the car and made the trip back to our hotel for another plate of spooky on A&M. The 10 p.m. show was *The Ghost and Mr. Chicken*, starring Don Knotts—one of my all-time favorite 'horror' comedies from 1966. (No I wasn't alive then, but we'd bought the DVD a couple years ago.)

Knott's plays a small town reporter who spends the night in an old mansion on the anniversary of a murder in the house so he can write a story about it. After being scared stiff, or shakily as only Don Knotts can, by several haunting incidents (namely an organ that plays by itself) he uncovers the mystery surrounding the cold case. It was more silly than frightening and good fodder for the imaginations of a dreaming mind. So that night my dreams centered on creeping around an old house.

6 SONG AND DANCE

It was 8:37 a.m. Halloween morning when we arrived at Razzmatazz Studios (a.ka. The Davis Playhouse) for our day of observation. Our dads dropped us off after a quick breakfast at the local Jack in the Box and headed up town to the courthouse for the Thachne trial. Bart and I walked in the front door of the old antebellum* and poked our heads into the cubical room where animators were hard at work in their little boxes. *Think outside the box*, I thought, *Why, they won't even let me out of the box.*

"Go on up," said Iwerks, "Jon's expecting you." I nodded and Bart and I backed out of the room and hit the stairs, taking the left turn at the top toward the CEO's office. The man sat in the library browsing a book on Disney animation, but looked up as we approached.

"Good morning Peter, Bart. Happy Halloween."

"Hi, Mr. Barbor," we said in unison.

"Oh, call me Jonathan," he said, closing the large book with a thump. "Walt Disney, still the standard."

I would agree," I said. "Even his first feature-length animation, *Snow White and the Seven Dwarfs*, stands the test of time."

"It almost didn't get made. No one believed in him," said the CEO. "Called it 'Disney's Folly.'"

"And look who had the last laugh," said Bart.

"*Fo Troo*," I commented, "It's almost seventy-five years old!"

"Classic," said Jonathan rising. "Anyway, let's head down stairs and meet the team."

After descending the stairs we hung a right into the workroom and Jonathan introduced us to the various artists — animators, shaders, lighting specialists, effects coordinators, painters, and those who specialized in rendering and networking, etcetera. Each of them was happy to explain their skills and demonstrate their work. Some of them teased us about being ghost hunters, others shared stories about the hauntings—nothing we hadn't already heard. All were good natured and amiable. Several had candy dishes on their desks laden with Halloween sweets and we were offered more than our fill. It was kind of like trick-or-treating. At last Jonathan gave us his leave and permission to explore with full reign of the place. The team planned to knock off at 3 p.m., so we sat about observing what we could.

"Well," said Bart looking at his watch with a sigh, "it's 10:52."

"Yup," I said gazing off in space.

"About an hour to lunch time," he said. "We didn't bring anything."

"You ate enough candy to put four diabetics into a coma."

"I'm still hungry," he said.

"Why am I not surprised?" The antique grand-father clock in the veranda struck eleven, tolling as many times.

"Yup," he said, "an hour until lunch." More minutes passed and the boredom was palpable. At last I couldn't take it anymore. Absolutely nothing was happening in the way of hauntings.

"What say we do some exploring?" I said.

"Yeah, sure," said my friend as he got up. "Better than sitting here listening to my tummy rumble." I led us over to the other side of the staircase to the hall between it and the auditorium. The wall was bedecked with a couple of plaques and several photographs. The first photo in the series showed the Davis family in all the glory of pre-Civil War sepia tone. This was followed by some black-and-whites of the opera's heyday and various Presidents of the Women's Opera Guild (WOG).

Further down the wall they progressed to color and the last photo was of the current WOG President, Becky Krabach, a high-society type woman in her late forties, I would say. From there we turned and went into the auditorium to poke around on the stage for a while.

Looking up from the deck, I noticed the fly loft was pretty empty. No scenery or theatrical light-ing equipment hung from the battens above, just the usual curtains—legs, tormentors, borders, the teaser, and the tabs—along with a large, rolled up, motorized projection screen directly behind the grand drape which was still open to the seating area. A black drape took the place of the usual cyclorama at the back (or upstage). There were two pair of theatrical ellipsoidal spots hanging from the front of house (or first batten) rail, two right and two left. The stage floor (or deck) was painted black and a trap (as in trap door) was placed about mid-stage. I tugged on the ring that served as a handle and the door wouldn't budge open.

"The trap won't open," I said to Bart.

"Is it locked?" he asked.

"Might just be stuck," I answered, "I wonder if it only goes down the two foot stage depth or if there's a basement."

"Sparky didn't mention a basement," said Bart, grunting while trying the ring, which still wouldn't budge.

"Come on," I said, "let's check out the backstage area."

"And the kitchen," he added. "I'm..."

"Hungry, I know." We found the center opening in the upstage curtain, descended the four steps into the wide room behind and wandered back toward the kitchen's double swinging doors. Bart charged through first and came up short of fully crossing the threshold. I ran into him from behind. There, in the center of the large industrial kitchen, on the stain-less steel prep table was a black cat—dead as a door nail. Though *'Mind!'* I thought of the Charles Dickens line from *A Christmas Carol*, which I'd done on stage last Christmas, *'I don't mean to say that, of my own knowledge, what there is particularly dead about a doornail. I might have been inclined, myself, to regard a coffin-nail as the deadest piece of ironmongery in the trade.'* The feline was flayed open, blood oozing onto the table. We gasped in succession.

"I just lost my appetite," said Bart, holding his stomach.

"That would be a first, *padnet**," I replied, "but I don't blame you."

"What *is* this?" he asked.

"It's a dead cat, dude."

"Duh, what's it mean?"

"It means either someone doesn't like cats or…" I trailed off.

"Or what?"

"It's a warning."

"I hope it means someone doesn't like cats. So, what should we…?"

"We should report this to Jonathan."

"Sounds like a plan," said Bart. We turned around and hightailed it down the hall and up the stairs. At the landing we hung a left through the library and rapped on the CEO's door.

"Come in," said the voice on the other side of the door. I turned the handle and we went in. "You boys look like you've seen a ghost. Have you?"

"Uh…" said Bart.

"Not…exactly," I said, windily.

"Then what exactly?" asked the CEO.

"A cat," said Bart.

"A dead cat," I specified.

"Were you in the alley way?" asked the CEO.

"No, it's in the kitchen" I said, "…on the prep table."

Jonathan shook his head. "Let's take a look," he said getting up. "Show me." With that the three of us left the office in route to the kitchen. I held the door open for the CEO and he went in. We followed.

"Where?" he said. The cat was gone and so was the blood!

"So the cat was here you say?" said Jonathan pointing to the stainless table.

"Yes," I replied. "Slayed, splayed and filleted with blood oozing out."

"There's no trace of blood now," he said, looking closely at the table and wiping his finger across the shiny surface.

"I see that," I replied.

"But it *was* there," said Bart.

"I believe you," said the CEO, "but it's a first. There hasn't been anything like that before." He scanned the floor and tried the doors. He checked the trash can by the door, but seemed to have found nothing. Bart whipped the pantry door open and stepped to the side like he was some sort of one man SWAT team or something, then peaked around the casing.

"See anything?" I asked.

"Food," he replied. I rolled my eyes.

Jonathan looked at his watch. "Goodness," he said, "it's nearly 1 p.m., have you boys eaten?"

"No," answered Bart. "We forgot to bring lunch, but we could walk down to Slim's and get something in a moment."

"No need," answered the CEO, "I'll order something in. You two, like Chinese?"

A parody song by Tim Hawkins* entered my mind just then: *'The cat's in the kettle at the Peking Moon,'* and I smirked just as Bart said, "Sure."

Jonathan put his hand on my shoulder and said, "Good."

"But what happened to the cat?" I asked, not wanting to let the mystery go unsolved.

"You can puzzle about that over lunch," said Jonathan. "Come on." He took his hand from my shoulder and led us out through the lobby. Bart and I stopped at the elevator; Jonathan kept moving down the hall, but called back, "I like to take the stairs for the exercise, I'll meet you up top. No hurry though, it'll take a half hour for the food to arrive."

"Sure," I yelled down the hall and then spoke to Bart, "I want to go talk to the animators—or at least see if any of them look guilty." Bart shrugged and we spun right, then left around the wall into the workroom. Each of the artists was hard at work, but most of them took a moment away from their computers or drawing desks to offer a kindly hello—and more candy. Neither of us mentioned the cat as we wove our way through the cubicle maze. One of the ladies sat in her office chair, arms across her chest with a smirky-look of satisfaction on her face. She seemed to be doing nothing else but look across the walkway at the cubicle across from her's. I followed her eyes and saw that the office into which she gazed was empty. She gave us the shush sign and beckoned us to come into her space.

"Hi, I'm Sandra. Lillian's gone to the restroom," she said in a hushed tone pointing across the way. "I've been waiting to do this for a while. Sit here with me and look busy, but keep a lookout."

"Here comes a lady," whispered Bart.

"Sit, sit" she said hastily. We did and soon the woman entered her cubicle and let go with a loud oath. Sandra held in her laughter, but I could tell it wasn't easy for her. I wondered what was so funny and then, looking, I saw what had upset Lillian. A bottle of nail polish was tipped and spilling out polish onto a piece of art on her desk.

"Wait a minute," said Lillian, "This isn't my color! Who's been in my office?"

Sandra couldn't hold it in any longer and started laughing out loud. Lillian whirled in our direction. "YOU!" she bellowed through clenched jaw. "That plate was just about finished, Sandra! Why were you doing your nails in *my* office?"

Sandra rose still smiling broadly, "It's just a gag, Lil. Pick it up." A puzzled look crossed Lillian's face and she reached for the bottle and plucked it from her desk. The 'spill' came up with the bottle and Lillian, too, began to laugh. We chuckled at the prank with them. *That was good,* I thought.

"I bought it from a novelty shop down on Decatur two weeks ago," said Sandra to the other woman. "I've just been waiting for the right moment to use it on you."

"Well," said Lillian jovially, "you got me, but, rest assured, I will get you back, Sandy. And I don't just get even, I up my revenge." It was time to make our exit, and we got up.

"Nice one," said Bart as we left the cubicle.

"*Fo troo*," I replied.

☠ ☠ ☠

We made our way through the rest of the office space making chit-chat with all the employees when the front door opened and a young Chinese man poked his head in. He carried several white paper sacks. "Baba, here? He order Chinese," he said.

"Upstairs," answered Iwerks. "Go on up." The boy nodded and bound up the steps, disappearing from sight. Bart looked at me and, from his expression, I knew he was thinking 'food!'

"Should we go up?" I asked him. "Or wait until he calls so we don't look too eager?"

"I am eager," he answered.

"That much is obvious. Come on, we'll take the elevator." We passed back through the room, nodding at Sandra and

Lillian, on the way to the lift and punched the call button. While we waited for the car to arrive I asked Bart if he knew Chinese food might not always be what they say it is. He looked at me all puzzled-like. The elevator dinged and the door slid open. A foggy haze drifted out and inside hung an effigy of a black woman. Bart screamed in shock and we both took a step back. Written in blood on the mirrored rear wall of the car were the words:

if you sing, i will dance

A moment later Danny G., the Razzmatazz computer whiz, ducked around the corner.

"Everything okay?" he asked. Bart pointed into the elevator car and Danny came around for a look. He gasped and we all stood there staring at the stuffed dummy hanging from a rope within. "Better tell the boss," he said at last.

"Uh," I said, after sniffing the air (*not theatrical fog*), "we were just going up, we'll let him know if you will stay here and... and..."

"Guard the body," he said. "Sure." Just as we turned to head down the hall to the stairs he spoke again, "We can just ride her up, if you want."

"No thanks," said Bart, "but you can."

"Will do," he said. "Meet you up there."

We knocked on the CEO's door, were bidden to enter, did so and told him of our new encounter. His office was alive with the tempting scents of steaming pork fried rice, egg foo yung, sub gum yuk and chow mein, but the food would have to wait a bit longer. Jonathan went down the hall with us, examined the elevator, and called the police from his cell before we walked back to his office to eat and talk. Bart chowed down on the chow mein, while I poked some pork fried rice around on a paper plate.

"I think," said Jonathan, "that the ante has been upped."

"Yeah," I said, "what do you mean?"

"This kind of thing...well," he returned, "up until now, there's been no bodies, feline or otherwise."

"The cat," I said, "a thought occurred to me. Just a while ago Sandra played a joke on Lillian that involved a fake spilled bottle of nail polish."

"And?" said the CEO, looking up from his subgum.

"The cat, how it disappeared, blood and all," I said, "It could have been a fake, too. There would be traces of blood, if it were real blood, but it was completely gone in an instant. Not enough time to clean up a mess like that. I think the blood might have been latex."

"Yeah," interjected Bart, "we never touched it."

"You might be onto..." said the CEO just as there was a knock on the door. "Come in," he said. The door opened and in stepped a police officer.

7 GREENROOM GHOST

The offices had cleared out at 3:20. Jonathan was the last to leave. He left the remainder of the take-out in his office mini-fridge and said we could heat it up with the microwave that sat on top of it when we were hungry again. He bid us safety and farewell. Nearly two hours later our dads arrived back from court and we filled them in on what had happened during the day. We gave them the police report, though the forensic results on the writing weren't yet back from the lab.

Our fathers were quite concerned and nearly insisted that they stay with us overnight or that we come back to the hotel. In the end I convinced them that we would be okay and that they were only a few blocks away and that we would call if anything truly dangerous were to happen. Bart and I settled into the old house close to 10 p.m. We'd set up our sleeping bags on the cushioned window seats in the greenroom though we weren't planning on sleeping anytime soon. I rang up Reed to fill him in. He told us he'd watched the docudrama and suggested we do the same.

"You're what?" he exclaimed at the other end of the line—or, more correctly, signal.

"You know, like I said, staying the night in a totally creepy haunted house."

"You guys have all the fun," said Reed. I laughed and he added, "You guys need me on this and you know it."

"Oh, you'd just wet your pants, wuss."

"It's, like, boring here. My folks are out at a costume party and I have to stay home and watch my little sister and hand out candy."

"And you'd rather stay at a haunted house on Halloween? What kind of fun is that when you have...?" I said reclining on the greenroom's wrap-around cushion.

"Don't mess with me! It's total dullsville here. I'd give anything to be in your shoes."

"Yeah, yeah," I said. "Look, *padnet*, we'll call if we need anything else."

"Why am I always the phone guy?"

"Happy Halloween."

"Same atchya, but you're the wiener."

☠ ☠ ☠

Armed with nothing more than flash-lights, and Bart with a take-out box of cold egg foo yung, we prowled around the old theater like we were the two Hardy Boys—minus the Chinese food. Our flash-lights were handily tucked into our waist-bands, because some of the lights were on in the work-room, veranda and library, but there if we needed them.

"What first?" asked Bart with a wad of egg halfway in and halfway out of his mouth.

"We never did really explore the kitchen or pantry," I answered.

He slurped in the foo yung and said, "Lead on, dude." Down the hall, behind the stage we hung a left into the kitchen. I flipped on the light switch and the room was illuminated. Stark fluorescents mir-rored off the stainless surfaces. No cats. Good. We circled the prep table and went to the pantry door. Bart pulled the door open and searched for the switch along the inside wall with what appeared to be some trepidation. I pulled out my flash-light, clicked it on and swung the beam inside the door-way. Bart peaked in and found the wall switch and flicked it on.

"Hmm," he said as I scanned the small room—well, small as in about twelve by twelve. On the shelves surrounding the space and running floor to ceiling (except where there was another door at the back) there was a smattering of industrial-sized canned food items as well as larger storage tins and plastic tubs. A dull single bulb hung from the eight foot ceiling. A pungent smell mixed with the aroma of spices filled the room. A bit of flour seemed to have been spilled upon the floor near the door.

"Looks like a sparingly used pantry," I said, crossing to the door in back. A bar spread across the door's face, wedged into four L-brackets—two on the door and one on each side of the wall—serving as a 'lock.' I lifted the bar out of the brackets and tried the handle. The door didn't budge and it was then that I noticed a deadbolt knob above the handle. I gave it a spin and tried the latch again. The door swung open to the outside. Four cement steps led down to a concrete driveway than ran to a gate at the side of the yard. The moon hung full in the night sky above the broad, gangly oaks that stood proudly in the yard. Dark thready clouds moved across the lunar face. I closed the door and reset the locks. "Goes outside," I said.

"I saw that," said Bart, standing in the center of the pantry. I joined him. Turning off the light and closing the door we crossed the kitchen floor. Just as we were passing the prep table, where we'd earlier found the dead cat, a piercing scream erupted from behind the door we'd just exited. Both of us nearly jumped out of our shorts. Bart dropped his take-out and rushed from the room to the back stage area, but I turned and ran back to the door clicking on my flashlight as I did so. Call me fool-hardy if you must, but I flung the door open and raised my light, both as a weapon and a source of illumination. Nothing was there.

"Bart, Bart," I called. "Come here." A moment later I heard slow footsteps behind me and I turned around to see Bart approaching with apprehension. "There's no one in here, *padnet.*"

"We both heard the scream," he said. "It...it came from in there." He had not yet come inside.

"Seriously, there's no one here," I reiterated and he cautiously entered. I could see that the back door was locked as I had left it. "Odd," I said flipping on the light and once again scanning the room. There were footprints in the flour dust on the floor which I pointed out to my friend.

"*I* didn't step in that," he said.

"Neither did I," I said, looking through the shelves, "And don't step in it now. The print can be used as evidence."

"What are you looking for, now?" asked Bart.

"A hidden speaker or something. Help me search. You look at that wall," I said indicating to my left as I moved to the wall on my right shining my flashlight up and down to provide greater light in the poorly lit areas of the room's nooks and crannies. "By the way, you sort of lost your lunch back there," I said, shoving a few of the larger tins aside to look behind them. I could hear Bart doing the same.

We moved methodically toward the back door caught up in our search when all of a sudden the bulb over our heads popped and went out. At the same time the door to the pantry slammed shut. Again we jumped, Bart squealed and my bladder suddenly wanted to pee. For the record, I did *not* wet myself though my heart con-tinued to pound rapidly in my chest. Our flashlights were still on and I shone mine at Bart—he looked eerily white.

"Well," I said, "there's always the door to the outside."

"Yeah," said Bart almost breathlessly, "but here's the...uh, th-the thing, ss-someone—or ss-something—was in here and, b-by the way, has shut us in." He took a deep breath, "The point is, since they didn't come and go through the out-side door, there has to be..."

"...another way in and out," I completed his thought. "Logical. Let's find it." We continued our search for a door and/or speaker and continued to find nothing for a good ten minutes. I rubbed

my eyes and temples, feeling tense and
tired.

"This is getting us nowhere," Bart
said at last, slumping down to sitting
position by the door against the only
place in the wall without a shelf. I heard
an odd click as he did so. He noticed it,
too, and cocked his head.

"Get up Bart," I said crossing to him
and extending my hand in aid. He grabbed
it and rose to his feet. Behind him the wall
came away from the corner about an inch.
My eyes must have widened a bit because
something registered in Bart and he turned to see what I had seen.

"Holy secret door, Batman!" he exclaimed in a whisper. Letting go of Bart's hand I
reached out to the crack in the corner,
wedging my fingers behind it and pulled.
But the wall didn't move. Bart looked at me
then set has hand on the left of the short
wall and pushed. About two feet of panel
receded by where he'd pushed. I looked at
him and shoved the panel to the left. It slid
further sideways into a recess.

I swung my light into the space beyond
and saw a very small room, not more than
three feet deep. To the right there was the
wall. I cast my beam to the left and found a
ladder leaning nearly against the wall not
four feet in that direction. I swung my
beam upward and saw that the ladder
went up through a small trap in the ceiling.

"Don't even think about going up there," said Bart. "It looks like a trap."

"Ha, ha," I said to the pun. "And you know I'm going."

"Ah, yeah, well, I'll stay down here and make sure no one locks us in here."

"Sounds like a plan," I replied. Bart came into the small enclosure and leaned against the opposite wall as I put my flashlight in my mouth and put a hand on a rung of the ladder before me. As he did there was another click. I turned my head to look at him and he smiled. "What is it with you?" I said.

"Just lucky, I guess," he replied coming away from the wall and sliding his fingers into the crevice created by yet another secret panel. I stepped toward him and pulled at the joint on the left. We shone our flashlight beams into the room beyond and I stepped in. I saw a door to my left, which I opened. It led into the backstage area/hall between the stage and kitchen.

Bart stepped in behind me and said, "Well, we know how this 'ghost' gets around."

"*Fo troo, padent,* that we do."

"You still going up the ladder?"

"I think I will," I replied. Bart stepped aside and I shimmied past him back into the secret room. He got behind me, but stayed at the bottom with his foot against the secret panel. I assumed that was to keep it from closing. I climbed, again with my flashlight in my teeth and, reaching the top, wedged myself through the trap. I found myself in an identical room to the one below. Pulling myself up from the floor I walked to the two steps to the far wall and gave it a shove. It clicked and I slid the panel aside like we'd done to the other two. I found myself in a closet packed with clothing, went to the door, opened it and saw an office before me. It was an office I hadn't yet been in. *Must be the VP's office,* I thought.

I stepped back through the closet and called down to Bart, "Leads to the VP's office. Come on up." A moment later I heard Bart climbing the ladder and soon he joined me in the closet. We entered the office and I found the light switch and switched it on. I walked around the desk, Bart following closely, and I sat down in the swivel chair. I looked at the desk clock which read 11:58. The night was getting on and I could feel my body wanting to slump into the chair and catch some shuteye. I looked blurrily at the clock as it clicked to 11:59. "Almost midnight," I said.

"Ah," said Bart, "the witching hour. On Halloween. Nice."

"Do you have to say such things?" I retorted. But then a random thought crossed *my* mind and I *had* to say it. "'Darkness falls across the land, the midnight hour is close at hand, creatures crawl in search of blood, to…'"

"Stop it!" cried Bart.

"What don't you like Michael Jackson?"

"Not at the moment, at least not just now, if you don't mind."

"Well, *you* started it" I said, looking again at the clock. "It *is* nearly mid…" The clock clicked from 11:59 to 12:00 and at precisely that moment a woman's laughter echoed from outside the office door. The lights flickered and went dark and the grandfather clock in the hall began its strike of midnight. My heart thundered again as I flicked on my flashlight. There was nothing to it: I had to find out what was going on, so I sprang to the door only to find the hallway empty.

Hearing the sound of footfalls on the stairs, I ran through the short hall past the fly rails and turned left to look down into the dark-ness. Seeing no one and nothing, I dashed down the staircase in pursuit of who knows what. At the bottom of the landing I stopped and, hearing steps behind me, turned quickly around only to find Bart in descent. I turned back around and shone my light wildly about. Bart joined me in the veranda.

"Why did you leave me up…?" he began, just as laughter again pealed around to our right somewhere from the workroom.

"Come on," I whispered, starting toward the office space. Weaving quickly through the cubicles, I tripped and fell headlong onto the carpeted floor accompanied by a great clattering sound. Bart stopped behind me. I quickly rose to my feet and noticed Bart standing there with wide eyes, his flashlight pointing to the floor near where I'd stumbled. I looked down and in the illumination of his flashlight beam I saw what had frozen him in his tracks. There on the floor, inches from us, lay a pile of human-like skulls and bones!

I gathered my will and pulled Bart around the skeleton pieces. Upon closer examination I decided I could pick one of the skulls up—they just didn't look entirely real. In my hand I could tell it was merely a plastic prop. "Alas, poor Yorick," I said, holding the skull in the palm of my hand, "I knew him well..." (another quote from *Hamlet*). "It's only a theatrical pro..." Just then a sinister female laugh echoed from the greenroom (a.k.a solarium). I dropped the prop and we quickly made our way through the rest of the maze and into the room with the bay windows.

The space was lit by an eerie blue light from the moon coming in the windows. Our sleeping bags were cut to threads. I heard a tinkling sound like a multitude of coins shaken in a glass, and looked up to see the chandelier rattling violently. On the ceiling, in the beam of my flashlight, I saw scrawled in crimson, the words:

dare to slumber

in my resting place?

8 BREAK A LEG

We stood fixated, mouths agape. The chandelier ceased shaking and the sudden silence felt unnerving. It occurred to me for the first time that Bart and I were alone in the house with a...with something or someone who clearly didn't want us there. I felt the strange presence of danger that seeps through your bones and tightens your throat and chest. I was scared. *'Do not be afraid for the Lord, your God is with you.'** The scripture I'd memorized from my childhood popped into my brain and I repeated it in my mind over and over again until Bart broke the silence.

"And I was sort of tired."

"Aye," I said, "...for in that sleep of death, what dreams may come?"

"Will you quit it with brooding *Hamlet*?"

"Sorry, how about *'be strong and courageous**?"

"Yes, better."

"And we'd better get cracking at solving this mystery," I said slapping him on the shoulder. I tried the door off the hall that led outside. It was locked. I looked to the other side of the hall. You remember, that little door in the five foot wall? It was under the back of the stairway. I moved to it and gave the ancient glass handle a turn, but it, too, was locked. I turned around and saw Bart scanning the hall. I tapped him on the shoulder and he flinched. "Let's check out the other offices upstairs."

We moved around the wall and went down the narrow hallway between the stairs and the workroom and, arriving at the threshold, ascended the staircase to the top landing. Passing the elevator to our right we entered the CFO's office. I tried the switch, but the lights didn't come on.

"Dude," said Bart, "has it occurred to you that we have no idea about a motive for this 'haunting'?" Bart said the last word using air quotes. "It's obviously just small potatoes."

"Small potatoes?" I questioned as we moved across the room to the closet.

"Yeah, with the Voodoo Virus thing it was terrorism. With Marsh Monster it was, like, thousands of dollars in treasure. What's the motivation here? It can't be anything big."

"Why not?" I said, stopping at the closet door and pulling it open. "There could be treasure in this house, or some long lost secret someone doesn't want uncovered—

like a murder, like in *The Ghost and Mr. Chicken.*"

"I just don't get that feeling," said Bart.

I peered inside, swinging my flashlight right then left. "Actually, neither do I, but ...bingo! This closet is deeper on the right." I stepped in and pushed on the left hand wall and a panel opened just as I expected. The small space behind the fake wall had no other exits or ladders—it was just an empty hiding place except for a little gizmo attached to the wall. "Thing is, there *has* to be a reason for trying to scare us and Razzmatazz out."

"I get that. I'm just trying to figure out why." I examined the gizmo which I saw consisted of a hand crank attached to an odd-shaped cog or rig. Next to the crank a thin, taut fishing line ran up and down, attached above the crank to a screw in a chunk of two by four nailed to the wall. The mono-filament line ran down to the floorboard where it disappeared between the wall and floor.

"Me too," I said, turning the crank. The cog spun and twanged against the fishing line, causing it to move back and forth. *Hmm*, I thought, *must move something.* I couldn't for the life of me figure out what it was. "Come in here Bart."

He poked his head in. "Look at this," I said, giving the device another whirl as he stepped in. "What do you make of it?"

"It's gotta move something," he said. "Looks like it might shift something by a fraction of an inch in a repetitive fashion."

"What? Like shaking?"

"Yeah, yeah," he answered.

"The chandelier downstairs in the greenroom?"

"Oh, yeah. Sure."

"We'll have to check that out," I said closing the panel, turning around and leaving the space. Coming out of the office we turned right toward the library and I stopped and turning back. I walked back toward the CFO's office keeping my eyes on the wall that encased the elevator.

"What?" said Bart.

"I think this elevator shaft is deeper front to back on this floor," I said, "I'm sure of it."

"Deeper?"

"Yeah, by a couple of feet," I said indicating the space behind the door, "This way." I thumped the wall and it popped open. I pulled the panel back and shown my light inside. Indeed, there was a narrow passageway. Stepping in I walked the five feet to the other side and pushed the oppo-site wall. Nothing happened. "Looks like just another little hidey-hole."

"Nice," said Bart. "Now what?"

"Jonathan's office."

☠ ☠ ☠

"So," I said as we walked through the library, "let's think this through. Someone plays the ghost to rid the house of the new renters. Though there were ghost rumors and minor 'hauntings' when it was a theater, there didn't seem to be the same intensity or motivation." I stopped at the door and pulled it open. "Was the specter fine with the house being a theater?"

"That would be my guess," said Bart as we entered the room and moved toward the closet.

"So our ghost wants it to be a theater again?"

"Again, that's my best guess, but the question is *who*?"

"Yeah, we don't really have a suspect," I said pulling open the closet door and looking in.

"Someone with Razzmatazz?"

"Not likely, they seem to want to be here." The space, filled with hangers of expensive suits and dress shirts, was even, both left and right, but I decided to try the walls anyway. I stepped to the left through the glut of garments and pushed, and a panel snapped open. Behind the wall was another small room. I took the two steps toward the far wall and gave it a rap. It sounded hollow, but nothing opened. I rapped on the right. Nothing. I rapped on the left. *Hmm, solid.* "How about

Sparky? This was his home for nearly twenty years?" I was examining a seam that ran up and down the wall from floor to ceiling. "And he could miss his job as the theater tech."

"Yeah, maybe he feels his space has been invaded and wants his job and home back." I wedged my fingers into the seam and pulled right, then left. A short portion of the wall moved to the left. I continued to push. "But, he has been so cooperative and doesn't seem like the type."

"Which could be a ruse, besides, he would likely know this place inside and out." The wall continued to move left and I continued to push, stepping to-ward the opening. I soon found myself in the library. A portion of the bookcase had swung open on a pivot. I stepped back through the opening and into the closet once a-gain. Bart had been at work on the oppo-site wall and had discovered a secret panel.

"The bookcase opens," I said. "What'd you find?"

"Looks like a passageway," said Bart, "There's a door on the right and a hall to the left. I see light coming from that way."

"Well, let's explore," I said, gently shoving him into the space, "If I'm right, this is the hall to the upper floor of the turret. The door on the right is the one that was locked in Jonathan's office."

"So," said Bart as we moved down the passage way, "What about one of the council members? What about Lurch?"

"You may be on to something there. He's so mysterious and grumpy and he did give us the warning to be careful—as if to scare us." We stepped into an octagon room. Moonlight shown in from the floor to ceiling windows on the walls to our right, illuminating the u-shaped desk that wrapped around three walls on our left in front of a curtained twenty-four by twenty-four window. On the desk sat a sixteen channel NSI light board, a laptop computer, a DVD player, a video switcher and a small and ancient SUNN audio board.

On the only non-windowed wall was a mirror—about twenty-four inches by thirty-six inches. Under it was a small vanity on which sat an electric razor and other items a man would use to spruce up. A small fan and several theatrical lighting fixtures hung from a rail stretching from wall to wall. "But then again, why didn't Sparky mention this control booth?"

"Better, question: Why didn't you think to ask? *You*, of all people, had to know a theater would have one."

"I guess...well, I wasn't thinking theater," I said, poking around the control equipment. "But your question about Sparky seems valid, however, the screams—the laughter—have been female."

"The councilwoman then?"

"Possibly, but she seems bent on keeping the renters or at least collecting the remainder of the lease." I pulled the curtain over the control desk aside and peered out. Below I could see the auditorium and stage cast dimly in the light streaming in from the outside windows.

"Also a smoke screen, perhaps?"

"Maybe, but those screams and laughter could still be merely recordings."

"They sound pretty real to me."

"Yeah," I said," but I think I'd like to see the council's voting record on the takeover of the theater."

"We could have our dads pick up the transcripts at the courthouse while they're there."

"Those would be at City Hall," I corrected, "I'll give them a call first thing in the morning."

"Sounds good."

"You know," I said as the old grandfather began to toll the one-o-clock hour, "there's one place we haven't explored."

"What's that?" asked Bart.

"The trap in the stage floor. What, if anything, is there underneath? I have a sneaking suspicion that there's a basement to this place and that that door under the staircase has another set of stairs leading down."

"Oh, great," he said, "a dungeon."

"The pit of despair," I croaked like the hunchback in *The Princess Bride.* Bart moaned.

"Come on," I said, making my way down the hall and through the bookcase passage with Bart following behind me. Once we were in the library I closed the bookcase and we set off toward the stairs, Bart in the lead. He was first to step into the stair-well and took the steps rapidly without using his flashlight. That was a mistake. In the beam of my flashlight I saw him tumble about halfway down and go to his knees with a wild grab to the banister. He let out a yelp of pain. There on the step beside him I saw what had caused him to trip—a sneering, clown-faced doll.

Bart rose to his feet with a wince of pain as I arrived at his position. "You all right?" I asked, but knowing from the way he clung to the rail and kept his weight off one leg, that he'd turned his ankle.

"Twisted my ankle," he said as I looked down at the hideous doll. *Chucky,* I thought as I picked it up. Pinned to the doll's clothing was a note and I cast my light on it and read:

don't clown around, come on down

I threw the doll down the stairs and it crashed against the front door in the veranda and started to laugh—*hahahahaha hahahaha*—in that creepy Joker laugh from the original Batman with Jack Nicholson. "Can you make it down?" I asked.

"Yeah, sure," he answered, hobbling down the steps.

9 STAGE DIRECTION

Down on the main floor we rounded the stair-way hall to the left on the auditorium side of the staircase. As we reached the back wall, laughter erupted from the theater's PA system. We cut right and went up the stage steps and looked out into the seating area. Above us, in the window of the darkened control room, stood a semi-transparent, shimmering woman of African descent, her clothing and hair flying wild.

"You haven't got my hint," came a distorted voice over the loudspeaker. "I *don't* want you here! Go away, all of you, and let me rest in peace." Bart nearly swooned as he came up behind me.

"Why?" I yelled, "What are you hiding?"

"This is my theater," said the apparition. "You are in danger." Bart grabbed my arm and I could feel him trembling.

"It's nothing…" I said to my friend in hushed tones, "nothing but Pepper's Ghost."

"Who's Pepper?" he croaked.

"It's not a who, but a what," I explained under my breath, "a theatrical trick. The mirror, fan and lights in the control booth. The person who wishes to appear as a ghost stands to one side of a darkened space in front of a mirror positioned at a forty-five degree angle from a glass pane as the light is brought up. They appear in the glass as a transparent being. It's an old, old effect. They use it in ballroom scene of the Haunted Mansion at Disneyland."

"Well, then if that's human, we'd better go up there and capture our 'ghost,'" whispered Bart.

"My guess is we'll be too late. I suggest we continue our quest."

"But, but, but..."said Bart.

"Hakuna Matata—no worries. Come on." We went back down the stage steps into the wide hallway, coming to the little wall with the door under the staircase. "I'll go to the kitchen and get a butter knife to jimmy the lock," I said.

"I'll stay here," said Bart, "and watch for spooks."

"You do that," I said ducking into the backstage area. In the kitchen I searched the drawers and finally came up with the tool I was looking for. When I got back, Bart was standing next to the door and it was opened.

"How'd you get that open?" I asked.

"It wasn't locked."

"Yes, it was," I said stepping up beside him and looking in. Indeed, a staircase led down into the darkness.

"Wasn't."

"Well, it was when I tried it earlier."

"You're sure?"

"I know it was, which means..."

"This could be a trap."

"That someone wants us to go down there."

"And *why* do I get the sinking feeling that that's just what we're going to do?"

"Because you know me so well."

"I know, you're crazy."

"However, I am not so cracked as to have us both go. You will stand guard up here."

"That makes me feel soooooo much better."

"I thought it might," I said aiming my flashlight down into the gloom. "Here goes, hold my phone, just in case." I handed him my cell and put my foot on the first of the rickety wooden steps and it squealed under my weight. *Lord*, I prayed silently as a took another step, '*Yay, though I walk through the valley of the shadow of death I will fear no evil, for You are with me.**' Down I went, Bart standing at the top of the staircase be-hind me, adding his light to mine.

Clomp, squeak, clomp, squeak, I went.
Bart's light illuminating the steps and
casting my long shadow eerily on the
staircase in front of me, my light swinging back and forth over the dark space
before me. A dank smell filled my nostrils
as I descended into the abyss.

The floor of the basement area was
crowded with stacks of crates and various
scenic pieces. Against the walls leaned
mildewing theatrical flats—painted scenes
of Gothic stone arches, Victorian walls and
garden terraces. Reaching the bottom I
moved to my left, away from the staircase.
There, near what would be center stage,
was a hydraulic lift, its frame stretching
upwards to the trap door in the stage
deck.

The noise behind me was sudden and
sickening. Thudding, screaming, crashing.
I looked around to see Bart careening and
flailing down the staircase, screaming
wildly. Then I heard the door slam at the
top of the stairwell as he hit the bottom
with a final thud. Rushing to him, I bent
down to see if he was okay. He labored for
breath, the wind knocked from his lungs.
At last he gasped for air and moaned.

"Bart, are you okay?"

He gasped again and managed to grunt
out, "Someone pushed me!"

"Are you okay?" I repeated. Female
laughter peeled from above.

"I think...I'll live," he answered, "for now," as he rolled to his hands and knees. "Ouch."

"What's wrong?"

"Bruised some ribs. Might be cracked. And my wrist hurts." He sat back and winced at the pressure on his previously injured ankle. I rose and rushed up the stairs, taking them two at a time. I, of course, found the door locked.

"I think it's time we called our dads," I said, "Give me my cell phone."

Bart felt his pockets, "I don't have it."

"Whataya mean?"

"I thought I had it in my hand. I seem to have lost it and my flashlight in the fall."

I waved my light around the space at the bottom of the stairs and found my phone on the floor. Picking it up I saw immediately that it was broken. The face of the screen was shattered and the battery was missing. Searching I found the battery and put it back into the cavity of the cell. It was to no avail, my cell was not going to function. "Great," I said despairingly. "Now what are we going to do?"

"*You*, my friend, will think of something," said Bart struggling to his feet. "You always do." I picked up his flashlight and attempted to click it on, which it did not.

"Well," I said, "we only have one flashlight now and I do believe mine is dimming."

"When your batteries die, use mine."

"Good thinking, Bart. However, I do think we should reserve our use. Do you mind if I switch this off for a while?"

"Sure, let's sit in the dark creepy basement."

"What's the worst that could happen?"

"Oh, I don't know. Get eaten by rats. Stabbed by our mysterious friend?"

"Fiend," I corrected, clicking off the light. The darkness was complete—as black as the inside of a witch's caldron. Blacker than night. And my mind? It was black as well.

10 WAITING IN THE WINGS

We sat alone in the dark basement for what seemed like hours (though I'm sure it was just minutes) listening to one another breathe and the occasional scurry of what had to be rodents—mice or rats. My mind was working, but it wasn't working well. The need for sleep clouded my thinking skills. I tried to think of movie scenarios that might get us out of this. Bart and I called them my 'movie moves.' None seemed helpful and I must have begun to nod off.

"I don't understand," said Bart out of the black-ness, breaking the silence and jarring me awake.

"Only one of our supposed suspects is a woman and she isn't black. If the apparition we saw was a black women...then..."

"That doesn't rule our suspects out. You've heard of stage makeup, I assume? Besides, it may not be one of our suspects at all or it could be an accomplice or conspirator. And on top of all that, our priority is really just getting out of here."

"About that," said Bart.

"Yes."

"Do you think we could break the door down?"

"Maybe with a battering ram or a hatchet."

"Well, why don't we step out to Lowe's for one of those." That's what we did for our last caper.

"Unless there's one handy in the corner," I said, "we'll have to come up with another plan."

"Couldn't we just use the trap lift?"

"No electricity, remember?"

"No, I mean stack some of these crates and crawl out."

"That would be great if it weren't locked."

"But it would have to be latched from this side, no? And maybe it isn't locked at all."

"Bart, I believe that would be worth a try. I certainly don't have a better idea." I switched on my flashlight and helped my friend to his feet, seeing him wince again in pain. "You gonna be okay?"

"I have to try, don't I?"

"Tell you what, you can help me empty the crates so that they are easier for me to move. How's that?"

"Let's do it."

☠ ☠ ☠

My flashlight glowed with only a dim amber light as we moved to a wooden box near the lift. I opened the lid and found it loaded with heavy prop swords and guns. The two of us pulled the fake weapons from the crate and cast them quickly a-side, each clanging loudly on the cement floor. When the box was empty I shoved it across the floor and wrestled it onto the lift platform just as my light flickered out. I beat it against the palm of my hand, nudging it back to life and handing it to Bart along with the other flashlight I'd stowed in my back pocket. "Time to change the batteries," I said. Bart opened the chamber of his former light and re-moved the batteries in prep for when mine died altogether.

We walked to another crate and I opened the lid. Bart shown the dimming flashlight inside and we saw a variety of neatly folded medieval costumes which we quickly re-moved, casting them aside. We finished the job just as the flashlight dimmed out. I could hear Bart bashing the instrument against his hand in an effort to bring it back online, but his efforts were in vain. "I'm changing the batteries now," he said through the darkness. I could hear him unscrew the cap on the battery chamber and slowly—methodically—slide the batteries in. A minute later he clicked the light on and I went to work at stacking the second crate on top of the first. When I turned around I could see a fog rolling down the stairs. It wasn't a creeping fog, it was descending the stairs rapidly at high volume. "We've got a mounting problem," I said, "Look behind you."

"Tell me that's just theatrical fog, and not poisonous gas."

"It looks like dry ice fog, CO2, carbon di-oxide."

"Harmless then."

"Generally, yes, but enough of it will displace the oxygen. It's heavier than air and will cause the oxygen to rise out of the basement if the volume is great enough."

"Meaning, like, we will not be able to breathe?"

"Excellent deduction, Watson*. I suggest we hurry." We scrambled to a third crate. *Two would be enough,* I thought as I opened the lid. *Eight foot ceiling. Hmm, that's four feet or so, and I'm five foot, six inches.* "I'm pretty sure I can reach with just two boxes," I said, "Shine the light up here." I pulled myself up on top of the two stacked crates in the lift and stood as the fog continued to rise, which was now about nose-level with Bart standing on the floor. I had to crane my neck to the side to keep my face from smashing into the trap door. *Yeah, high enough.* I looked at the latch—a simple sliding mechanism (a bar through a bracket) that kept the hatch from opening downward. If I slid the latch, the door would fall open and it would swing to the side where it could be latched open on the ceiling in another bracket.

"Bart, you are absolutely brilliant!" I said tugging at the bar. It slid with only minor resistance and the small door swung down. But the opening was blocked; something sat over the trap exit. I pushed upward at the obstacle which did not budge.

"Get up here," I said. "There's something heavy blocking the way. I need your help." Bart climbed up to join me and, when he was standing, I told him to push for all he was worth. He was taller than I and put his shoulder to the task. It pained him and he grunted with effort. The obstacle budged upward slightly. I turned the flashlight off and slid it into my pocket so I could use both hands.

"Push and slide," I said, "To my right." Again we shoved with all our might and the barrier lifted. We tried moving the heavy object to the side. It wouldn't budge. The carbon di-oxide gas was at our waists now and rising fast. Sweat trickled down my back from the exertion. "We need a lever and fulcrum," I said turning on my light and shining the beam downward.

"We aren't going to find anything in that fog," commented Bart, "It's thick as pea soup."

"That's so cliché."

"That's what people say. And what's a fulcrum, anyway?"

"It's the point on which a bar—a leveraging tool—rests and pivots."

"Couldn't the bar that holds the trap door open or closed be used as a lever?"

"For guy who doesn't even know what a fulcrum is you are one smart dude, dude."

"Thanks," said Bart, "I think."

The fog was up to our necks as I slid the bar from the brackets. I sat it atop our shoulders and held it in place with my left hand. "Now lift and I'll try to wedge it under the barricade. I wish it were longer for more leverage, but it will have to do."

Again we shoved upward for all we were worth as the fog rose up to our faces. I could barely see now. As I felt the obstacle rise I slipped the bar into the gap. "Lift, lift," I said, "pour it on."

Bart heaved with me and I continued to work the lever further into the crack. Finally our strength gave out as we labored in the thinning oxygen. "Now," I said, "pull down on the back end of the bar and wiggle it to our right." We groped for the end of the five foot bar and took purchase, tugging with all our might. The obstacle began to move upward and we twisted the back of the bar to our left. I was straining with effort. "Move the bar back to the right quickly in a downward motion on my cue —the count of three. One, two, three." We let the pressure off and twisted the bar quickly back to the right as we did. "Lift and twist to the left again." It was easier to breathe now since we were close to the opening where air now seeped in. "Again."

Two more tugs and a larger gap appeared, letting in a thin, pale light. "Pull the bar back in here," I said. We wiggled it back and forth and pulled toward us finally freeing the bar. I pushed it through the lit gap. "One more time, but to the left, back end to the right, to move this thing out of the way." Bart followed my instructtions and the obstacle slid reluctantly aside another foot. I wedged my body— hands and face first—up into the opening, until I had a shoulder through. I was facing the obstacle, whatever it was. "Get behind me," I yelled down to Bart. "Push on my back."

When I felt Bart in position I strained forward and again the object slid reluctantly inch by inch. There was now e-nough room to slip out, but instead I dropped back down through the opening into the dense fog that was now pouring out of the hole above me. "Bart," I said into the haze, "put your face out and get some air." He rose up beside me, accidentally knocking me aside and I tumbled off the crates. Throwing my arms out before me to break my fall I hit the floor with a crashing thud. I felt my forearm snap and cried out in pain.

"Peter, Peter," I heard Bart yell into the dark, foggy abyss.

"I'll...be up in...a minute," I grunting, clamoring to my knees and then to my feet. I felt around for the boxes and, finding them, pulled myself upon them with a sheering pain shooting through my arm. I stood and asked Bart to help me through the opening. He lifted me like I didn't weigh more than a feather and I crawled out of our would-be tomb. "Wait a minute," I said, sitting my hiney into the hole against the lip of the opening and putting by feet against what I now saw was an upside-down desk laden with two dozen cinder blocks. I shoved with my legs until they burned as the desk inched away from me. At full extension I rolled to my side facing the stage floor, panting.

11 EXIT, STAGE LEFT

B art's head popped out of the hole, followed by his arms and he pulled himself to the stage deck next to me and sat with his legs dangling below. "We made it," he said taking in fresh air. Me? I was feeling woozy and clammy, breathing shallow, which meant I was experiencing shock.

"Bart, I need to get to a doctor. My arm's broken. Shock's coming on."

"Uh, yeah, right," he said, swinging his legs from the trap. He scooted toward me and reached out his hand, touching my forehead. "I'm going to help you turn over, dude. How do you feel?"

I tried to describe the feeling as Bart rolled me to my back. He lifted one of the cinder blocks off the desk with his single good hand and placed it on the floor near my feet. He lifted my feet from the floor and placed them on the block. "Hang in there, *pad-net*. Let me get you something to keep you warm." He placed a couple fingers at my carotid artery on my neck, noting my slowed pulse.

"Don't leave me, Bart. I'm warm enough."

"Sure, buddy." He took off his outer shirt and laid it over my chest as the grandfather clock struck four. "How's the arm?"

"Throbbing."

"Okay. Rest. I need to make a 911 call. I'll need to go into the other room."

"No, no," I pleaded, "Let's just get out of here."

"You're not in any condition to..."

"There's a phone booth about three blocks from here; by the Jack in the Box. I can make it."

"Our dad's hotel isn't much further away. Could you do that?"

"I don't know. It seems like a lot of extra time and effort. I don't know."

"Okay, okay. I'll help you up." He rose from the floor and reached out to take my hand. I extended my good arm and he leaned away, pulling as I placed my feet on the floor. I was standing now and Bart let go. He bent down to pick up his shirt which he'd placed over my shoulders. We supported one another making for the door off to stage left which led outside. Arriving, Bart turned the deadbolt and reached for the knob.

"Exit, stage left, even," I said, imitating the cartoon character Snagglepuss. *I still had it.*

"Heavens to Murgatroyd," he quoted back, pulling the door open. The cool night air brushed over my sweating skin and a chill ran down my spine. We descended the steps to the yard and made for the gate. On the sidewalk we proceeded clumsily north along Second Street toward St. Charles Avenue. Jack-o-lanterns and other holiday décor decorated the porches and yards of the ritzy antebellum mansions along the way. A particularly stoic Gothic* manor featured a graveyard scene behind its wrought iron fence.

"Looks like the Disney World Haunted Mansion," I said.

"*Fo troo,*" commented Bart. "Beware of hitchhiking ghosts."

Arriving at St. Charles Avenue, we turned east toward the Jack in the Box one block down. I was feeling increasingly cloudy and disoriented, but Bart kept us on task. Arriving at the callbox, Bart helped me down to the sidewalk and hastily placed the emergency call after which he bent over me. "You doing okay, *padnet?*" he asked. I grunted a reply of some sort. A few minutes later the ambulance arrived and we were whisked away to Tulane University Hospital which was about four minutes away. Bart gave the EMT our dad's cell numbers and they were called while we were in route.

☠ ☠ ☠

I don't remember much of the treatment procedures, but I was resting quietly in a recovery room when our fathers arrived. The room was a double and I awoke to the sound of voices. I opened my eyes and saw Bart in the bed next to me speaking with his dad. Mine sat in the chair next to my bed listening. My arm was bound in a splint.

"Good morning, son," said my father. "We've been praying for you."

"Thank you. What time is it?" I asked.

"Nearly six," he answered, standing. "Happy Day of the Dead."

"Since I'm not dead," I mused, "it is a happy day."

"Indeed," said Bart's dad walking over to my bed. "It sounds like, from what Bart has told us that death might have been a strong possibility."

"Yeah, again."

"Peter," said my dad, "I'm glad you're okay."

"I'm not exactly feeling okay," I said. "Has a squad car been sent to...?"

"Yes, no one was found. You have suspects, I hear. You think we should round them up?"

"No, not yet," I answered, "I have a better idea."

"And what is that?" asked Bart's dad.

"I'll put it together for you in a minute," I answered, "but first I need to outline some footwork." (That's the term law enforcement officers use for tracking down information.) Dad whipped out his notepad and, preparing for my list of instructions, sat back down and crossed his legs.

"For starters we need the voting records of the City Council. Transcripts of any meetings involving the sale or proposed sale of the Davis House may also be useful." Dad jotted the items in his notebook and I continued. "Find out the lab results of the bloodied handwriting. Call a meeting of the Council, have it convene tonight at the house. I need Jonathan and Sparky there as well. We're going to stage a little 'show.'"

"Oh!" said Bart, "like bringing the courtroom to the haunted house like they did in *The Ghost and Mr. Chicken*."

"Yes," I answered, "And like *Sleuth* and *Haunted Honeymoon*..."

"And *Clue*," interjected Bart, "A movie move! I knew you'd come through."

"Exactly," I said, "and, by the way, Agatha Christie's *And Then There Were None*, also known as *Ten Little Indians*. Oh, and back to our to-do list, see if you can have the head of the Women's Opera Guild join us as well. Her name is Becky Krabach, I believe. Threaten subpoena if you need to, but I'll need each of these people present. And finally, get a search warrant and have the offices of the council searched for any and all thumb drives and CD ROMs; have them secured as evidence."

"That might be a problem," said my dad.

"Not if attempted murder is..."

"I'll see what I can do, but I'll need to file charges and name names."

"Dennis Jenkins, Jaynie Harrison and Burt Burkmann should do," I said.

"And Jonathan Barbor," interjected Bart.

"I don't think so," I replied.

"But he didn't tell us about the control room and the basement. He's withholding something."

"I don't believe that was his intent. I think he just assumed that Sparky would have showed us everything. But, on second thought, have him join us, just in case."

Bart nodded, "So, why didn't Sparky show them to us?"

"*That* is a good question I intend to get answered. To do that I need to stop by the local theatrical supply store, an Office Depot, a hobby store and a magic shop, plus a voodoo supply; and we'll meet back in the house a couple hours before the meeting, so make the meeting late. I also need someone to check out some possible purchases made by…" Just then an olive-skinned nurse entered holding an iPad.

"Hi," she said through a beautiful smile, her brown eyes twinkling, "Am I interrupting anything?" As she stepped closer I saw her name tag. It read: Mandy.

"No, not at all," said Warden Davis, "What did you need?"

"I have the discharge papers for the boys," said Mandy, tossing back her brunette pony tail. "Well, actually, I don't have any papers, just this iPad. It's our new thing, but, anyway, if you'll sign it with the stylus the papers will be generated at the desk."

"Don't you just love technology?" said Bart.

"I guess," said the nurse handing the tablet to my dad who read it over while Amanda continued, "Do you have any questions?"

"No," said Warden Davis, pointing to my dad's leg splint boot, "Been there, done that—elevation, ice, keep it dry—we know the drill."

"Accidents run in the family?" she asked rhetorically with another beautiful smile. She looked about twenty-five. *If only I were older.* But then, I had Carla who was equally stunning (*and* much closer to my age). "You'll need to make an appointment for a cast," she said, "I assume you have a clinic back in Houma. You do, don't you?"

"It's not *that* backwoods," said Bart's dad. Our dads signed 'the papers' and Amanda took the tablet, reminding us that we could go any time and to pick up the printouts at the nurses' station before leaving us. I sat up and swung my feet over the side of the bed and Bart did the same. We gathered our stuff, checked out at the nurses' station and left the hospital. Back in the car we divvied up the footwork as we returned to our dad's hotel room.

12 ALL THE WORLD'S A STAGE

That afternoon we were all very busy. My dad rented a second car, hit up the local cop shop to secure a search warrant and then went to City Hall to gather evidence—if any. Bart's dad took us to the theatrical supply house where I picked up some 'show' equipment and asked about recent purchases involving various make-up items, then we made the rounds to the neighborhood's Lowe's to pick up some stuff and see about the purchase of a goodly amount of cinder blocks. We also hit up a hobby store, an office and art supply place, as well as a magic shop and Dr. Zombies Voodoo Supply (where they give Haunted History Tours) in the French Quarter*. Meanwhile Warden Davis managed to wedge a dozen phone calls in between stops. I also put in a call to our friend Beth back in Houma, requesting her assistance.

By 4 p.m. we'd completed all but one item on our to-do lists, leaving only the work I had to do back at the Davis House.

The meeting had been set up for 8 p.m., so after grabbing some lunch at the local Taco Bell we met dad at the car rental place where he'd turned in the sedan he'd rented. Beth, who'd drove over from Houma, met us at the restaurant right at 4:30 as I'd requested. On the way to the Davis House we filled my dad in on the meeting to come.

"Both Jonathan and Sparky said they'd be there and all but one of the six council members will be, too," said Bart's dad. "The mayor and Turlet—the sixth council-member—are on vacation out of the country, have been all week."

"*Ten Little Indians*," said Bart. "With the four of us that makes ten."

"Let's hope we're not killed off one by one," I said, remembering the movie's plot.

"Sho nuff," said Bart.

"So, dad, do you have the jump drives?"

"I do, I gathered almost a dozen and many times that in CD ROMs."

"How about the records and transcripts?"

"I have the records, but not the transcripts. However, I have something better; all the council meetings were recorded for closed circuit TV and have been put on the web in a searchable database."

"That should make things a lot easier," said Warden Davis as we started the bumpy, bone-jarring drive over the Garden District streets. Bart held his ribs and grimaced.

"Good, good," I said. "Mr. Davis, what about..."

"Our 'shopping list'?" he said.

"Yeah," I answered, "Any leads?"

"Maybe, but it's only empirical evidence at best, nothing hard and fast."

"Speaking of evidence," interjected Bart, "how went the Thachne trial?"

"Conviction," answered my dad, "He'll do at least twenty for murder and more."

"Any claims on the treasure?" said Bart enthusiastically. I remembered that we might be due some serious cash for uncovering the Marsh Monster plot.

"We won't know that for at least a few weeks, could take months," answered Warden Davis as we pulled up to the curb at Razzmatazz.

"Ah," I said, "'let slip the dogs of war.*'" Bart's dad shut off the engine and we extracted ourselves from the car as Bart's dad beeped the key fob and the trunk popped open. We each took a load from the compartment and Warden Davis shut the lid. Bart and I, it seemed, were regulated to a half load, due to our injured arms.

☠ ☠ ☠

We entered the side door leading to the stage from the grounds. The power was back on, which I assumed was due to the police investigation and their switching the breaker back on. The desk and cinderblocks were gone and the trap was shut.

"Who cleaned up?" asked Bart.

"Don't know," said my dad. "The local police found nothing of what you boys described from your, uh, stay."

"You mean," I asked, "all the evidence has been...?"

"Removed," finished my dad.

"Convenient," said Bart as we sat our loads on the deck. The old grandfather chimed in at 5 p.m.

"Well," I said, "we'd best get crack-a-lackin.' We have a lot to do."

"Let's have a word of prayer first," said Bart, "I feel uneasy about this."

"Don't we all," said my father, "That's a good idea, Bart. We bowed our heads and each of us asked for the Lord's guidance, forgiveness (since what we were about to do was a bit sketchy), and protection. We also prayed our culprit would be revealed. I closed with:

"The word says to, *'trust in the Lord with all your heart... and He will direct your path.*'* Lord, we ask You to direct our steps. In Jesus name, amen."

"I guess I'll be upstairs in Jonathan's office," said my dad leaving the stage. "I'll go through these flash drives and search through the council meeting videos."

"Okay, thanks Dad," I said grabbing up the rented micro-sized fog machine with my good arm, "Bart, you're with me. Mr. Davis, you know what to do."

"Ten-four," he answered, leaving Bart and I as he proceeded through the auditorium.

"What about me?" asked Beth, "Where will I be working from?"

"You remember what I told you on the phone?" I asked her.

"Sure," she answered.

"The room is upstairs to the left of the landing. Go down through the auditorium to the front door, you'll see the staircase when you get there. Bart will be up to set things up for you as soon as he has a chance," I said, reaching down for a sack from the theatrical supply store. "In the meantime, here's your kit." She took the bag and left the room.

"To the solarium?" said Bart, picking up several other articles.

"Lead on!" I replied.

☠ ☠ ☠

We made a couple of trips to and from the stage back to the former greenroom with supplies. On our third trip it occurred to me that we hadn't checked out whether the gizmo in the upstairs hiding place had anything to do with the shaking chandelier. As Bart was busy running rubber tubing under the cushions of the window seats I looked up and walked around the hanging light. At last I spotted the tiny filament attached to one of the lighting structure's arms and running up through a small hole in the ceiling among the cobwebs. It was nearly in-visible. I figured it poked through the floor above and ran under the office's carpet to the hidey-hole. *Ingenious!*

Warden Davis entered the room laboring with the big screen TV from Jonathan's office, "Where do you want this?" he asked, huffing.

"Set it down on the cushions over there," I said pointing to the window behind me as Bart finished up what he was working on. His father sat the TV down.

"I'll bring down the desk monitor as soon as your dad's done checking through files," he said, "Anything else you need?"

"I don't think so," I answered, "Unless you want to help Bart get that thing hooked up to a computer. You can use the laptop from the control booth upstairs."

"Sure thing," he answered and left for the room off the CEO's office.

A few moments later there was a knock at the door. "That will be the furniture rental place," I said to Bart, "Can you get that?" Bart left the room for the front door and a within few minutes he arrived with a couple of hefty guys in coveralls hefting an oval oak dining room table. "Right here," I instruct-ed, "Under the chandelier in the center of the room." They sat the table in place and one of them said they'd be back momentarily with the chairs and rental agreement.

Bart's dad came in with the laptop from the control booth just as they left. "Your dad's done with the files. There was nothing incriminating on any of the jump drives or CD ROMs, but he did find some interesting things among the council videos and voting records. He's burned some footage onto a DVD and he'll be down with me in a moment. He's unhook-ing the monitor now."

"Okay," I said, "we'll need that laptop wired to the TV..."

"I'll give Bart a hand," he said as the rental guys came in, each carrying two chairs in each hand.

"Around the table please," I said. When they were in place one of the men left as the other pulled some papers and a pen from his front shirt pocket.

"You wanna sign dis'?" he said.

"Mr. Davis?" I said. Bart's dad looked up from the work with his son and made his way over to the man just as the other returned with the final two chairs. He carried them both in one hand and under the other arm he carried two table leaves (for making the table bigger). He had a sand-wich hanging from his mouth.

"T'anks," said the first man, obviously Cajun from his inability to pronounce the *th* sound, when Warden Davis handed him back the paperwork.

"No," I said, "Thank you."

"Dats what I said," he laughed. The men exited as I flopped a large flip chart on the table along with an x-acto knife and pencil. My dad came into the room with a DVD in one hand and the OLED monitor under his arm.

"Oh," said Bart's dad, "thanks for saving me another trip."

"No problem," said my dad.

"Can you lay that monitor face down on this flipchart?" I asked as I flipped it open. When he did I asked him to repositioned it in the center of the pad and drew around it with the pencil and put them aside. I open-ed the x-acto packaging and asked my dad to move the monitor away. He did so and I cut around the line I'd made as Bart went upstairs with an arm-load of gear and my dad went to assist Mr. Davis. I busied my-self with the first of several projects I'd come up with for staging the 'show of the cen-tury.' *But will it all work?* I thought as I cut into another sheet of the flipchart. *Sure it will.* I was encouraging myself. *Seems that 'all the world's a stage,' indeed.*

We worked for another couple hours completing the rigging required for our little show and I'd checked with Beth to make sure she was ready and gave her some last minute instructions. After that we had about thirty minutes left to review the video footage dad had burned to the DVD. That took about fifteen minutes and a couple sequences were quite amusing (in a hair-curling sort of way) though much of the content made me sad (which I will explain later). We sat back for a well-deserved breather and to await our arrivals for the meeting.

13 SHOWTIME!

Jonathan was the first to arrive and was met by my father at the door. The CEO wanted to go to his office for a minute, but Dad said that he couldn't, as I'd instructed, and led him into the greenroom. The others arrived over the course of the next twenty minutes with Sparky coming in last, my dad directing them all directly to our meeting room and the seats we'd assigned them. The meeting began at 8:08. All were in attendance as requested and seated as I had planned. We did a round of introductions and I began my opening speech.

"We requested your presence..."

"Demanded," said Harrison.

"*Required* your presence here," I continued, "because we believe we're close to solving this mystery. However, we need more information from some of you and from someone else who's presence we will soon request as well."

"Wait a minute," said Lurch in voice so low in the register it made my chest rumble. "All the chairs are full. Who else is coming?"

"I'll get to that," I answered. "Please bear with me. First of all I'd like to establish each of your whereabouts last night. We'll begin with you Jonathan and move around the table to the right."

The CEO shifted in his seat and began, "Well, after a meeting with a client over dinner I went home, took my kids out trick-or-treating and went to bed."

"And what time did these events take place?" asked my father.

"The dinner meeting concluded at 7 p.m. or so, I got home shortly thereafter and we went out trick-or-treating at eight and we were done by about 9:45. I put the kids to bed a read a chap-ter of Brock Eastman's new book to them then took a shower. I was in bed by elev-en."

"*Unleash*?" asked Bart, "from the *Quest for Truth* books?" I rolled my eyes. Bart was a voracious reader, but the topic was irrelevant.

"That's the one."

"Okay," I said, "we can convene the book club meeting later. Who can corroborate your whereabouts?"

"My family—wife and kids."

"Thank you. Councilmember Burk-mann?"

"My wife and I went to a costume ball until about 2 a.m. It was at the City Manager's place."

"And..." I began.

"I have the receipt for my tux right here in my wallet," Burkmann cut in, going for his back pocket, "My wife went as Thing and I went as Lurch from the *Addam's Family*." He half smiled, something I'd never seen him even attempt up until then. *How appropriate*, I thought. Frankly, I wasn't surprised—it was the perfect character for him. I couldn't help but won-der what his wife looked like—in real life.

"The receipt proves nothing," I said. "I assume the City Manager and others at the party can substantiate your alibi?"

"Yes, I'm sure they will."

"Thank you. Councilmember Harrison?"

The councilwoman shifted uneasily in her chair. Stealthily, I watched her eyes. *Was she uncomfortable?* "I was at the same party," she said, her eyes darting right and left.

"How long were *you* there?" asked my dad.

"Oh," she said with a flip of her hand, "I left early; all the politics were getting to me."

Jonathan chuckled and Councilmember Stewart, to her left, blew silently through his lips and rolled his eyes back.

"Mr. Stewart," I said, "You have a comment?"

"Oh, no, no, no," he blustered.

Harrison glared at him.

"Ms. Harrison," I said, "Is there something we should know? Would you like to elaborate on when you left the party and where you went after?"

"I really don't have to say."

"No, you don't," said my father, "but your cooperation would be appreciated and may..."

"This isn't a court of law!" she burst out.

"No," said my father evenly, "it isn't and we would like to avoid having you appear at one, but if you'd like..."

"Don't you threaten me!" Her eyes where wild with fire.

"Dad," I turned to him and spoke in a hushed tone, "It's okay. We know how she can get riled up. Don't press it."

"What do you know, boy?" Her words were vehement—hostile. We'd intended for her to overhear and she did.

I couldn't help but smirk. I picked up the TV and DVD player remotes from the table before me, "I have a few short clips that I wish to show," I said pushing buttons. The TV came on and the DVD's menu showed on the screen. I scrolled to the first icon and clicked. The video played a quick montage assembled by my father from council meeting recordings. It went like this:

- Councilwomen Harrison swearing a blue streak—several clips edited together.
- Harrison taking off her shoe and banging it on the boardroom table.
- Harrison swearing and throwing a notepad at the mayor.
- Harrison dumping her water glass over councilmember Stewart's head.
- Harrison storming from the council chambers.

The room was quiet as all eyes turned to Harrison who was seething silently as DVD bumped back to its main menu. It was Mrs. Krabach who spoke first. She leaned to the councilwoman across the table from her, "You *are* quite a spirited woman." Lurch cracked a small smile.

"I have a lot more spirit than the rest of the council yahoos," she answered. "So," she continued, fixing her eyes like daggers on me, "What was the point of that little charade?"

"Merely establishing the fact that you have, shall I say, a difference of opinion," I said. "In fact, one of the issues that you feel so passionate about is this playhouse, isn't it Ms. Harrison?"

"Yes," she said, "I, unlike the rest of the council, see value in supporting the arts."

"Indeed," I said. "You have been the only councilmember to faithfully foster support for the arts. You have consistently argued that the city invest a portion of the municipal budget for the support of theater, public sculpture, and the symphony."

"Yes," she said proudly, "and they never have!"

"And, you voted against the city's takeover of this house a couple of years ago, and..."

"The raising of the Opera Guild's rent. Yes, yes, I saw through their smokescreen. I knew the motive behind their closed wallets."

"And what is that?"

"They never cared for the arts. They were concerned only with lining their own pockets. In the same meeting in which they raised the rent, they also voted themselves salary increases. The motive? Why, greed, pure and simple."

"Okay, then," I said, "Why did you leave the party and where did you go afterward?"

"Like I said, I was fed up with all the hot gas and you don't need to know where I went."

"Fine, but I think you'll want to sing a different tune soon enough. Stewart," I said, shifting my eyes to the councilman, "Where were you last night?"

The councilwoman slumped in her seat, obviously glad to have the pressure move to someone else as the councilman began. "I didn't go to the ball. I wasn't invited. The city manager and I don't see eye to eye. Anyway, I was building a Habitat for Humanity house—with my wife and several other volunteers—downtown until nine, then we, my wife and I, went to a night watch service at my church. I was home by elevenish and in bed soon after. You can check all that out." *Contrasts* was the word that came to mind.

"Mrs. Krabach, how about you?"

"Well, first I'd like to thank Jaynie for her continued support of the Guild, not only in her capacity on the City Council—at least she tries—and for her personal support and donations as well." She smiled and nodded at the councilwoman. "And *I* was at the final performance of our show, Marschner's *Der Vampir*, until after ten. It was showing at the Mahali Jackson Theater for the Performing Arts. After that we had a closing gala at the Hotel Monteleone until 1 p.m."

"And after that?"

"Home to bed."

"And...?"

"There was no one at home, if that's what you mean. My husband is away on business."

"And Mr. Jenkins," I said to Sparky.

"I was at the same show and gala."

They're in cahoots, I thought, "I suppose you're corroborating for one another?"

"Well, I suppose, but there are others who saw me there."

"And afterward?"

"I took a room in the hotel. I'm afraid I was a bit...well, a few sheets to the wind. I *do* have the bill."

"So," I said looking around the room dramatically at each of the suspects, "None of you came to this house last night?" All shook their heads.

"Then I want to introduce you all to the final member of this...uh, party. Are you ready? No, I suppose not. How could you be?" I paused for dramatic effect and once again asked in silent prayer for the Lord's guidance. '*The Lord is my strength and salvation; whom shall I fear?*'

14 SMOKE AND MIRRORS

Although recent 'hauntings' have certainly been the work of a human, there *is* and *has been* a genuine ghost haunting this house since the turn of the century. Bart," I said turning to him, "would you like to fill us in?"

"I'll keep the history brief..."

Councilman Stewart butted in, "You don't expect us to believe that, do you? This is the twentieth century, for crying out loud."

"Nonetheless," said Bart, "you can soon judge for yourself. May I continue?" He looked around the room. While Stewart harrumphed, no one else commented. "Well then. This house was built for the Edward Davis family. After the Civil War they retained...uh...servants—blacks, descendant from the slaves that served the family before that. They were provided servant's quarters—the outbuilding on the grounds—meals, and a subsistence 'salary.' One of the servants—the house maid

—a seventeen year-old—was molested and killed, presumably by one of Davis' sons, though nothing went to court (such were the times) and nothing proven. The women's name was Sarah Davis, since slaves took their master's last name. Her ghost has haunted this house since her death. She seeks justice."

"That's a load of bunk!" said Stewart. I was in agreement, but I couldn't let on— even though I really hated to mislead these people.

"Be as it may, the presence—her presence—has been documented by, what many believe is, a reliable source. Peter."

I picked the remote up from the table and clicked for the next video segment.

An overcast sky backed the shot of the Davis House, surrounded by the wrought iron fence. Eerie music played. The camera zoomed in on the plaque attached to the fence near the front gate—a voice-over explained the ownership of the Opera Guild (at the time) and described the theater's use. Another shot of the house filled the screen and craned down through a large oak tree on the grounds. A third shot dollied slowly through the theater's seating area. The voiceover said that employees all over the opera house had experienced strange activity as the shot panned up to the dimly lit stage.

The camera cut to the host of the Ghost Hunters *cable show standing in the theater. "A lot of the activity takes place in the theater where children take summer classes," he said. The shot dissolved slowly to show Becky Krabach gesturing to the seating area.*

"So, this is our theater," she said, "And patrons won't sit in that seat, H6. The kids won't sit in it."

"Do they say why?" asked the host.

"They, they just say it makes them uncomfortable."

"And they don't know why?"

"And they don't know why." The eerie music peaked with a flash of light, cutting to another exterior shot showing the house's turret with a single lit window in the second story. The shot dis-solved to an interior view of the greenroom then to another shot of a second woman dressed in black.

"There's an angry young black woman," she said, "She doesn't want to be bothered. She gets so annoyed." A new shot showed the same woman as if seen through a camera—framed with a red 'REC' icon in the upper right corner. "The kids are loud, they-'re hyper...all I know is that ghost didn't like 'um."

The eerie music kicked in as the screen went black and dissolved slowly to another moving crane shot of the exterior. "What else happens here?" asked the host. A new shot showed Krabach once again.

"One patron told us—she was seated in G6—she told us she heard laughter behind her." The video cut to a tilting shot of the empty theater seats and then back to the host.

"Was there a show in progress at the time?"

"Yes," answered the image of Krabach.

"Was it a comedy?" The TV Krabach laughed.

"I'm asking about the laughter," said the host. "Was there anyone seated behind the patron?"

"No, no," said Krabach. The video cut to a dolly shot moving through the curtain as the eerie music swelled once again.

"When they annoy her," came the voice of the second women as the shot dissolved to her, "she might do...something...to scare them. When she gets annoyed, she gets an-noyed." A final tilting shot of the theater seats filled the screen with the final cre-scendo of the music and the screen went black.

The screen snapped back to the menus page.

"*That* is *not* a reliable source," said Stewart.

"Yes it is," said Krabach, "the show documents hauntings all over the world."

"Bunk!" exclaimed Stewart.

"People," interjected my dad, leaning over the table, "we need to proceed with the work at hand. Bart, go ahead."

"We have contacted this ghost." Bart paused for dramatic effect and scanned the faces of everyone in the room before proceeding. "Sarah, wishes to speak for herself."

"Okay," said Stewart, "This is getting out of hand!"

"Oh, shut up!" screamed—you guessed it—Harrison. Stewart kowtowed and Bart continued.

"In a few moments we will hold a séance. Peter." The room was silent except for the rustle of hind ends squirming in their seats and the distant ticking of the house's grandfather clock. I picked up the remotes and shut down the electronic devices, arose and walked to the flip chart propped up on one of the greenroom's wrap-around cushions.

"This," I said, flipping back the pad's cover, "is a newspaper image from 1889 of Sarah Davis. Sorry for the grainy quality, newspaper photos weren't very good back then and I had it blown up. Bart, if you would be so good as to kill the lights at the breaker while I light the candles." Bart nodded, got up and left the room as I moved to the table and lit a match. I moved slowly around the table lighting the ring of

candles—one for each person present—
that I'd earlier arranged in the table's center around a shallow clay pot.

"I will need your silence," I continued,
"during the course of these procedures," I
said, moving back to my seat and bending
down to get the bag below it.

I set the sack on the table and opened
it. *Sorry, Lord*, I prayed silently once again.
Reaching inside I pulled out a tattered,
seemingly ancient, voodoo doll. "This," I
continued, "we found in the servant's
quarters. We were led directly to it, hidden
under the floorboards, by a mist." Stewart
looked like he was about to say something, but instead flinched. I assumed
Harrison had stomped his foot under the
table. "It belonged to Sarah—the young
girl..." I paused again for dramatic effect,
then continued in a slow measured cadence "...that was...murdered...in this
very room." The lights went out as if on
cue, which it was. Harrison gasped.

☠ ☠ ☠

Bart arrived back at the table soon
after and took his seat. I sat and placed
the doll in front of me on the table, "This
doll is our link to the past—our link to
Sarah's spirit," I said. "Please place your
hands flat on the table." The reluctance
was obvious, but eventually everyone

complied. "Now remember, absolute silence." *Were they going to buy this?* I thought. Spiritualism was common enough in the Big Easy that they might assume I'd at least dabbled in it. Frankly, I hated doing this—even though I knew I was pulling off nothing more than a theatrical hoax, nothing but a show—for the Bible forbade talking with the dead.

"And now," I said, "I must hold the relic." I picked up the doll and tried to clutch it ceremoniously. The wicker figurine was illuminated in the candlelight. "Sarah, Sarah," I began, "We know you are angry with us and we want to right this wrong. We call upon you to join us and resolve the issues. Sarah, do you hear us?"

The silence was palpable, though I could clearly hear the tick tock of the Grandfather clock in the hall. "Sarah," I continued, "Your blood cries from this very room, it cries out for vengeance, for resolve, for justice." *Was I being too dramatic?* "Sarah, I am going to place your doll in the center of the table now. Will you join us through it?" I rose and walked around to the side of the oval table and reached over between Lurch and Jonathan, placing the doll in the clay dish. I walked slowly back to my seat and sat down. "Sarah, the doll is in place. Come to us, come to us now," I cried in a loud voice.

Tick tock went the clock, *tick tock, tick tock, tick tock...*

BONG!

The clock struck the first of the hour's nine tolls and everyone jumped. The old grandfather continued through eight more tolls. Silently I counted off four more seconds and then whispered down toward my chest like Brick from the TV show *The Middle,* "*Sar-rah.*"

Another second passed and a sudden flash of fire erupted from the dish. Again everyone flinched. I knew that behind me now fog rolled from the seat cushion on which sat the flip-chart. I could feel the tension in the room as the smallest glow of light shimmered from around the silhouette of the image on the flipchart. I knew this was happening as all eyes turned to the photograph. I kept my eyes forward, trance-like. Then the image began to fade to color, slightly out of focus and faint. "*Sar-rah.*"

"I am here." The voice came from the pad.

"Speak Sarah," I said. "Speak your mind." *What if this little trick actually called up a demon? 'We wrestle not against flesh and blood, but against principalities and powers...' 'And He shall give His angels charge over thee...'*

15 NOT A GHOST OF A CHANCE

*I*t's *working, it's working*, I thought as the image grew lighter and more focused and the mouth formed the words, "Davis, I want Davis," the audio coming directly from the tablet. "Give me Davis."

"There are ancestors here," I said, "but the one who murdered you is long dead."

"Long have I waited," said the voice. "Too long have I waited for revenge."

"Is revenge a dish best served so cold,* when these are innocent of your blood?"

"Who are dese who are descendants?" asked the voice.

"I will have them stand," I said, "but please do not harm them; they are my friends."

"At last, those who will answer," said the voice with a sigh of relief.

"Mr. Davis, Bart, please stand," I requested and they got up slowly from their seats their hands at their sides as if at attention.

"Ah," said the voice, "A young one. How old?"

"I am sixteen," said Bart.

"So young, almost my age...when I died. Would you answer for the crimes of your ancestor?"

"Take me, take me instead of my son," cried Warden Davis.

"Ah, so much love," the voice mocked.

"If I could take your place in death, I would," answered Bart. "My life for yours, but we know that such an exchange would not bring you back. Would my death appease you? Would it help you rest? If not, then I ask to live."

"I feel dat is a noble answer and so...I will let you live, but still justice must be served. Feel my wrath!" Bart's left arm flashed into a sudden flame, he twisted and cried out in seeming shock and pain, threw himself to the ground and grabbed his arm which had just as suddenly extinguished. His father rushed to him and picked him up into his arms.

"You have struck my son," he yelled in anguished tones, cradling his son. "Are you satisfied?"

"I feel remorse," answered the voice with sadness, "I should not have done dat. I am glad dat I did not kill him. And yet...I am sorry, is dere somet'ing I can do?"

"Sarah," I said, "there *is* something. I need an answer."

"What do I know dat you seek?"

"Do you see all in this house?"

"I do."

"Then answer me; who has played the ghost here?"

"I am the ghost."

"I know, but who has played the ghost. Who among us has impersonated you?"

"I t'ink no one among you, but another."

"Who then? Do you know?"

"I do, but not in name, the false one is a female, I would put her age at..."

"I did it! I did it!" cried Mrs. Krabach, standing quickly to her feet. All eyes turned from the image to the Opera Guild President.

"It was not you," said the voice. All eyes returned to the image. "This one was young-er."

"It was me," screamed Krabach, "I...I hired someone." With that she broke into sobs and Bart and his father rose from the floor. Bart pulled his shirt off with the arm he had hidden under it. The shirt fell to the floor, a false arm and hand still filling the left sleeve. He walked to the table, reach-ed under it and pressed a button. The moving image disappeared from the flip-chart, leaving only the black and white printout.

"What is this?" said Sparky.

"A bit of theatrics and nothing more," I answered, "a trick. I am sorry. Bart, will you get the lights?" My friend left the room as Mrs. Krabach composed herself—her emotional outburst turning to a look of confusion.

"Wha, wha..." she stammered.

"Mrs. Krabach," I said, "you have not spoken truthfully."

"I..I.."

"You didn't hire anyone, did you?"

"But I...no, it was me, I played the ghost."

"But why?" asked my father, "Why, Mrs, Krabach? Why?"

"To scare away the tenants," she confessed, "to get my theater back."

"*Your* theater?" said Stewart as the lights came back on.

"But you didn't stage the hauntings, did you? Who was it?" I asked. The woman looked around the room, her lips pressed tightly together as Bart reentered. "The ghost that appeared to us in the control room window was a younger woman," I explained, "possibly in her late twenties and she was either black or in makeup, but definitely younger." Krabach remained tight-lipped.

"This," said my father looking the opera lady directly in the eye, "will go to court if the truth doesn't come out here, Mrs. Krabach. And we *will* find out the truth. We have bloody fingerprints to analyze." (We didn't, but he was fibbing.) "Who are you protecting?"

"This is *my* theater!" said the woman. "My daughter cut her acting chops here. She's going onto New York next year. She's going to be a star...a shining Broadway star, I tell you!" She said nothing more and the room was quiet with her. After a moment it was Sparky who spoke up.

"Becky does have a daughter who has been acting here since she was twelve," he said, "She's twenty-eight now. And...she's African-American."

"Was it your daughter who played the ghost?" asked Bart.

"No, no, no," whimpered Krabach.

My father rose and walked to the opposite end of the table where he placed his hand on Mrs. Krabach's shoulder. "Tell us," he said tenderly. My dad was good.

"Leah," the woman again broke into tears, "Leah..."

"Leah Keeler," said Sparky, "from a former marriage."

"I only wanted her...I wanted her to..." the woman snuffled, "She just needed...a good start..."

"Did you put her up to playing the ghost, Mrs..."

"I didn't mean for it to go so far," she said with an edge of remorse, "Things just got out of hand, that's all. I just wanted the theater back. It isn't right that the City took it from us. It isn't right." My father reached to his belt and snapped his walkie-talkie from its case as the woman babbled on incoherently.

"You can come in now," he said into the device.

"Ten-four," said the talkie, "We're on our way."

My father clipped the device back into its holster and spoke to the O.G. President, "Mrs. Krabach, you're being placed under arrest for attempted mur-der..." The woman broke into sobs once again as my father continued, re-citing to Krabach her Miranda rights*, "You have the right to remain silent, any-thing you say may be used against you in a court of law, you have the right to consult with an attorney and to have that attorney present during questioning, if you have no attorney one will be provided at no cost to you."

16 THE SHOW MUST GO ON

I blew out the candles as Becky Krabach was taken away by the NOPD (New Orleans City Police). The smoky wisps lingered like lazy ghosts in the silent room. "How did you know it was Mrs. Krabach?" Jonathan asked leaning toward me across the table.

"I didn't. I had no idea."

"Then..." began Lurch.

"I knew—at least I was pretty sure—that I could flush out the culprit from among you with, well, a little, shall we say...razzmatazz."

Jonathan laughed.

"You thought it was one of us?" asked Harrison .

I laughed, "*You*, in fact, were my prime suspect—beings that you were..."

"So, uh, passionate?" asked Harrison.

"You could put it that way," said Bart, "You consistently showed signs of aggression and hostility." Stewart rolled his eyes furtively.

"But," I said, "Burkmann was also under suspicion as was Sparky. Each had possible motives."

"So you didn't suspect Krabach at all?" said Jonathan.

"She wasn't even on my radar until I met her," I confirmed, "It didn't occur to me, though it should have. I didn't know she had a daughter, though I did learn, from some footwork, that it was a young, African-American woman who had purchased a truckload of bricks from the Lowe's in town. I knew there was likely an accomplice. And, by the way, I don't fault Krabach for wanting the theater back, but I do regard her motives with distain. They were selfish."

"All crime is selfish," said my father. "Usually motivated by greed." The scripture *'For all that is in the world, the lust of the flesh and the lust of the eyes and the boastful pride of life, is not from the Father, but is from the world,'* came to my mind.

"There was, however," said Bart, "a degree of heart in Krabach's motive. She was obsessed with her daughter's success."

"A true stage mom," I added.

"So, will you press charges?" asked the CEO.

I looked at my father, "I don't believe I will. She really meant no bodily harm. She wasn't trying to kill us, just scare us. And her daughter..."

"...was merely acting on her mother's instruction," said Bart, completing my thought, "she probably didn't know that theatrical CO_2 would displace the oxygen in the basement."

"Huh?" said Burkmann.

"It's a little known fact," said Bart proudly.

"So," said Jonathan, "What *will* you do?"

"I will address that after a short recess," I said, "We've been at this for quite some time, and, frankly, I have to use the restroom."

"You know where it is," said the CEO.

☠ ☠ ☠

Back from the facilities, I stood and addressed the assembly once again, "I understand from my research, that this house was actually given to the opera guild in 1955, but that at a later date—because the guild was barely making ends meet and because of the house's high maintenance needs—that the City Council offered a 'management deal.'"

"Yes," said Sparky, "that's how I understand it, too. The City's offer looked good. The city parks department would take over ownership and provide the necessary restoration and upgrades, as well as on-going maintenance and janitorial services, to save the Women's Opera Guild from losing the building under the promise that the guild could rent the building perpetually."

"Exactly," I said, "and I would like to point out two further facts. One, the required restoration and upgrades—which included ADA* compliance—were imposed by city ordinance, and two, that the legalese in the contract covered the fact that the council could raise the rent at will. And, finally, this is an assumption based on those facts: The City's intention all along was not to aid the guild or 'save the arts'..."

"Now wait a..." Stewart melted under the gaze of Harrison and didn't finish.

"It's track record has never supported that aim," I continued, "but, rather, to take control of the building in order to drive the Opera Guild out. It didn't take even six months for the City Council to not just incrementally, but rather, astronomically raise the rent to such a point that the Guild could not possibly comply."

"In other words," added Sparky, "the guild was suddenly up a creek without a paddle."

"Right," said Harrison. "This, in essence, is what happens to small theater all over the nation. The city makes such restrictive and burdensome demands that the companies can find no place to set up shop. Buildings can't be converted to theater space because they can't meet the costly conversion costs imposed upon them. It's like the municipalities don't want the arts to thrive when the arts are what make cities more livable."

"But,' said Jonathan putting his finger in the air, "this facility already meets building code as a theater. At least it has to be grandfathered* in."

"Be as it may, the WOG can't meet the rent," interjected the councilwoman, "and, even so, the place *is* occupied at the moment."

"Well," said the CEO, "I think I have a solution to that."

"Oh?" said Harrison.

"They can still use this facility," stated Jonathan. All eyes were on the CEO, several of them raised in anticipation. "I know they manage to pull off one or two operas a year at the Jackson, but they can reinstate the smaller plays here, too."

"What? Have you decided to move out after all?" asked Lurch.

The CEO laughed, "Oh, no, no, no."

"Then how can...?" questioned Bart.

"It's simple," said Jonathan, "we only use the space during the weekdays; performances take place nights and on weekends, do they not?"

"True," said Harrison.

"And half of the building is not used that much during the days we *do* work," added Jonathan, "The theater/auditorium portion stands empty most of the time."

"So," said Harrison, lighting up, "you're saying..."

"That I love the arts—our company could share the space."

"You're kidding me!" exclaimed Harrison.

"I am perfectly serious," said the CEO. "In fact I think my board would agree to do so rent free." Harrison appeared dumbfounded, so the CEO continued, "There are only some minor details to work out so that our schedules mesh, but yes, I think it could work very well."

"That would be a godsend," gushed Harrison.

"Fine," said Jonathan. "I will convene a meeting of our board next week and have an agreement drawn up. I suggest that we also meet with the Opera Guild at earliest convenience."

"You mean," said Sparky, "as soon as Krabach's out of jail?"

"Or until a new president is appointed," said Bart's dad.

"If need be," I said.

"Then so be it," concluded Jonathan. "Is this meeting adjourned? Quite frankly, I am totally bushed."

"I second that," said Bart. "I'm ready to go home."

"All in favor?" I laughed and every hand went up with confirming 'Ayes' all around. "Then this meeting is adjourned."

17 CURTAIN CALL

The room cleared and Bart went to relieve Beth of her post upstairs. Our fathers began carting the big screen toward the elevator. The CEO lingered, gazing out the window into the dark. "So, how'd you do all this?" asked Jonathan turning and walking to the flipchart.

"Just using my skills," I answered wandering over next to him, "Num-chuck skills ...bow hunting skills... computer hacking skills..."

"Some skills, a real *Napoleon Dynamite*, huh?" he said as Bart returned with Beth who was peeling away her nose putty. "Oh," chuckled the CEO, "and here's our ghost." I introduced them to one another and Jonathan complimented her on her performance to which she thanked him.

"Peter's the real brains though," she said kindly.

"Yeah," he said, "He was just about to explain to me how it was done."

I ripped the newspaper printout page from the flipchart revealing Jonathan's very thin flat screen nestled within the cavity I'd cut. This caused him to laugh most heartily. Bart flipped up the seat cushion exposing the fog machine, "A little smoke and mirrors," he said, "nothing more."

"Add a video feed," I said, "...some makeup, flash paper*, a hobby rocket firing kit to ignite the paper and a whole lot of theatrics and, well, there you have it."

"Well done," commented the CEO looking under the table where Bart had been seated, "You had me fooled. That false arm on Bart...wow! I can see now how he was working the controls, so to speak, with his real arm. Ingenious, really."

"Thank you," I said. Our fathers returned and continued the work of dismantling our 'show.'

"Yeah," said Beth removing her wig. "Peter's pretty amazing. Bart, too." Did I perceive a coy glance there? *Hmm, Beth is sweet on Bart?* "Would it be alright if I go upstairs and take off the rest of this make-up?"

"No problem," I said. "Thanks Beth, you were great."

"Well, it was fun," she said, "but I'm not the actor you are."

"Oh, I think you're at least twice the actor I am. You were totally convincing. Totally Amy Adams."

"You really think so?" she said, blushing.

"I wouldn't have called upon you if I didn't have faith in you and, well, I have more now. Why don't you come out and audition for the next show?"

"You really think I should?"

"I *know* you should. *Godspell* is next and then *Blithe Spirit*—that should be a real natural for you."

"*Blithe Spirit?*"

"It's about a haunting,"

Beth laughed, "Thanks. Peter. I'll go upstairs now."

"And, uh...I'll go disassemble the video stuff," said Bart. *Maybe he was sweet on her, too.*

"You were all great," said the CEO as Beth and Bart left the room.

"Thanks," they called back over their shoulders.

"Well," said the CEO, "it's been a long day, I think I'll head out, if that's okay?"

"Sure," I said. "We're heading home in the morning. I'll drop the key by before we do."

"Thanks," said Jonathan walking over and squeezing my shoulder as our fathers returned, "I can't thank you enough. Do you have hospital bills?"

"We have insurance," said my dad.

"May I pay the deductibles, please?"

"That would be commendable," interjected Warden Davis.

"Well, it's the least I can do," said the CEO. "Send me the bill and I'll cut a check. And for your hotel bill, too."

"Thank you," said my father, "You don't have to do that, we were..."

"No, no, no, thank you," returned Jonathan, "I want to. Just send me the bill, please. I'll see you in the morning." He turned to go, "Oh! And breakfast, it's on me." He pulled out his wallet and handed my dad a crisp one-hundred dollar bill. "This should cover it. Try the Please-U on St. Charles, it's the bomb."

"The bomb?" I said, "Old expression, but I like the idea."

"You would," said my dad with a hardy chuckle.

"Then it's good night," and with that the CEO left. My dad walked over to me and wrapped his arm around my shoulders, careful not to squeeze my broken arm.

"You know, I'm proud of you, son. I wish you wouldn't get all broken up on these adventures, but, well, kids get hurt all the time in other hobbies like football and BMX and stuff. I guess there's no difference. Anyway, you did good and I'm proud of you."

"Thanks dad," I said.

"I'm proud of you, too," said Warden Davis, "And I think I want to let my son know I'm proud of him, too."

"He's upstairs," I said, "but...ah, knock first."

"Right-o," said the warden, "I'll just wander on up there."

☠ ☠ ☠

We spent the next hour wearily gathering our equipment and loading it into the car, then left for our hotel. On the way we stopped for a Taco Bell fourth meal. (Hey, it was cheap, fast and tasty.) I was as beat as I've ever been by the time we reached the hotel. It was 11 p.m. That night, well, I slept like a log nestled in a feather bed set on a cloud. We all did.

18 ENCORE

After dropping the key by Razzmatazz (and receiving more thanks from Jonathan) we hit Please-U and had an absolute gastronomical delight—grits and cheese, biscuits and gravy and fritters that were indeed the bomb. Over breakfast our conversation went something like this:

"Well," said Bart, "I didn't make Zumstein's harvest party."

"On the other hand," I replied, "we *did* miss a couple days of school."

"You know, we'll just have to make it up, anyway."

"Straight up," said my father with a smile.

"That's the trouble with homeschooling," said Bart.

"*Fo troo,*" I replied with a laugh, "but it *is* flexible."

Bart, as was his custom, conversed with the waitress and made her feel spec-ial. Our bill was less than $60, so we left a nice tip and had enough left over for lunch on Jonathan when we would get back to Houma. We spent the rest of the morning returning rental items be-fore heading toward home— Beth in her 'roller skate' (GEO Metro) and the rest of us in Dad's family sedan.

☠ ☠ ☠

Bart and I slept all the way to Houma. Warden Davis woke us up just as we drove into the parking lot of Big Mike's BBQ Smokehouse—a family favorite. Dad had called ahead to our moms and they were there waiting for us—to, uh, hug on us and make a big fuss about our injuries. (They did. For about five minutes. Right there in the parking lot. Moms!) The big pig painted on the barn wood building smiled down at us as we—finally—ap-proached the entrance. Several motor-cycles were parked out front and Freddy 'Flame' Sauvageau was just pulling off his helmet.

"Eve'nin' Sheriff," he said fluffing his long black hair with his tatted arm. Don't get the wrong idea, Flame was a good folk —amiable and full of heart—one of those Christian biker guys that did a lot of char-ity work.

"Hey, Flame!" said my dad, "What's the good word?"

"Dat would be the Bible, Sheriff."

"Straight up," said Warden Davis.

"Hey, boys," said the biker, giving us the peace sign. "You two is growin' like weeds."

"Flame on!" Bart and I said in our customary greeting to our old friend.

"What about them aliens?" he said.

"Huh?" asked Bart.

"The UFO sightin's, you know?"

"No, we don't," I said. "Something new? We've been out of town over the weekend."

"I wasn't going to mention it," said my mom, "but I suppose you would have—did—find out anyway." My dad let out a sigh.

"You boys want to eat or what?" said Bart's mom.

"Is the Pope Catholic?" said Bart, "Do…"

"…the Bayou Boys solve mysteries?" I finished, though he was probably going to say something about bears pooping in the woods. I turned to Flame. "Can you join us and fill us in?"

"Sure," answered Flame, "for a minute. Me an' da boys is meetin' at seven t' make plans for our holiday toy run. I got a few."

We rolled inside the open beamed structure where Arcadian-style, slow-smoked meats, prepared for days in the smokehouse out back, and all the fixin's were served from a long line of steam tables and found our seats near the patio. License plates from all over the country decorated the rustic walls. Mike Lewis, owner and master chef, waved a hearty hello from the kitchen window.

Yvette whisked up to our table to wait on us as we sat. "Good to see the Davises and Myers again, you, too, Flame," she said. "What are ya having t' drink today? The usual? Sweet tea all around?"

"Sweet tea good?" asked my mom looking around at each of us. She noted our nods and answered to the Southern-Cajun gal, "That will be fine."

Flame took Yvette's hand, "Dere ain't nuthin' sweeter dan you, buttercup, but I'll try and swallow some a dat swamp water."

"Oh, Flame," returned the waitress batting her eyes, "ya set ma heart on fire. Sweat tea it is, folks. I'll be right back. You folks know da drill," said Yvette, "one price, all ya kin eat." And with that Yvette left us with a smile and Flame watched her wiggle off.

"Flame, I don't know what...," said my father.

"...it is with my fiery charm?" he said with a smoldering look, "Ha! The good Lord done made me fiiii-ine. Yvette ain't bad neither." He laughed. "Okay, so, here's the thing on them you-foe's. You ready fer dis?"

"Fire away," said Bart.

"Now, mind you, some folks is sayin' it's just swamp gas."

"That's what Bart blames his gas on," I interjected.

"Peter!" said my mom, "Mind your manners." Bart beamed. *How could he be so proud of his foulness? He could drop a skunk at twenty paces.*

"For all I know," continued the biker, "it prolly is, but dere's been plenty a folks dat seen um, doe I ain't."

"What do they say they look like?" I asked.

"Some say great balls a fire twirlin' in da sky. Two, t'ree at a time. Some say saucers, others globes an'..."

"Where?" asked Bart.

"Over da Gulf yonder of Lake Timbaliar Bay."

"That's not far from where Grams lives," said my mother, "by the heliport base."

"Could it be the rigs letting off natural gas," asked my father, "or something the military is working on?" The Gulf of Mexico had thousands of oil drilling platforms.

"I don't believe dats so," answered the biker, "The military denies any, ah, projects. And, whatever it is, it's too big and too floaty to be a gas discharge."

"Well," said Warden Davis, "if the military *is* working on something they would deny it."

"Floaty?" asked Bart as we got up and approached the line of deliciously smelling smoked meats, corn on the cob, cowboy beans, beans and rice, beans and...*Man, I hope Bart takes it easy on the beans....* bacon, grits, fried okra, and... Need I go on?

"Dey hover, dart an' move aron' quick, like. Least dats what I heard."

"Reed has got to be in conniptions," I said.

"Do ya think?" said Bart laughing. "It's a wonder he hasn't called us."

"Oh," said my mom holding her plate out in front of her for baked potato so large you could shove a football into it. "Reed's away, up at Branson, in Missouri. It was a surprise."

"I know where Branson is," I said. "Home of the amusement park Silver Dollar City. And a great surprise if I do say so."

"Dat's right," said Flame, "I did a stopover dere on da way upta Sturgis las' year. Lot a fun."

"Sturgis!?" mom questioned, shocked like.

"It's a bike rally..." said the biker. "Two cobs please."

"I know that..." said Mom.

"Oh, you mean: What was a church boy like me doin' at a place known for its hellions?" He held out his plate for some smoked chicken with a crooked little smile on his face.

"I didn't mean to..."

The biker laughed, "Dats okay, ma'am. Da Christian Motorcycle Association always makes an appearance. Great place for evangelism."

"I'm sorry," said my mother. I saw my dad smirking as a heap of coleslaw was piled on his plate.

"T'ink nuthin' of it," he said with a wave of his hand. "We look da part, but don't play it. Get dat all da time."

☠ ☠ ☠

We returned to our seats after piling our platters high with scrumptious barbequed goodness just as Yvette returned with a tray laden with tall iced teas. "Anyt'ing else I kin do fer ya?" she said.

"We're good," said Bart's mom. "Thanks, Yvette."

"My pleasure," she said sashaying off as Flame watched with interest. My dad cleared his throat and brought the bikers attention back around.

"What?!" he asked in mock surprise, "She ain't married! Can't a single guy admire God's creation?"

"So," I interjected, "about these UFO's?"

"Seriously boys," said my mother, "Please, don't get involved in another dangerous…"

"Adventure?" said Bart.

"Danger is, after all," began my dad with a wink, "their middle names."

Flame laughed until our moms extinguished his joviality with icy eyes.

Dad cleared his throat, "Shall we say grace?"

All thumbs went up but Flame's.

Above: A photograph I took of the Davis House theater in the Garden District of New Orleans, Louisiana that was featured on the original cover of ***Playhouse Phantom***. The photo has been altered in Photoshop (night for day, sky replacement, and window lighting).

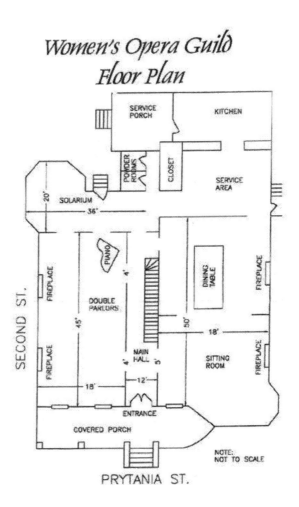

Women's Opera Guild Floor Plan

Above: The actual floorplan of the Davis House theater in the Garden District of New Orleans, Louisiana.

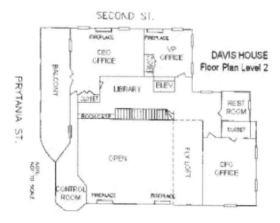

Above: The Davis House as imagined in the previous story. **Following pages:** Current pictures of the Davis House interior.

433

Above: Photographs of the Davis House interior.

Above: Pictures of the Davis House interior.

GLOSSARY/ENDNOTES

Chapter 1

- NOLA: <u>N</u>ew <u>O</u>rleans, <u>L</u>ouisian<u>a</u>

- The Big Easy: Another name for New Orleans, especially the French Quarter

- Sweet Potato Pumpkin Pecan pie (recipe follows this glossary)

- Gallery: A porch
- Na'lins (a way to say New Orleans)

- Roberto Thachne: The villain in *Marsh Monster*, the second book in the Bayou Boys Adventure series

- *Voodoo Virus*: The first book in the Bayou Boys Adventure series

Chapter 2

- *Marsh Monster* was the second book in the Bayou Boys Adventure series
- "Where y'at?": A common greeting in New Orleans, meaning "How are you doing?" or "What are you thinking?"

- Fly loft: the space above the stage where things (like curtains and lighting) are hung

Chapter 3

- *étouffée*: a Cajun dish made with a roux (gravy) meaning "smothered"

- Saints: The New Orleans football team

- *Flue du luce*: The symbol of New Orleans, Louisiana; literally French for "flower lily"

- *Fo troo*: For true

- Redemption: The saving grace of Jesus Christ, to be forgiven and bought by sacrifice

Chapter 4

- *'to be absent in the body is to be present with the Lord'* II Corinthians 5:8

Chapter 5

- Walt Iwerks: A made up name paying tribute to Walt Disney and Ub Iwerks, the chief animator of Mickey Mouse

Chapter 6

- Antebellum: Meaning literally "before the war" and a reference to a style of architecture—specifically houses of the Civil War period

- Tim Hawkins: A Christian comedian and musician; you can see his work on YouTube

Chapter 8

- *'Do not be afraid, the Lord your God is with you'* Deuteronomy 31:6
- *'Be strong and courageous'* Deuteronomy 31:6 and several passages in the book of Joshua

- *Padnet*: A Cajun term meaning "friend" or "buddy"

Chapter 9

- *'Yay, though I walk through the valley of the shadow of death, I will fear no evil'* From the 23rd Psalm

Chapter 10

- Watson: Sherlock Holmes sidekick

Chapter 11

- Gothic: Another style of architecture

Chapter 12

- The French Quarter: An area of New Orleans, the old city

- "Let slip the dogs of war" a phrase used in *Star Trek VI: The Undiscovered Country*; it is an old military order from the Middle Ages to direct the soldiery (in Shakespeare's [Julius Caesar] parlance 'the dogs of war') to pillage and chaos; also from *The Black Book of the Admiralty*, 1385; and *Ordinances of War of Richard II*

- *'Trust in the Lord with all your heart...and He will direct your path'* Proverbs 3:5 and 6

Chapter 13

- *'The Lord is my strength and my salvation; who shall I fear?'* Psalm 27:1

Chapter 14

- *'We wrestle not against flesh and blood, but against principalities and powers'* Ephesians 6:12

- *'And He shall give His angels charge over you..."* Psalm 91:11

Chapter 15

- 'Revenge is a dish best served cold' The popular expression comes from a French diplomat. It has been in the English language since at least 1846, via a translation from the French novel *Mathilde* by Joseph Marie Eugène. The familiar wording appears in *The Godfather* a film by Mario Puzo (1969) and is quoted as if from an 'old Klingon Proverb' in the film *Star Trek II: The Wrath of Khan* (1982) and in the title sequence of the Quentin Tarantino film *Kill Bill: Vol. 1* (2003).

- Miranda Rights are a set of warnings given by police in the United States to criminal suspects in police custody (or in a custodial interrogation) before they are interrogated to preserve the admissibility of their statements against them in criminal proceedings.

Chapter 16

- *'For all that is in the world, the lust of the flesh, the lust of the eyes and the boastful pride of life, is not from the Father, but from the world.'* I John 2:14

- ADA: The American Disabilities Act

- Grandfathered: Meaning compliant retrospectively before other laws or codes were in affect, thus allowing operation under the laws previous to the code

Chapter 17

- Flash paper: a highly flammable paper that burns rapidly with no smoke used by magicians

RECIPES for dishes described in the stories of this volume (developed by from authentic Southern Louisiana recipes by the author for his book *Big Papa Zee's Cajun & Caribbean Cookbook*).

Sweet Potato Pumpkin Pecan Pie

Prep: 20 min. Bake: 40 min. + cooling Yield: 8 Servings

Ingredients
1 can (15 ounces) solid-pack pumpkin
1 cup mashed sweet potatoes
3/4 cup packed brown sugar
1-1/2 teaspoons ground cinnamon
1/2 teaspoon salt
1/2 teaspoon ground ginger
1/2 teaspoon ground nutmeg
1/4 teaspoon ground cloves
3 eggs, beaten
1-1/4 cups heavy whipping cream
1 can (5 ounces) evaporated milk
1 tablespoon rum flavor (opt.)
Pastry for single-crust pie (9 inches)

PECANS:
2 cups pecan halves
1/2 cup packed brown sugar
1/4 cup heavy whipping cream
Whipped cream

Directions, next page>

Directions

In a large bowl, combine the first eight ingredients. Add the eggs, cream, milk and rum flavor; mix well. Line a 9-in. deep-dish pie plate with pastry; trim and flute edges. Pour pumpkin mixture into pastry. Bake at 400° for 40-45 minutes or until a knife inserted near the center comes out clean. Cool on a wire rack.

In a small bowl, combine the pecans, brown sugar and cream. Spread into a greased 15-in. x 10-in. x 1-in. baking pan. Bake at 350° for 15-20 minutes or until toasted, stirring once. Cool completely. Top pie with sugared pecans; serve with whipped cream.

Holy Trinity Jambalaya

8 C chicken broth*
4 C white rice
1 bunch celery, diced
2-3 medium onions, diced
3 medium bell peppers, diced (various colors)
1 pkg. Andouille sausage, sliced (about 4 sausages)
1 lb. cooked chicken breast, chunked
3 Tsp. **Big Papa Zee's Ragin' Cajun Seasoning**
Salt to taste

First make a rich stock (see full directions page 8) by pouring the broth into a two gallon pot, throw in the chicken breast and put on high heat. Cut the bottom and tips off the celery and toss that into the pot. Now skin the onions and put the remains in the pot as well. Cover and let boil to make a rich stock. Dice the vegetables (the holy trinity of celery, onion>

and bell peppers—a staple of many Cajun dishes) and set aside.

Slice the sausage and set aside. Remove the chicken from the stock and chunk it up; set aside with the sausage. Strain the stock off all vegetable matter and measure the liquid to eight cups (if required, add water to make up the deficit). Add the chicken, sausage, and rice to the pot. Heat up a frying pan with a little olive oil and sauté the vegetables with the seasoning until the vegetables begin to turn translucent. Add them to the pot, which should have returned to a boil, reduce the heat to simmer and cook until the rice is tender and absorbed most of the liquid. Makes 8-10 servings.

Chicken or Shrimp Étouffée

2 lbs. boneless, skinless chicken OR shrimp (you may also use crawfish if desired)
4 C low sodium chicken broth (or rich stock)
1 C all-purpose flour
1 C unsalted butter
1 bunch celery, 2 med. Onions and 2 med. Bell peppers, diced
4 C prepared rice
Salt, to taste
1 Tbs. **Big Papa Zee's Ragin' Cajun Seasoning**

Shake the chicken (shelled shrimp or crawfish) in the seasoning and cook until done. Set aside.. Note: this dish is best prepared outside due to smoke and splatter. Make a roux with 1 cup of butter and 1 cup of flour. Once it has reached a golden brown color,>

slowly, while whisking, gradually add in the broth or stock to combine and dissolve. Bring the mixture to a rolling boil and simmer, uncovered, over low heat for 15 minutes to thicken. While it's simmering sauté the vegetables and seasonings in a skillet over low heat until they become wilted and translucent. Add the vegetables into the sauce and simmer 15 minutes. Add in the prepared meat or seafood and skim any grease from the surface. Serve over prepared rice.   *Serves eight.*

Red Beans and Rice

8 C of low sodium chicken broth
2 C rice
2 C red beans
1 medium onion, finely diced
4 stalks celery, finely diced
1 C of finely diced Andouille sausage or ham
2 Tbs **Big Papa Zee's Ragin' Cajun Seasoning**

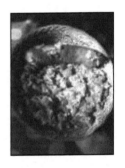

Soak the beans overnight in water and drain when you are ready to prepare the dish. Add them to the broth in two gallon pot and set the burner on high to bring to a boil. While the pot boils, dice up the meat and vegetables. Throw them in the pot along with the rice and seasoning and return to boil. Reduce heat and simmer until the rice and beans are tender. It should be soupy. Serve immediately with your favorite meat dish.   *Serves eight.*

Southern Sweet Tea

Two gallons water
20 tea bags
A pinch of baking soda
3 C. Sugar

Put one gallon of water into a two gallon pot and bring it to a boil. Turn it off and throw in 20 tea bags, cover and let steep for one hour. Remove the tea bags, throw in a pinch of baking soda and three cups of sugar. Stir until the sugar dissolves; add in one gallon of cold water. Serve over ice. What isn't served may be refrigerated for up to a week or frozen (and thawed for later use).

<Twenty tantalizing taste-tested recipes that will have your taste buds dancing a *fais do do*. $5.99

ABOUT THE AUTHOR

Gregory E. Zschomler is the author of a dozen books (many of them for young readers) and the editor-contributor to a few others. He has traveled the U.S. widely and "let the good times roll" in Louisiana where he's experienced the  Honey Island Swamp tour, walked the Garden District and The Quarter, been guided to local haunts, visited Houma and eaten as much Cajun goodness as he jam in his pie-hole. He loves Jesus and all things Disney. You can friend/follow him on Facebook and Twitter. He blogs at: **gregoryezschomler@blogspot.com**

PLAYHOUSE PHANTOM

Made in the
USA
Lexington, KY